The Guardians
And the Heirs of the Brown Dragon

The Guardians
And the Heirs of the Brown Dragon

Katherine M. L. Smith

iUniverse, Inc.
Bloomington

The Guardians and the Heirs of the Brown Dragon

iUniverse books may be ordered through booksellers or by contacting:

iUniverse
1663 Liberty Drive
Bloomington, IN 47403
www.iuniverse.com
1-800-Authors (1-800-288-4677)

ISBN: 978-1-4620-2072-0 (sc)
ISBN: 978-1-4620-2074-4 (hc)
ISBN: 978-1-4620-2073-7 (ebk)

Printed in the United States of America

iUniverse rev. date: 7/27/2011

This book is dedicated to:

The Valley Family, particularly Joseph and Isaac,
who gave me inspiration and memories and
taught me to be young at heart always . . .

. . . and to Miss Nicolosi, my English tutor
who gave me encouragement and
a stronger will to succeed.

Part One

Heroes Introduced

Chapter 1

The West Coast was silent. The night sky stretched like a glittering tapestry over the shadowy ocean as waves lapped quietly at the shoreline. Massive, dark rock formations stood soundless around the coast where gigantic walls of rock shot straight up towards the cliffs and the grassy land above. Indented in these walls were several smallish caves, hollowed out by ancient underground rivers when the world had been young. The caves reached far back into the depths of the earth, but whatever lurked deep down in there never came up. Even if it did, such a creature would flee at the sight of a certain family of dragons nesting in the entrance to one of these caves.

The biggest dragon slept in the front of the cave, half his nose poking out to scent intruders. Behind him, settled on a nest of rocks, dried seaweed, and bits of this and that, was his mate. She breathed easily and quietly, so as not to disturb the seven balls of fuzz curled up beside her. These were her dragonets—her young. She kept them close, lest someone or something should happen to sneak by her mate and try to get at her babies. Such an event, however, was rare. Nobody dared to mess with a fully-grown male dragon and his protective, equally-lethal mate.

One of the balls of fuzz squeaked in his sleep and stirred. He was smaller than the others, blue, with delicate wings. His foot twitched. Then he gasped and jerked awake, knocking his head on his mother's elbow and disturbing his siblings curled beside him in the nest. Rubbing his head, the little dragon blinked huge brown eyes and tested the air with a highly-sensitive, forked tongue. The vibrations were still and silent. The rest of his body, however, was covered in a cold sweat.

"Umphy? Are you alright?"

The little dragon turned. The eldest of his siblings, Possa, was awake and staring at him.

"I think I was dreaming again," he said softly. "My stomach hurts."

"What was it?" Possa enquired curiously. It was a well-known fact that dragons did not have the gift of night-thought, commonly referred to by humans as *dreams*. A dragon who dreamed was considered to be insane and an outcast. But Possa had not the heart to tell her elders about her darling little brother. She was curious to know what dreams were like. She pressed him again for answers.

Umphy trembled. "I saw the white lady again. She stood beside a very tall tree with silver veins and gold-rimmed leaves, and three rivers flowed from it, going north, east, and west. The riverbed going south was dried up."

"The Tree of Life!" Possa said reverently. The Tree of Life stood in the very center of the land of Balské, in a garden protected by very powerful spirits. Its rivers fed the three most prominent areas of the land, like a constant blessing. "Go on, Umphy. What happened next?"

"The lady stood beside the tree by the dried up riverbed. She said, 'This will run again when the crown is complete.' And then she pointed upwards, and . . . and suddenly I was up in the tree, high off the ground, and sitting on a branch near the top of the tree. Surrounding me were eight identical branches all parallel to each other in a circle, like the rim of a crown, and there were—" Umphy looked at his sister. "Possa, they looked like owl-holes, but they were all the same size and shape—as if something was meant to fit inside. And I thought—it was funny, but I thought—"

"What?" Possa gave her brother a small push.

"I thought to myself, the crown is missing its jewels."

Possa was quiet for a minute. "Did she sing to you again?"

"Oh, yes." Umphy dutifully recited:

Let he who seeks find not
And he who asks first knock.
The mountain dark, the people dread
Who live beneath the rocky ledge.
They guard me, keep me safe from harm.
Lest evil come and cast its charm.
Find me, take me, if you can:
I solve doors and puzzles, heart of man.
Where to find me? The wise man knows.
Find him where the blue stone grows.
Use me well when thrice the sun
Makes its turn on its fifth run.
Then let me lead thee, guide thee on
Behind the wall of silver-stone.
I'll take thee to three golden halls
And on beyond the valley falls.
There, silver bells are hung in rows
And brightly gleams the red-red rose.
The tree is tall; the dragon brown
Within that hall who lives deep down.
The empress white; her satin gown
Ripples eight beneath her crown!
The day on which I shall awake
Will be the day the foe's life I take.
And set me once again within the hand
That forever more will rule the land.

"When the lullaby ended, I saw a flash of amber eyes and a wave of fire. My stomach hurts awfully." Umphy clutched his stomach and winced. Of all seven dragonets, he was the youngest, a runt from birth, and naturally sickly. His dreams had begun only within his third year of life; he was not yet four years old. All dragons marked their stages of life according to the years they lived; the first ten years were bolora years, and the next ten were keldora years. When a dragon reached the age of twenty, he or she was free to seek a mate and become a master and mistress. Dragons usually mated once for life, and gave birth to two broods of never more than ten at a time. Weaklings, runts, and mortally-sick dragonets were cast off from their clans in order to ensure the healthy development of their species. Umphy's mother, however, was an unusually kind-hearted drakona. She was the protective shield that guarded him from the fate other runts faced at birth and continued to look after him as he grew older. Nevertheless, with his dreams and illnesses, Umphy continued to walk a very thin line. Only Possa knew of his dreams, and only Possa would ever know of the stomachaches that accompanied them.

"Wait here." Possa slid over the side of the nest and hurried down the dark tunnel. She returned a moment later with a dark green plant. "Eat this," she said, climbing back into the nest and handing it to her brother. "It will make you feel better."

"Possa, when you become a keldora, you should think about apprenticing yourself to the healers," Umphy smiled and munched the plant. It had a strong, pungent smell and almost bitter taste, but his stomach felt better afterwards. "You're so clever with herbs."

The pretty young drakona made a funny face. "Too much learning for my taste. I've already asked for permission to go adventuring across the oceans. Papa says that if I behave myself, he'll take me to the islands in a few years. Then I can venture out on my own, officially." Possa watched her brother anxiously. "I might take you along with me, if you want."

Umphy snuggled up beside his sister. "I'd like that. But papa would be very angry if I didn't try to make my own way in the world."

She folded her wing over him, like a tent. "Baby brother mine, you might never leave these coves. You were born a runt, remember? Besides, you don't even know what you want to do in life, or what path you want to take. The only things you enjoy are playing your flute and exploring." She tweaked his nose. "And you have night-thoughts."

Umphy sighed. He already knew that his life would never measure up to a normal dragon's. But he felt in his heart that his path was something special and unlike any other's.

"The lady in white is trying to tell me something," he declared firmly. "Someday I will go adventuring on my own, like you, and I'll find her. I'll be a great hero, you just wait and see! And I'll bring you a beautiful golden statue from a faraway palace."

Possa laughed. "You've got your head up in the clouds, Umphy. I'd love to have a golden statue in my cave. But I'd rather have you, safe and sound, than all the golden statues in the world."

When morning dawned at last, the early mist lifted, revealing a pristine day. Spring was in the air; the Sunstar dragon clan had survived another harsh winter, and now they welcomed the warmth of the sun, eager to soak up its light and heat. The tide was out, exposing tide-pools and a smooth blanket of golden sand for miles up and down the West Coast, which was famous for its beaches, magnificent tide-pools, and exotic sea-creatures. The sun shone warmly upon the glittering waves of the sea, and gulls chased each other around the cove, searching for bits of fish and crab.

In the cave, tiny yawns announced the waking dragonets. One by one, several carefully poked their noses around the edge of the cave, sniffing the air and testing it with their tongues. Then, squealing with glee and tumbling over each other in their haste, the little dragons raced out to the tide-pools. They enjoyed collecting tiny mole crabs that buried in the sand, or the infant hermit-crabs that nestled in the seaweed patches. Seashells, sea-glass, driftwood, and varieties of seaweed littered the foam-speckled tide-line. The sand was wet enough to build sand-castles. When the tide was out, it was the perfect time to go play and explore.

Umphy sat on the beach with his flute and played for a small audience of gulls that hopped closer to listen. Possa had ingeniously crafted the flute out of smooth white driftwood and given it to her little brother for his second birthday. Umphy was somewhat of a music prodigy, and even the clan Matriarch had remarked once that his talent was unique and remarkable. He was fluting a childhood nursery rhyme when his older brother Kestern snuck up behind him and yanked sharply on his tail. "OUCH!! Kestern, knock it off!"

Kestern snorted. "Come on, dimwit. The tide's out. I thought you'd like to go out to the plateau today with me."

"I can't go," Umphy muttered angrily, clutching his flute tightly to his chest. "You know darn well I can't go." It was just like Kestern to make fun of him like that! The dragonets practiced their flying skills from the height of a hundred-foot plateau that rose out of the sea close to the coves. Umphy, however, was far too young, and his wings, delicate in their fibers, were not yet strong enough to take the wind. Umphy's mother had repeatedly told him never to approach the plateau, and Kestern bullied and teased his little brother for being the runt of the family. Umphy was frustrated by his incapacities and his brother's teasing did not help. But today Kestern only shrugged and smiled good-naturedly.

"Suit yourself. I thought you'd like to at least try. But if you're too scared—"

"I am not!"

"You are, too! Look, I bet today will be your lucky day. Come on, what's it hurt to try? I'll rescue you if you fall or something."

Umphy carefully laid his flute down on the sand. "If you promise . . ."

"Sure," Kestern's yellow eyes twinkled. "I'll even give you some pointers on how to fly."

Inside the cave, the female dragon, Rana, watched her little ones playing and smiled. A dragonet's young stages of life were most important for learning to trust their senses and to develop various motor skills and flexibility that would aid them in battle someday. Experience was a dragon's most powerful teacher.

Rana's mate, Eitelve Firetongue, stood beside her and covered her tenderly with a wing. He was a large, powerful dragon with horns that sprouted from his head and curved wickedly down around his jaw. Muscles rippled beneath the black sheen of his scales, and yellow claws gripped the earth. Few other dragons ever crossed him. He was not a purebred Green Dragon, nor had his kin been a gentle species. Opposites dwelled in him; he was violent and temperamental like a storm at sea and yet as kind and gentle as a summer breeze. But he had always been aware of himself, inside and out, and suppressed his raging emotions in order to be a protective husband and responsible father. "Did Umphy go to play with his siblings?"

"Why should he not? He's old enough to look after himself." If Eitelve was a smoldering volcano, his mate, Rana, was the soft rain that calmed his temper. She and her mate had been divided once over their youngest son. Runts were an impediment to a clan, but Rana opposed her husband's traditional view of the deadly solution and raised her son like her other children. Nevertheless, Eitelve still fretted and worried in his strong, silent way.

"Age does not always incur wisdom. Umphy is curious and irresponsible. Lately, we haven't been able to keep him still for five minutes before he is off snuffling after some new interest."

"His mind is opening to the world."

Eitelve raised one eyebrow skeptically. "I hope so, for his sake. We cannot afford to have mindless youngsters in the clan, Rana. Not now. But neither can we have curious dragonets who snuffle after every hermit crab that walks by. These are dangerous times we're living in."

"You speak as though you've heard some news." Rana willed herself to stay calm. Eitelve turned away from his wife to watch the dragonets playing outside. He seemed hesitant.

7

"I was speaking to Deral of the Rockflower clan. He lives closer to the southwest."

"I remember him. He took a mate from our clan almost ten years ago, Ophria. She was my childhood playmate. I remember she said that Deral lives too close to the land of Hebaruin for her taste."

"It is his beneficial location. He has a spy-chain down there; creatures report just about anything and everything to him, and then he passes the information along. He thought I should know."

"Know about what? What is it, Eitelve?"

"There's talk down there, love. Talk of the Black Dragon. Of Morbane."

A heavy silence hung in the air. *Black Dragon, Black Death,* Rana's father used to say. *And when there is Black Death, Black Hope as well.* The Guardians feared the Black Dragon of the South more than any other foe. Rana came and stood beside her husband, shoulder to shoulder. "What did Deral say?"

"The South has had recent earthquakes and volcanic eruptions. The Tree of Death is shifting. They say Morbane is restless."

"Eitelve, stop beating around the bush and tell me. Has Morbane risen?"

There was a long silence before the master replied to his mate.

"Not yet. But they say soon."

High up on the rocks, Umphy watched Kestern dive off the rim of the plateau and soar around the ocean waves, hooting as loud as he could. Umphy trembled in anticipation. He knew that his own wings were too weak for flight yet, but his courage and will were both strong as iron. He felt as though he could conquer the world! He could hardly wait to try flying.

Kestern came soaring back with a hoot and a holler, smiling in mock cheerfulness at his brother. The wind had picked up slightly, but Umphy was grateful for that. It would lend him aid for his wings.

"It's your turn," Kestern offered, with the innocence of a newborn lamb.

"How do I do that?" Umphy asked, all agog.

"Take a giant running leap and spread your wings. Catch the wind with 'em. You'll have the time of your life, I promise."

"Is that a squall coming up?" Umphy pointed to a thin line of gray clouds on the horizon.

"It won't touch us for several hours yet. Come on, what are you waiting for? Don't be nervous. Hurry up and jump!" Kestern's look of brotherly affection turned into one of impatience.

Umphy took a deep breath and ran full-speed ahead at the edge of the plateau. He spread his wings and took a mighty leap into space, feeling, for a brief instant, the warmth of the sun on his face and the wind through his fuzz.

Then he began to fall.

Umphy, panicking, tried to flap his wings, but the underdeveloped skeletal structure and thin-veined webbing was not fit yet for flight. Umphy felt a searing pain through one wing as a tendon snapped brutally, and both wings crumpled like paper as he fell like a stone a hundred feet to the cold water below. Umphy screamed and clutched for support, but his paws clamped down on nothing but air. A rush of wind passed him, and then pain shot through his body as he hit the pounding waves of the sea below. Salt water filled his nostrils as he inhaled sharply, and then he couldn't breathe and the world went dark as he sank like a stone.

Chapter 2

"I am pleased and proud to recognize those young ones in our clan who have successfully achieved the rank of keldora today."

A large, elderly drakona stood on a small ridge overlooking the beach of the Eastern shore. She was the Matriarch of the Firespring Clan. Advanced in wisdom and strength, she had seen her share of life, love, and even war. She was the natural leader. The other dragons looked up at her with grave respect. Standing in front of her were six fine-looking dragonets. They faced their elders with fierce pride and joy as the firm voice of the Matriarch boomed out over the sands.

"We all know why we celebrate this ancient custom of the Recognition. Each dragon passes through stages of life. In their young bolora years they learn by experience and grow in knowledge. We now gladly accept them into our community as proper adults, to begin their next stage of life: that of keldora, in which they will choose their path of life and continue to grow as adults. But I would say a few words to you all in commemoration of this great day."

One of the new keldoras, a tough-looking dragon with mischievous gray eyes, grinned and spoke out of the corner of his mouth to the bigger dragon beside him.

"Here she goes again, Tarragon. I told you she'd do it."

The other dragon merely chuckled and tried to keep a proud, straight face. Despite having heard this speech numerous times before, it never really bored him.

"Friends and Beloved Kin, let us, for a moment, remember our heritage. Long ago, when the world was newly created, our

Ancestor, the Brown Dragon, was given the gift of Guardianship. His descendants have inherited that power in their blood. It is what enabled us to be Guardians of the land of Balské, peacemakers, lovers, and defenders of all that is right and just. Our race flourished like the jungles of the midlands, and all things living respected us. We cultivated light and beauty, and brought the Sweet Magic into being, a Great Power that only served the Illuminator, Enovan. Some dragons had the ability to turn their spiritual gift into a physical reality, like a pearl in an oyster. The Orb built up layer by layer inside a dragon's stomach, to eventually be given birth later in life. The keeper of the Orb was given long life, riches beyond their wildest dreams, power beyond measure, and success forever.

"But then," the Matriarch growled, and her eyes grew dark. "The Black Dragons came. They dared to make war against us and brought their lies, terror, and plague to the land! They desired our Secret, and killed many dragons to find it. The seven Orbs were stolen and placed in the iron crown of the Southern Emperor, and he drove the cursed Black Dragon, Morbane, to worse acts of atrocity. The land was burned and thousands died by the sword. The realm of the South, Hebaruin, built up a dark kingdom. The Black Dragons drove us away into hiding, and here we have stayed for over two thousand years. And so, even as we linger here in fear, we hold on to hope, for there is a prophecy."

"Oh, great, here it goes." The keldora beside Tarragon rolled his eyes impatiently, and Tarragon chuckled, chiding his friend out of the corner of his mouth.

"Oh, shush, Jorgan. I like this part."

The Matriarch seemed to grow taller in her storytelling. Her neck stretched upwards, and she stood rigidly, chanting loudly, her wings spread in submission to Fate.

Seven will be lost and found again.
The eighth shall be the sign of hope.
When they are placed within the Tree

*Thy spirit will be renewed upon the earth
The weak will shine forth to aid the mighty.
The mighty will rise to guard again.
The twain will slay the Evil Worm;
Evil will fall, his people will scatter,
And peace will walk abroad once more.
And a New Spring will come to Balské.*

"Two dragons shall be born—the heirs of the Brown Dragon. One shall hold the Eighth Orb, and the other will hold within him the spirit of the Brown Dragon. The Heirs of the Brown Dragon shall bring the Guardians back to the land when evil is destroyed and the Eighth Orb is placed within the Tree of Life.

And that is why I say that we must take pride in these young ones, for our future lies with them. They will uphold and cherish the prophecy, and perhaps even see its fruition in their time. But as for me, I am growing old, and will be with you only for a little while yet. So I am proud to announce that I have chosen a successor for myself, one whom I will train, and that you will one day look to for guidance."

There were murmurs of surprise among the dragons. As a rule, Matriarchs did not choose their successors. Instead, older drakonas who had given birth to and raised their last brood fought each other for the position. The honor a Matriarch carried was very great, and though she could neither mate nor give birth again, she held the authority to direct the community as she saw fit, ruling over it in her age and wisdom. Only when she passed away could another drakona take her place. The dragons murmured and wondered who this fortunate successor could possibly be.

The Matriarch stretched her neck towards the row of keldoras beneath her. She breathed deeply, and fire shot from her nostrils, scorching the back of a young female, whose eyes widened in pain, but said nothing.

"I have given the Lady Padina my mark. Let her and these others go forth now to bring their talents and visions for the future to this community, so that we may continue to live in peace and in hope for the day when our heroes will rise and bid us follow them to glory against our enemy!"

"That was very good," Jorgan said a little while later, as the clan dragons mingled with one another, talking and congratulating the new keldoras. "I clocked that speech a little under half an hour."

"And you made such a fuss," Padina laughed. She was a pretty young dragon with soft brown eyes and sleek, muscled limbs.

"Easy for you to say! You got made into the Matriarch's successor! That's an honor most females would die for, Padina. And it's so rare."

"I can't say I wanted it," she replied with a sigh. "I was actually hoping to apprentice myself to the healer."

"Don't be ridiculous," snorted Jorgan. "Then you probably would have ended up marrying a male like Venier, and you know that would break my heart, honey."

She swiped a paw at him playfully. "I shan't marry anyone, leastwise Venier. He's too bloodthirsty for me; he hangs around that nasty Razot too much."

Tarragon chuckled. "Padina, just saying that will break all the male hearts in our clan. You're a very pretty young female!"

Padina blushed. Tarragon was by far the strongest keldora, as massive and silent as an ancient cliff that has withstood the pounding of a sea in a storm. For all his youth, he was unusually large and healthy, with rippling muscles and a proud glance that made all the females sigh longingly. But he was also very quiet, and preferred the company of a few rather than the many. Society and its rules and traditions bored and frustrated him terribly. He longed to prove himself a hero amidst the stiff-necked elders of his community to show them that the old codes were dead, and it would only be the young and daring that could leave a mark on history. His radical ideas both shocked and pleased his peers, and, of course, made all the females think very highly of him and his independent nature.

"Oh, Tar," Padina said shyly. "You know you've always had my favor."

"Hey, what about me?" Jorgan protested.

"You're a brother to me, Jor."

"That's what comes of having muscles," he sighed, looking enviously at Tarragon. "I don't get it. What did your parents feed you, anyway? You're almost full-grown, and you're as old as I am. It isn't fair. How am I supposed to marry a good-looking lass if I've got you for competition?"

"I'll just have to marry outside my clan," Tarragon chuckled. "Or you will. I hear the Green Dragons of the West Coast have particularly docile, clever females."

"Honestly!" Padina tossed her head. "The way you two carry on—anyone would think you had marriage on your minds. You cannot marry until you master a female in battle. We're naturally superior because—"

"Because your protective instincts are higher, yes, we've heard it before." Jorgan rolled his eyes. "But it doesn't hurt to plan ahead, does it? Besides, I wouldn't like to marry right now anyway. I'm apprenticing myself to the flight instructor. I'd like to train young dragonets in the art of speed-racing."

"You would," Padina rolled her eyes. "What about you, Tarragon?"

"I'd like to travel," he said thoughtfully, though he did not tell his friends the whole truth of his ambitions. Tarragon wanted, more than anything else in the world, to be a father. He admired his own paternal guardian for his kindness, gentility, intelligence, strong sense of justice, and protective instincts. Tarragon himself was a natural leader among his peers and the younger dragons. They gravitated to him because of his strength and humor. He knew how to take care of them. They trusted him.

"Traveling—now there's an idea," said Jorgan enthusiastically. "Tarragon, we should both go. We'll fly away and be heroes in a distant country and come back covered with ribbons and medals of honor. Then we'll *both* have a fair chance at marriage!" He turned hopefully to Padina. "If we came back decorated, would you let us duel over you?"

"Duel away," Padina said airily. "But I really don't intend to marry."

"Darn. My heart's gone and broke. How's yours, Tar?"

"Still hale and healthy," the young dragon laughed. "It has to be, if I'm to live under Matriarch Padina!" He ducked to avoid getting swiped.

"Tarragon? Where's my lad?" Tarragon's father, Gaunta, wove his way through the crowd and nuzzled his son's cheek. "There you are. Well done, my boy! I'm so proud of you. Congratulations, Padina. And to you, Jorgan. My, aren't you all fine-looking keldoras!"

"Thank you, sir," Padina said politely. Gaunta was smaller than most male dragons, having been born a runt. It was a stroke of good fortune for him to wed the daughter of a prominent Green Dragon Master. A wizard had hatched her from an egg, brought her up, and arranged the marriage himself. Tarragon had never known the name of the wizard, though he was sure such a man must be very clever to have brought together two fine dragons. The fortuitous match earned Gaunta some small respect.

"Tarragon, your sisters have a present for you," Gaunta lifted his wing to reveal all three of the keldora's little sisters, who clumped together and held up a hunk of raw deer meet.

"For YOU!!" they chorused in tiny squeaks.

"Oh, gosh!" Tarragon gasped. Keldoras were formally allowed now, as was custom, to eat "land meat." Gaunta's eyes shone brightly as he explained how he had caught the deer and gave a bit of it to the females to give their big brother. Tarragon thanked his sisters and inhaled the delicious scent eagerly. He had every intention of sharing it with his friends, when a shadow fell over them.

"Are you sure he's earned that, Gaunta?" The cold, sneering tone could come from but one dragon in the clan: Razot, an unusually large and powerful dragon rumored to be a Black Dragon crossbreed. "After all, this little one has nothing to his name but mere size and his mother's treasure. Why waste good stuff on him?"

"I think, Razot, that this is my son, not yours, and I'll do with him as I see fit," Gaunta replied coolly, ignoring the look of surprise and indignation on Tarragon's face. Everyone in the clan knew full-well that Razot was jealous of Gaunta's marriage to the prettiest drakona, and so now doubly jealous of the strong, healthy keldora who was well-known for his fighting abilities—who could present a threat someday. Razot turned an ugly, mocking face back to Gaunta.

"Hard to believe he's your son," he sneered. "After all, such a fine-looking lad with those strong limbs could never have been born of some crazy old man's pupil and her runt husband!"

Gaunta's eyes flashed. At this point, all conversation in the clan had died down, and all heads were turned in the direction of the speakers. Tarragon's mother started to move forward, but one of the females held her back. A challenge had been offered. It was now Gaunta's obligation to accept the challenge or be disgraced. Not even his wife could interfere.

"Leave Dana out of it," Gaunta said quietly.

"Why? Afraid you won't be able to properly defend her?" Razot taunted, looking for a fight.

"This is not the time, nor the place."

"I'd say it's perfect. Little Tarragon will have a chance to learn from the best." Razot flexed his muscles. "And Dana just might discover what she's missed all these years!"

"I said, leave my wife out of it!" Gaunta snorted violently, and his eyes flashed again. Tarragon had dropped the deer meat in confusion and fear; his sisters huddled about him, trembling, as they watched the interaction between their father and the dragon they all feared and hated.

Razot struck so suddenly that Gaunta was knocked off his feet, a wound gouged into his hip. Obliged to protect himself, Tarragon's father staggered to his feet and assumed a fighting stance. The rest of the dragons immediately pushed Tarragon out of the way in their rush to see the fight. Tarragon found himself on the outside of the circle of hooting dragons, his arms clutched around his sisters.

"He'll murder him!" Padina's voice shrieked above the din. "Somebody stop them!"

"It's too late; the code says that a master must fight to the death to protect his wife's honor," said another dragon. Tarragon glared at the speaker.

"My father can't fight Razot and win! *I'll* fight him!"

"Stay out of it, young Tarragon," said the elder quietly.

Tarragon was seething with rage. The Code of the Guardians stated very clearly that once a dragon offered another dragon a challenge, it was to be met with dignity, and no other creature could interfere. It was nature's way of weeding out the weaker dragons. But Tarragon cared nothing for this rule. It was an unfair fight, and Tarragon hated unfair fights. He was used to interfering between bullies and their victims when a challenge was made, a habit that constantly got him into trouble. But Tarragon's protective instincts were unlike any others in his clan. He pushed his way through the crowd and into the inner ring where his father battled Razot.

He struck the pose for combat and bared his teeth.

Razot laughed. "What have we here? If it isn't little Tarragon, come to save his daddy! Looking for your first kill, eh, keldora? Gaunta, this really *is* humiliating for you."

"Why don't you face me down, eh?" Tarragon snapped. "You think it so high and mighty to pick on weaker males and helpless females and young dragons. Why don't you try me for size?"

Razot chuckled loudly. "Shouldn't you be doing something useful, rather than fighting your father's fights?"

"You're afraid," the keldora taunted. "You're nothing but a murdering scumbag and a half-blooded Black Dragon's spawn who couldn't find a proper mate! Corward!"

There was a dreadful silence among the other dragons. Tarragon had just violated two codes at once: he had interfered in a fight, and he was now boldly disrespecting a full-grown adult. But Tarragon thought nothing of this.

Razot's eyes were murderous.

"So," he hissed. "The son of Gaunta is a liar and an insulting little fool as well as an arrogant idiot." He pawed the ground and jerked his head up and down impatiently like a wild animal barely able to restrain himself. "Get that little streak of green slime out of the ring, Gaunta, or I'll fry him where he stands!"

Tarragon did not move. "If you kill my father, I'll tell the whole world that you're a murdering crossbreed! You're nothing but mud beneath a real Guardian's feet!"

"MOVE YOUR SON, GAUNTA!" Razot's voice became a roar.

"Tarragon, go back to the cave!" Gaunta pleaded. But his son boldly stood his ground.

Razot lunged forward, and Tarragon felt sharp teeth close over his leg as the furious adult tried to viciously drag him away. Tarragon cried out and twisted, slashing viciously over Razot's muzzle. The pressure on his leg lifted, and the keldora scrambled backwards, assuming the stance for combat. Razot hesitated for only a moment before charging forward. The two dragons slammed together like boulders, on their hind feet, grappling at the shoulders. Bystanders gasped in amazement. Razot was the only undefeated dragon in the entire clan. His fighting skills were infamous. Until now, no one had ever seen another dragon—much less a keldora!—match the strength and power of Razot in battle. Every muscle in Tarragon's body stood out as he pushed against his foe. Razot bit into the young keldora's neck, a move that usually took other opponents off guard. Tarragon flinched and then hooked his leg underneath

Razot's, tumbling him to the ground. Another gasp went around the circle of onlookers.

Razot wrenched himself off the sand. His eyes burned murderously. Never before had he been tumbled like that, and by a mere keldora, too! Bellowing like a wounded bull, the enraged dragon thundered forward again. Tarragon braced himself once more and met the oncoming dragon on his hind legs. They slammed together again. Tarragon held his ground, every muscle bulging. Dust and rocks flew up as the two dragons grappled back and forth, blow for blow, biting and scratching. Razot pushed against him cruelly, applying his entire weight. Tarragon felt his legs begin to buckle as the larger dragon pushed him down slowly.

Suddenly, the keldora dropped to the ground. Razot overbalanced and tumbled face-first into the rocky seashore. Spitting out sand and rocks, he turned furiously on Tarragon. "YOU LITTLE LIZARD'S SPAWN—I WILL KILL YOU FOR THAT!"

"ENOUGH!!"

The Matriarch had spoken. Every dragon froze. Razot halted where he stood, but Tarragon, infuriated, had to be restrained by at least three strong adult males. The Matriarch came forward, eyes blazing and stood between Razot and Tarragon. The scene was unheard-of. Though she was the only one with a right to interrupt a fight, this was the first time a Matriarch had ever done so. She faced Razot boldly, contempt dripping like venom from her tongue.

"The devil take you!" she snarled viciously. "Unworthy foe! If you come forward to slay a keldora, you'll have me to reckon with!" She flexed her muscles. Razot backed down. To fight a keldora was one thing, but to fight the Matriarch was the highest form of disrespect possible. "You are in black disgrace," the Matriarch continued. "Get your worthless carcass back to your dwelling and do not come out by the light of this day again! We'll deal with you later. Gaunta, stand by that rock and be silent. Your failure to protect your wife's honor casts deep shame over you. Tarragon, stay where you are!"

Tarragon did not have to be asked twice. He was by no means exhausted by his confrontation with the bully; on the contrary, he felt exuberant and lively. That changed when the Matriarch fixed him with her stern glare. There was a grave silence as she spoke again, her words and voice like the icy wind from the northern mountains.

"Look at me!"

He faced her boldly. Clear blue eyes met the flashing violet ones. "Are you proud of yourself? Thought you could handle a full-grown adult and save your father's shamed hide? Your interference might have been the death of you."

Tarragon's ire was up. "My father couldn't defeat Razot even on a good day, and you know it! Your stupid rules about defending his wife's honor would have killed him, and what then?"

"*Silence*!" the Matriarch hissed. Tarragon wilted visibly as she stalked up to him, her shadow completely engulfing him like a storm-cloud. She snorted and stomped her foot angrily. "You are in disgrace, Tarragon. Never have I had to deal with a more stubborn, rebellious little upstart in all my years of living! We will hold council and decide upon a fitting punishment. In the meantime, you are hereby ostracized from the rest of the clan, and no one may speak to you, nor may you seek out their society!"

Tarragon snapped his teeth and jerked his head to the right. It was a sign of his acceptance of the edict upon himself, but inwardly he fumed. Didn't they understand that if he hadn't stepped in to save his father, Razot would have killed Gaunta and taken Dana? He tried to look at his parents for help, and found, to his shock, that they both turned from him. His mother hung her head in grief and shame, and Gaunta limped dejectedly away, trailing blood from his wound. Tarragon suddenly felt numb and lost.

His new stage of life certainly wasn't getting off on the right foot.

Chapter 3

Umphy felt as though he were running through a dark forest, thick with weeds and low-brush undergrowth. At every turn he made, he found himself in a new, awkward position; sometimes he was running upside down, or floating on his back. Other times the landscape changed rapidly, and trees melted into monsters that snapped at his heels but never caught him. His feet seemed weighted down by iron chains, and he panicked, screaming out for his mother. His back ached with pain, and his stomach burned with an inner fire.

As he floundered around in the darkness, he thought that he heard voices above his head, inside the forest, and all around him.

"Such a stupid trick! It's just like Kestern to do such a thing!"

"Good thing Possa had been keeping an eye on them both . . . saved his life."

"He's good as dead now. His wings are shattered."

"Send for a wizard!"

"I won't have them. They are not wanted here. Neither is this one."

Umphy felt someone slip something into his paw and he instinctively clutched it, feeling the smooth white wood of his flute. Was that Possa leaning over him? He could not see her clearly; instead, he felt her tears falling on his nose and trickling down his jaw. She was crying. *I was going to give you a golden statue*, he protested, trying to speak, but nothing came out except a low moan of pain.

The sun was just beginning to set when Eitelve left the cave. Umphy was cradled in a sling about Eitelve's neck, his wooden flute clutched tightly in his paw. He was unconscious and did not catch the last glimpse of his home, nor the restless waters with its foamy waves and rocky crags. Nor did he hear the pounding of the waves against the shore, or smell the last of the salt air. Eitelve carried him up the steep slope rising from the shoreline to the hills above the sea, where cliffs of rock and overhanging grass overlooked the eternal stretch of blue water. At the top the master paused, looking from the bundle to the sharp rocks below. Then he shook his head and continued on.

When the sun had rising to its morning height, Eitelve finally stopped and settled his bundle on the ground. They were in front of the forest of Poloran, one of the most expansive forests in the west. Eitelve paused and looked down at his son. A struggle passed through him and several times he opened his mouth as if to say something, but words were useless here. He shook his head again and turned away gruffly.

He did not look back.

Umphy lay at the edge of the forest, regaining his consciousness slowly. He was terribly wet from his fall into the ocean, and his body ached, having hit the water with tremendous force. His wings, however, dragged helplessly, being torn beyond the attention of a mortal healer. Fierce pain shot through them into the little dragon's body. It was the first thing he could concentrate on at the moment. The second thing he realized was that he was all alone. His mother and father and six siblings were nowhere to be seen.

The little dragon began to cry helplessly. His worst fear in the world had been realized: as an injured runt, he was an impediment to the clan, and he had been kicked out.

A distant rumble between the overhead clouds reminded the little dragon that the squall he had seen earlier was drawing closer. He had to find shelter. His survival instincts kicking in, Umphy surveyed the forest before him hopefully. Perhaps in there he might find a place of refuge, or a helpful animal, and some food. His broken wings dragged painfully, but as he wandered into the forest, Umphy forgot his fear and pain.

What a beautiful, new world! He had never seen a chipmunk before, or seen such massive trees with their muscled limbs and long fronds! He had never before touched leaves, wood, or anything growing within the land, save grass. Mud squelched between his toes. Brightly-colored flowers brushed by his nose, tickling it. But the beautiful landscape was hushed and growing darker as he moved farther and farther into the heart of the forest.

As Umphy passed through the forest, he suddenly heard the far-off baying of hounds and the sound of horses as they crashed through the undergrowth. The noises were headed directly his way. Nervously, the little dragon looked around, and spotted a large bora tree, with a thick, knotted trunk and twisted limbs stretching high into the canopy above. Creeping over slowly, Umphy proceeded to climb a tree for the first time, and hid himself well in the foliage, having a dragon's natural talent for camouflage. The noises became louder, and then a group of humans burst into the woodland glade. Two men and a woman rode horseback, wearing clothes of animal skins and bearing dangerous-looking weapons. Sniffing the ground around the horse hooves were two hounds. They immediately followed Umphy's trail to the bora tree, and reared up on their hind legs against the trunk, howling. One of the men threw a rock at them.

"Yaahh, shut up! *Shut up*! Deh, your stupid hounds are after butter-fruits again!" he laughed, a harsh, coarse sound. The woman beside him snickered and notched an arrow in her bow.

"Just in case . . ." She took aim and let it fly; it stuck, quivering, into the very branch that Umphy was holding onto for dear life. He swallowed and forced himself not to cry out. Down below, the woman shrugged. "Nothing. This forest is barren. I told you so!"

The younger man spat on the ground. "It's that damned wizard. He's put a curse on it, I tell you! Give me my knife. I'll flay him to doll-rags, Darkness take him!"

"You're a fool," snapped the older man. "We have no powers that could ever match against a wizard's. You'd be doing yourself an injustice. We'll hunt in the plains. It'll be sporting to chase the herds." He gave a low, nasty chuckle.

"The plains are deadly grounds, now," the woman said flatly, and the two men turned to look at her. "Travel has been discouraged. The Southerners are moving again. They have stationed their guards at every inn and village gate along the road to the north, and if we kill for food outside our boundaries, we pay taxes to the South for robbing them of their meat."

"That ain't fair!" yelled the younger man. "We already pay taxes to 'em for use of their weapons."

"Ooh, poor you. Why don't you go and tell Fordomt how you feel?" crooned the woman. "I'm sure he'll feel sorry enough for you to put you out of your misery."

The young man spat. "I'd tell him to save his sympathy for those who will be overtaken by Morbane. He won't sit still for very long, eh?"

The older man chuckled grimly. "Enovan help the dragon he tracks down."

"You have nothing to laugh about," the woman snapped. "You'd best hope to the heavens Morbane stays locked in his muddy old hole beneath the Tree of Death. If he rises, that means only one thing: he's sensed the White Orb, the eighth and final. Fordomt will try to make a move on it as soon as he can locate it. He'll be sending out every witch, demon, monster, and ghost that he can summon. That's why the Southerners are stationed in the villages! Anyone with information on the dragon clans will be apprehended and questioned. The Green Dragons will be sought out again and routed through until the last Orb is located. Do you know what will happen then? War! And if Hebaruin wins, you'll have more to worry about than taxes," she told the young man.

There was a heavy silence in the air before the young man spat on the ground. "Yahh, never mind this political nonsense. I want meat on my table tonight. Let's continue our hunt. No forest is ever completely barren. If I can manage a squirrel, I'll count myself content!"

As the hoof-beats died away, Umphy slowly crept down out of the tree and started running in the opposite direction. After a few hours of wandering he broke through the darkened foliage to a small clearing. Moonlight filtered through the eaves of the trees to dance around the soft carpet of grass and wildflowers that grew abundantly between the rocks and on either side of a pretty little stream that trickled through the glade. Growing close to the stream was a perfect ring of mushrooms—a fairy ring! A place of healing and protection. The little dragon promptly plopped himself down in the center of the mushrooms and proceeded to doze.

"I say, young fellow, you *do* know there's a forest curfew, don't you?"

Umphy looked up, startled. A large black raven sat upon an overhead branch, looking down keenly at him. "I mean, really! The idea. Past your bedtime, young fellow, and you're in dangerous territory. Don't you know? I've seen grisly deaths out here that would turn any villain's stomach. I've seen large, hairy spiders, and gluttonous wolves, and other, older, uglier things that run amok in these woods at night! Don't be an idiot, young fellow, and go back. Run away to your mother, there's a good lad!"

Umphy burst into tears. The raven blinked twice, shifted uncomfortably, and then hopped from one foot to the other.

"Don't cry, young fellow, I can't stand it! I can't endure all that caterwauling! Egads, I didn't think I would set you off so dreadfully."

"I h-h-haven't got a m-m-mother!" Umphy sobbed, realizing for the first time how alone he really was.

"Oh, I say! Everyone has a mother. What's the matter? Did yours die?"

Umphy shook his head unhappily. "I've been b-b-banished."

"Banished! For what? Oh, I see, your wings are torn. I say, what rotten luck. I'd hate to lose my wings. They're valuable things. What's your name, my fine fellow? Might as well get it while we're chatting."

"Um-Um-Umphy." The little dragon's tears subsided and he wiped furiously at his eyes with both paws. The raven cawed with laughter.

"Umphy? What a strange name. I'm Arwos Ebonfeather; pleased and charmed to make your acquaintance, young fellow! I say, you look positively lost. Do you have any idea where you're going? No? Well, well, you're like me! I haven't a clue where I'm going, either! I used to work for a wizard over in the East. He adopted me after my folks kicked me out of the nest. Wonderful man! He taught me a bit of magic. I know a few incantations. But then he went and got himself an apprentice. Can you believe it? All those years I served him so darned faithfully—the man took on an apprentice! Ungrateful, that's what he was. After he kicked me out, I didn't know where I was going or what I was going to do. I just kind of wandered around, looking for some kind of meaning to my life. Do you know, traveling is the best way to get an education. I've learned many a lesson from vagabond Elves, gypsy caravans, city philosophers, and the best gamblers in the taverns." He smiled down at the young dragon. "I say, you really do look like you're in some pain, there. Did you know there's a wizard in this forest? He's somewhat of a hermit, but the best darn healer around for miles. He could fix your wings up, you know."

Umphy hesitated. His father had always disapproved of wizards and healers because their uses did not permit a dragon his independence and self-preservation. A dragon that could not support himself without help was no dragon at all. Umphy did not want to think of himself as so weak that he could not bear the pain and heal over the course of time. But Arwos, looking at him, guessed his thoughts precisely.

"Your wings won't heal overnight, you know. They're your strongest asset besides breathing fire. I'd take the advice of my new friend Arwos, if I was you, and go see the forest wizard immediately."

"Could you take me to him?"

"It would be an honor, young fellow." Arwos bowed. "We must be careful, though. I heard noises earlier. It seems that we have hunters in here again, and Enovan only knows what they'll do if they see you. Dragons are neither loved nor trusted anymore. You'd either end up as a sideshow amusement or the feature at a banquet, all dressed up with stuffing and an apple in your mouth. Come with me, but do as I say, and be quiet."

They quietly left the moonlit glade behind. Several times Arwos stopped, bidding Umphy to freeze, and then they would move on, the large raven fluttering quietly from branch to branch.

Suddenly, from out of nowhere, a huge black hound sprang forward with a blood-curdling, baying yelp, and sank its teeth into Umphy's wounded wing. The little dragon screamed and retaliated by biting the soft nose of the creature; it let go with a whine, and Umphy broke into a run. Arwos squawked and flew beside him, shouting out "Left!" and "Right!" every now and then so the little dragon could avoid hitting trees. But dragons were not gifted with long, swift legs, and the hounds were gaining on Umphy. He could hear the excited whoops of the humans behind him, and he began to cry in despair.

"AH-HA!! HAVE AT YOU, DEMON DOGS!! BEGONE!!"

There was a blinding flash, and Umphy screeched to a halt. Something flew past him in a flurry of green and gray robes.

"BEWARE MY MIGHTY WRATH!! FLEE THIS PLACE IF YOU VALUE YOUR SKINS!! BEGONE, LEST I SET THE SPIRITS OF THE FOREST UPON YE!!"

Umphy froze to the ground and covered his eyes. The noises went away—very quickly, in fact.

"There, that ought to do it. Well, well, what have we here?"

Warm, grandfatherly hands reached down and plucked Umphy from the ground. The little dragon found himself staring into two twinkling eyes of midnight-blue. Then the man spread a warm blanket over Umphy. Whether the cloth was enchanted or not, it had the desired effect upon the exhausted little dragon. He closed his eyes again and drifted off into a deep sleep.

The sound of thunder woke him up suddenly. The storm had finally hit, and there was a downpour outside. But Umphy was indoors, snuggled in a little nest of furs beside a cozy, crackling fireplace. His body ached, but the warmth of the little room in which he lay eased the pain. He sat up and looked around. The circular stone hut was well-thatched with dried mud and moss, built thick and warm for the cold winds that blew in from the northwest coast. The dirt floor was laid with colorful hooked rugs. Heaped bundles of dried herbs hung from the ceiling beams amidst copper pots and clay wind-chimes. Light from the little fireplace danced over the sparse oak furnishings, including a tall bookshelf laden with leather-bound books, scrolls, and rows of dusty bottles with odd labels: Dreamdust, Eyewater, Fernfingers, Lizardcheeks, and things like that. An appetizing aroma filled the little hut as a great black pot simmered and bubbled merrily over the fire.

"Hmm. You know, there's no sense in boiling the water with the raw birch leaves. It's best to let them dry first—"

"But you were supposed to add the 'shroom paste after the first batch of red-ant powder."

"And the hot-peppers. Did you remember the hot peppers?"

Umphy turned and saw an old man sitting in a chair, bent over an old book. He was cloaked in robes of green and gray, and his black boots were soiled with forest grime. He had a long white beard that reached below his belly, and ended at his knees. Upon his head was a tall conical hat, with no brim, and his eyes twinkled as he scoured the book. Arwos was perched on the man's shoulder. He looked comfortable enough, and was talking with the man as if he knew him. Umphy cleared his throat. The old man, still hunched over his books, did not even bat an eye.

"—birch leaves dried, and then mixed with chopped liver of a march hare and four—hm, better make it six or seven—cups of sugar—hello there, Umphy! Don't mind me; I'm exploring routes for an energy drink. With all the pepper and sugar, something ought to get people moving faster, eh? Don't worry. You're quite safe. Just rest for now, and our midnight snack will be on the table shortly!"

Umphy had never eaten anything besides a thick soup that his mother prepared using sea-water, fresh seaweed, the delicate white insides of fish, and the soft bits of oysters and clams. He was surprised and excited to be seated at a table with a wooden bowl and spoon as the man set out fragrant yellow cheese, crisp red apples, honey-butter, a loaf of white bread, a pitcher of creamy goat milk, and a bowl of plump, juicy strawberries. One by one, the man brought the bowls over to the pot by the stove, heaping them full of a rich, aromatic stew. When the grace had been said, the man beamed. "Don't inhale it all at once," he advised, and dug in. Beside him, Arwos splashed his beak in and began to gulp down the stew noisily, making a very annoying warbling noise in his throat. Umphy lifted his spoon and politely took tiny bites. The stew was a delicious concoction of salted venison, fresh vegetables, and a thick sauce made from the purest water and the richest herbal seasoning. Umphy was ravenous, and ate everything offered.

When everyone was quite full, and a heap of greasy dishes sat piled on the table, all three persons lay back in their chairs with contented sighs. The man looked over at Umphy, chuckling.

"I had a feeling that Arwos Ebonfeather was going to drag in something fascinating from the forest. He has the strange habit of finding the most interesting oddities and placing them on my doorstep. Not that you're odd, mind you. But I haven't seen a dragon for years."

"How did you find us?" Arwos asked. "We were at least a mile or so from your home."

"I was out picking mushrooms, and I heard the commotion," the man was idly picking moss from between the table cracks. "It wasn't all that hard! Just follow your ears, I always say. I traveled by incantation this time—thought it'd be quicker, and I was right. This is the third time this week that those ridiculous Deerskins have hunted around my territory. Some people! They never learn. I don't know why I even bother. But anyway, I'm bothering about you, young man! Arwos told me you're looking for a wizard to heal your wings."

"Are you a wizard, sir?"

"Well, sort of—I am not the same wizard that I was years and years back, but I daresay I can still do some handy-dandy levitation. I have lived here for many years since . . ." he tried counting the years on his fingers, messed up, and then gave up. "Well, never mind that! Let's take a look at those wings, shall we? What happened?"

Umphy explained about Kestern and the plateau. The wizard poked, prodded, and handled the torn fibers gently.

"Shame, shame, it's a terrible shame. And you're so young. Only a bolora, right? Not yet a keldora? I thought as much. Well, luckily they tore now and not later in life, when it gets more difficult to do the patchwork. I can have you mended in a jiffy. Young things like yourself always bounce back after a fall or two. No, don't try to thank me! Let me tell you, back in the days, I used to be a proper dragon's medicine man! They called upon me if ever the females were having difficulties in labor, or if they had torn wings or infant sicknesses. Let me tell you the story about the white dragon and her bad tooth . . ."

So the wizard worked with his bandages and medicines and salves, massaging and kneading, and healing gently with his skills while telling tale after tale of his "doctoring" in the dragon communities.

"What made you stop?" Umphy asked.

"The War," sighed the wizard. "During the Wizard Wars, I in my youth joined a band of spies for the Rebellion against the South, and we delivered information to and from the kingdoms in the north on the movements of our enemies. At that time, I fell in love." The wizard sighed again wistfully. "I almost married her, a golden girl with eyes like the pristine little violets of the mountains. However, she turned out to be the niece of a prominent official who was loyal to the South, and my entire group was discovered. Some of us were killed, and others were sent to be slaves in the mining pits of the South. I escaped with two others, though where they are now I do not know. I came here to this forest, deciding to be a hermit. And so I have been, for nearly a thousand years. Forgive me, Umphy, did I hurt you?"

"No," the little dragon winced as his stomach burned. "It's just my stomach, sir. It's been hurting for years. Mother always told me it was indigestion."

"Indigestion, my foot!" muttered the old man, running his hands over the dragon's stomach and feeling there within a growth of some kind. He looked up at the huge, innocent brown eyes. "It should be looked at by an expert," he remarked. "May I suggest my brother in Anthorwyn?"

"You mean Galdermyn," Arwos said. "Isn't he the most famous—"

"Noted most admirably for his spy-work during the Wars," said the wizard. "He was, I recall, the founder of the Jacerin."

"Who are they?" Umphy asked.

"Witch-hunters and demon-killers. Their roots go all the way back to a simple healer who cleared his town of a particularly deadly succubus. Galdermyn enlisted him and others as a separate military group that worked under no other authority but that of the wizards'. Each man is both healer and warrior. But the direct descendants of the original healer have died out. The last was a man by the name of Novanthelion—shame, I knew him, too. He was a good man—until the South got hold of him. That was almost twenty years ago," the wizard added thoughtfully. Then he shook his head. "I am quite confident that Galdermyn is the wizard you ought to see."

"But what's wrong with Umphy?" Arwos asked. "What's he got?"

"I can't possibly answer that right now. It appears to be a very bad infection."

Umphy's ears shot up in alarm. "Is there a cure?"

"I don't know. That's why I suggest you see Galdermyn. His knowledge of diseases and infections is greater than mine, as is his skills to heal them. I don't doubt that whatever it is you have, he'll be able to whip up a remedy for it. Now, we'll arrange for your departure immediately. I'll fill some food sacks. Oh, and Arwos, you're going with him."

"Now just a min—"

"You'll sleep here tonight. Get a full night's sleep and a good breakfast. Your wings will heal quickly with the salve I've administered. My advice to you would be to fly straight to the palace of Anthorwyn and ask to see Galdermyn. He doesn't live in the city itself; he dwells in the Green Tower on the edge of the mountains; he's not too far. The king will help you find him."

As the wizard went around finding blankets and pillows, Umphy whispered to Arwos, "What's Anthorwyn?"

"You don't know?"

"No. Is it a city?"

"The greatest in all the North! It's the home of merchants and traders, and a storehouse of weapons and warriors. Anthorwyn cultivates every art under the sun, and their food is to die for. You'll fall in love with their pastries!"

The whirlwind decision to send Umphy to the largest city of the North boggled the little dragon's mind. Never in all his born days had he ever imagined getting kicked out of his cave only to be sent on a grand adventure into human territory. Initial sadness at the parting from his family quickly turned into rambunctious excitement. In the twilight hours of the evening, when the squall had passed away and the stars came out overhead, Umphy completely forgot about his old home. The old wizard told wondrous stories of his days of youth and the marvelous creatures he'd encountered on his journeys. They drank hot, spiced cider and sang enchanting, lyrical songs, and as darkness flooded the hut, the wizard lit a fire and brought out his fiddle. Arwos and Umphy happily cavorted about, dancing and tumbling while the wizard played. But when they had all settled down, Umphy took out his flute and, at the request of the old wizard, played a song for them. The music dispersed into the warm night air like a waft of perfume released from a budding flower, reaching up as high as the stars. They twinkled down merrily upon the little forest in blessing.

Tarragon sat by the entrance to his cave and listened dully to the slap of the waves against the shore. His whole body felt numb as he listened to the conversation of the elders outside. His father sat outside by the shore and said nothing, staring out at the waves. His mother awaited the judgment with quiet patience, sitting with the other females. The elders would decide whether or not Gaunta was a fit master, since he had failed to uphold his wife's honor and protect his son. But they would also decide a fitting punishment for Tarragon, who had broken two codes and even spoken disrespectfully to his Matriarch. The young keldora strained his ears to hear the conversation.

"Such . . . foolish behavior!"

" . . . menace . . ."

"He'll cause trouble when he's full-grown, mark my words."

" . . . disturbance of the peace, breaking the codes . . . could have been killed . . ."

"Huh, that's hardly likely. Did you see the way he grappled with Razot?"

"I've never seen anything like it."

"He's a born warrior, that's certain!"

"But we cannot have troublemakers in this clan. He placed both his parents in a compromising situation; they had to defend him. This isn't the first time that Tarragon's been in a fight that wasn't his. His pride needs taking down a few notches! Furthermore, he is reckless, wild, and rebellious! Quite unmanageable. He will become as dangerous as Razot if we don't take special precautions. I say we let him learn to live on his own for a time, to cool his temper. If he's improved within three years, we will take him back and accept him in our community."

"But where shall we send him?"

"We'll make him live in the mountains. He will learn to hunt for his own food, defend himself from the cruelty of man, and keep himself pure of the evil that roams the land. If he survives those three years and has learned a lesson, we will take him back."

Tarragon put his head in his paws, wanting to cry, but no tears would come. Razot was getting away free as a bird, but he, Tarragon, who had stood up for his parents was receiving a punishment. The injustice of the situation made him sick. And he was terrified. A keldora who received banishment to the outside world of men and devils was as good as dead. The mountains were old places of refuge and haven, but dragons had not occupied those caves for years. And now he would have to live there, alone! All alone, by himself . . .

Tarragon began to cry.

Part Two

The Black Dragon and a Riddle

Chapter 4

The desert wilderness of Hebaruin was a vast expanse of sand; black, jagged rock; and burning heat. No river passed through its territory, but lava beds and pits of boiling tar festered in secret corners and open plains alike. Mountainous volcanoes, stretching hundreds of feet high, erupted daily. Beyond them lay the ruins of great temples, in which small black creatures made their homes. A depthless chasm divided these temples from a very high, black mountain range, into which was carved a magnificent castle, adorned with gargoyles, iron spikes, and flaming torches. At the base of the mountain sprouted the one piece of vegetation in the entire South. A lone tree, massive in size, twisted and evil in appearance, shot up from the rocky ground and shook its leafless, gnarled limbs to the red clouds above. Carrion birds sat silently. Around the base of the tree, scattered by the roots, were the bones of many victims, sacrifices made to the fruit of the Tree of Death, Morbane, who lived in a cave beneath the tree's roots.

Hebaruin had erupted into being more than two hundred years ago. Before the coming of the Black Dragons, the Southland was the Realm of Kilglede, the Joyful Land of Many Fountains. It had been a famous tropical paradise filled with exotic plants, animals, and water-geysers. Fed by one of the rivers from the Tree of Life, it was a luxurious, blessed country. But the Black Dragons set fire to its land, killing everything and drying up the pools and riverbeds. In destroying one empire of beauty, they turned it into another of death and destruction. Hebaruin attracted the wicked creatures and spirits who were already suppressed by the Guardians. They populated their new home quickly. From their ranks, Fordomt was born, a powerful spirit who took shape and flesh, reigning like an immortal god of war. And he did make war, seeking to expand his territory.

The Wizard War—as mentioned by the wizard in the forests of Poloran—was famous for its longevity and the great acts of magic that took place. The wizards rose up in protest against Fordomt, bringing men from the North, Elves, fairies, and other Sweet-Magic folk into the battle. Together they drove back the Southerners. The Guardians fought desperately against the Black Dragons, but the majority of them were defeated by Morbane and his kin, who had also slain the dragons carrying seven sacred Orbs. The remaining Guardians fled into hiding in order to regroup and build their numbers back up. The wizards and Jacerin were left to supervise the last few months of the great War. Galdermyn, the most powerful of all wizards, caused a vast black mountain range to erupt and encircle Hebaruin. The demons, witches, ghosts, and monsters were pressed back behind the mountains. And though they still crept forward to do their mischief in the troubled world, the wizards and the Jacerin continued to watch over the land. Yet they wondered when the Guardians would return. They were the key to the prophecy foretelling the destruction of Fordomt, Morbane, and all the evils of Hebaruin.

Meanwhile, Fordomt lay low and bided his time. He had what he had long desired: the seven Orbs were fixed in his crown, and all he needed was the eighth, not yet born. Let the Guardians hide and regroup! Let the foolish Northerners play and carry on with their politics and arts of healing! Let the whole land of Balské dwell in its little bubble of safety! Fordomt was not afraid of the wizards or the Guardians. What he feared most of all was the prophecy made long ago by Enovan Illuminator: that the two dragons would arise to oppose him and his Black Dragon. The Emperor was determined that no such thing should ever come to pass. His one advantage was Morbane.

Morbane was his hound of hell.

And he would use him!

The vultures and crows sitting upon the dead branches of the Tree of Death heard heavy breathing from within, and assumed correctly that the Black Dragon was going to rise. For several days he had been restless, slithering around in his den like a snake trapped in a cage. Now the earth trembled, and the carrion birds scattered into the air with vicious squawks of rage. A crack appeared at the ground by the roots and splintered to the edge of the chasm. The Tree of Death parted its roots, and black smoke billowed out. Flames licked the air and the ground shook as a mighty black paw, lined with razor-sharp claws, hit the earth.

Within moments, all of Hebaruin knew that the Black Dragon was awake and wandering the Southern Realm.

Umphy was certain that flying was the best thing in the world.

The wizard-hermit of the forest had spread his wings with a very powerful salve that not only healed the damage quickly, but imbibed the limbs with new strength and vigor. Though Umphy retained brown scars on the torn wing-fibers for the rest of his life, they were nothing in comparison to the pure joy of being able to fly for the first time. With a little early-morning coaching from Arwos and the wizard, the little dragon now flew as though he had been practicing all his life. It was sheer delight.

The trip to Anthorwyn, Arwos pointed out, would take nearly a full two weeks. Umphy was grateful to have such an invaluable traveling companion along. Arwos was older than he looked and seemed to have a bottomless store of knowledge accumulated over the years. He was well-traveled and experienced. He had a variety of interests, and he loved to converse about anything and everything. Umphy could not stop asking questions; his friend seemed to know every answer. In turn, Arwos was flattered by such adoring recognition of his skills, and remained patient with his new young friend.

Umphy had never known that Balské had such diverse landscapes. On a map, Balské was shaped like a stocking, and filled with smooth, open plains; rugged, vast stretches of mountains; deep, flowering valleys; lush, fertile forests; and magnificent canyons that spread for miles. Towards the South lay the desert wastelands and arid fields of high, blood-hued rocks and plateaus. Swamps and marshes lay closer towards the northeast. Each terrain was populated, and from each terrain came a gift of the land. The rivers and streams of the western mountains yielded veins of gold and silver. Those who lived in the plains were granted such rich soil that almost any kind of fruit or vegetable could be raised. From the forests and mountains of the north came timber and iron. The eastern hills and valleys produced special remedial herbs and potions that traders sold specially; also, the ports of the east were famous for their fishing industries and businesses with foreign countries, whose ships brought stores of wealth: exotic fabric, wild animals and birds, slaves, spices, and enough treasure to fill palace upon palace. From the south, however, no special gift came. That part of Balské had been long ago destroyed.

Most of the land below them seemed to be unguarded and safe for passage, but Arwos encouraged Umphy to stay in the air unless landing was necessary.

"We're high enough so that anyone below will mistake us for a pair of large birds—well, they'll mistake you, anyway!" he cackled with laughter. "Your eyes haven't been trained properly yet. The Southerners wear very distinctive clothing and armor, with helmets shaped like dragon-horns. I've seen them in guard stations in some of the trees, and they're moving in small groups down on the ground."

Umphy shivered. "Arwos, do *you* know why the roads are being guarded?"

"Hebaruinn—that's the Southern Empire, you know!—is getting restless again. Rumor has it that the Black Dragon down there has sensed the eighth and final Orb. You know all about that, of course!"

Umphy nodded. The eighth Orb, known better as the White Orb, was supposedly the most powerful of all the Orbs because it was the physical embodiment of the Brown Dragon's original gift. Whoever carried the Orb had a counterpart; another dragon existed whose soul was possessed by the spirit of the same Brown Dragon. When the White Orb was placed in the Tree of Life, the spirit of the Brown Dragon, kindled, would enable the other dragon to slay Morbane, and thus would two dragons bring peace to the land. It was all down in the prophecy ingrained in the education of every dragon from the moment of birth to the day of death. It was the hope that the Guardians clung tightly to. It was all they lived for.

"The Southerners are stationed along the roads in order to gain information on any dragons that happen to come into the interior," Arwos explained. "The North, of course, hasn't seen any dragons for over a thousand years, but sometimes a dragon is spotted near a village in the interior lands."

"I heard the hunters talking about Morbane. They spoke of the rumor. Is it true that if the Emperor finds the Orb there will be a war?"

"More than likely." Arwos looked glum. "Fordomt *will* send Morbane out—he's like a huge, Orb-sniffing hound. Once Fordomt has all eight Orbs in his crown—that's if he gets them—he will be able to make Morbane the most terrible weapon in the entire land. Nothing will be able to stand against him."

"Do you mean he's weak right now?" Umphy was astonished.

"Well, no, not exactly. Morbane is deadly, Orb or no Orb. He's much larger than a normal Green Dragon. Poison leaks from his claws. His scales burn like lava-rocks. His amber eyes can hypnotize and freeze you rock-solid. His strength is unmatched. But for all that, he has his mortal flaws just like any other dragon. If your legendary Brown Dragon were still alive, he would doubtless be the only one strong enough to fight Morbane and win."

Umphy had a sudden image of two incredibly powerful dragons grappling in the sky, drawing wounds that caused blood to fall like rain. He shuddered. Arwos continued. "If Fordomt gets the White Orb, Morbane will be an unstoppable force. Literally."

"If the Southerners found me what—w-w-what would happen?" The little dragon swallowed nervously.

"I don't know, and you don't want to know, either. There's only one way for them to check to see if you have an Orb inside you. And I don't mean that they ask politely."

Umphy shivered.

Around eventide, Umphy and Arwos descended into the forest to rest and find water. The little clearing where they landed was a hollowed-out plot of earth surrounded by an exotic array of trees with a canopy that stretched over a hundred feet high. The jungle-like forests of the North were spread over the vast mountains and hills, forming small valleys and canyons. Small towns nestled on the hillsides, and this, as Arwos explained, was a sure sign of the High Realms.

"Just breaking over these hills the land starts sloping more, and we'll come to a vast expansion of tiny hills and farmlands," he said. "And then you'll see a stretch of meadow right before the Evuinari Mountain range, and Anthorwyn is built at its base. We'll be there hopefully in only two days."

Umphy paid little attention to this. He was content to rest his wings and cool his paws in the little brook trickling from between the rocks. But what really caught his attention were the many ancient dragon statues that sat in the nearby forest and around the little pool of water, shrouded in shadow. Arwos pretended to take no notice, but Umphy climbed all over them, swinging from their horns and sliding down their tails.

"Hey, Arwos, look at me!" He hung himself from between the jaws of one dragon.

"You wouldn't think it was so fun if that thing was alive," the raven replied. "I'm going to go search out some fruit. You stay here and enjoy yourself."

Umphy grinned, watching his little friend flying off, and then froze. The stone tongue beneath him was moving . . . and some kind of liquid was dribbling down the little dragon's arm. The creature's gullet suddenly glistened and palpitated with a life of its own, and Umphy felt the teeth cutting like knives into his skin.

"ARRGHH!!"

The "statue" spat him out on the ground. "Oh . . . that is disgusting!" said a deep voice. "Almost as bad as finding slugs in your mouth on a Monday morning . . . yech!"

Umphy could not believe his eyes. The creature, only stone two minutes ago, was alive, with glistening gray scales and an audible heartbeat. Smoke rose from the dragon's nostrils as he yawned, and Umphy found himself looking into a red cavern, which he had so recently occupied, lined with razor-sharp teeth. The little dragon was suddenly aware of the rustling of grass and trees as the other dragons shook themselves free of fallen leaves and stretched themselves, rumbling with pleasure. The large, gray dragon cocked his head and chuckled.

"Looks like I shocked you clear off to the moon. Not afraid, are you?"

"N-n-no," Umphy squeaked. "Y-y-y-yes-s-s!"

"Ha!" the gray dragon laughed. "He can't make up his mind. Never fear, little one; I don't eat other dragons, no matter how funny they look."

Umphy wasn't sure if that last comment was an insult or not; at any rate, he was still undecided as to the hospitality of this creature.

"Y-y-you're talking," he finally whispered. "But . . . but you can't talk . . . you're a statue!"

"Statue?" the great dragon heaved itself up. Umphy gasped. The dragon was at least a magnificent thirty-five feet in length, muscles bulging and swelling with every move of his limbs, his neck stretching and contracting almost painfully, a thoroughly ugly face yawning, tongue outstretched to taste the air. "Hah!" it continued. "Statue! I must've played the part pretty well! No, little one, I'm a—"

"UMPHY! GET AWAY THIS INSTANT!" Arwos flew over hastily and placed himself between his little friend and the giant gray dragon, feathers ruffled, as if to scare away the frightful apparition. "That's a Stone Dragon! He'll rob you and beat you up if you give him half a chance!" He hopped up and down from one foot to the other, cawing loudly. "Go on! Beat it! Shove off, y'great stone lump of uselessness!"

"Well, well, well, what have we here?" chuckled the Stone Dragon. "I didn't know dragons were getting chummy with the birds. I can't stand 'em. They leave such a lot of nasty presents for me during the day."

"What's your name?" Umphy asked, feeling a little braver. Arwos looked funny, dancing around in front of that huge gray monster that could have swallowed him up. But the dragon seemed friendly. He grinned.

"Werso's the name. Werso Grayhorns. Umphy, is it? Umphy-what? Oh, you haven't got your formal dragon's title yet, eh? Well, time will tell. You're right lucky you came across me. I can show you were food and water are—"

"Don't be stupid," said Arwos furiously. "We're not staying here, we're going on to Anthorwyn!"

"Anthorwyn? You've crossed the border. Almost all of this forest is the city's territory, little raven. Don't you know anything about High Realms? Come, come, don't look so flustered," he said genially, for Arwos was ruffling his feathers in agitation. "What are you going to the city for?"

"None of your business," Arwos snapped.

"No need to get your feathers in knots, my friend. I merely asked because the famous Spring Festival takes place a couple weeks from now. It is the largest celebration in the North, and it is Anthorwyn's turn to host it this year. People from all over the North are flocking in to participate."

"Huh, well, we're not here for some party," Arwos snorted. "We're here on our own terms, and we're going into the city without your dirty double-crossing help, so scram."

"Oh, that's harsh." Werso yawned as the insult bounced off him. "You may need some dirty double-crossing help to get even your big toe inside the city gates."

"What do you mean?"

Werso lowered his voice. "There's something evil happening in the palace. I can sense the disturbing vibrations all the way out here. People talk of shadows that lurk in corners and eyes that follow them from street to street. Nobody walks the city grounds at night anymore. They speak of curses and demons. My herd and I are on the move now, and going to find shelter for ourselves. But if you want to try and make your fortune in Anthorwyn, that's your decision—and your funeral."

"Thanks for the happy advice," Arwos said dryly. "We'll bear it in mind. Come along, Umphy, we haven't got all night!"

"Good luck," Werso said. "All the same, I don't envy you at all. I wouldn't like to be in the palace. Not these days." And then, before their eyes, the landscape changed, trees rustled, and Werso disappeared. Umphy cocked his head, and then looked at Arwos.

"What's the matter with him?" he asked. "Where'd he go?"

"Oh, don't worry," grumbled Arwos. "Good riddance to bad rubbish, I say. Stone Dragons are a menace to travelers. We're lucky to be alive. And what's more, we've still got our stuff. For a Stone Dragon, Werso was awfully nice."

"Do you really think the city will be dangerous for us?" Umphy asked timidly.

"Nonsense. He was just trying to scare us. Stone Dragons love to play practical jokes! Just stick close to me, and I'll see that we both come out living like kings."

As they settled down for the night, neither the raven nor the little blue dragon noticed the man in the shadows. He watched them intently, keeping himself hidden between the trees. When he heard of their destination, he clenched his fists angrily. The light of vengeance shone brightly in his eye.

Chapter 5

The still white room enfolded in draperies of spun gold and silken blue held its priceless gem in its center, a woman seated upon an ivory chair, upheld comfortably by soft white eider-down pillows. Graceful, long hands lay in her lap; the slender, white fingers curled around the edges of a red, velvet-bound book. Her head was tipped ever so slightly on the pillows, relaxing against the back of the chair, her eyes closed, and her mouth parted slightly, breathing lightly. A mass of auburn-gold hair spilled from underneath a golden tiara, set with smoky-white crystals. She was sleeping peacefully, and the six handmaidens in violet-blue gowns who sewed quietly by her side dared not awaken her. One handmaiden paused in her sewing long enough to cover her lady more snugly with the silk blanket that had slipped off her bulging stomach—a telltale sign of an eight-month pregnancy.

The queen's name was Favia Unituriel, daughter of the third Northern kingdom, Haeroné. She was tiny, like a twelve-year-old child not yet come into the bloom of womanhood, but her face was strong and serene, mature beyond her thirty-eight years. She came from an ancient line of roving gypsies and mystic soothsayers, famous for their abilities to meld minds and become one with another creature. Unituriel was a powerful mystic, though she kept her powers secret for many years, choosing instead the life of a wife and mother. She had married King Feromar of Anthorwyn for the sake of establishing a peaceful contract between the realms. Her children were the king's only hope for a union with other kingdoms. She needed the best of care.

A young handmaiden dared to raise her voice to a whisper. "She's slept for a good part of the morning. Should we wake her up, now?"

"No, Masila," another replied softly. "We never waken her majesty unless there is an emergency."

Masila reached into her bag and brought out a small glass vial. "But the medicine is nearly gone, Elorani. The lord Gurthur instructed her to have the liquid once every six hours in order to prevent a miscarriage. Surely she'll want more soon!"

"Not today. That stuff only tires her. I've never seen her so low before. Why, when I was but a child, my lady was full of life and laughter, arranging games between the young swains and maidens, throwing evening dinner parties for her friends, and hunting with the men. Even when she married the king and became the queen of Anthorwyn, though she was more subdued, she was rosy-cheeked and happy. Now . . ." Elorani sighed. "Now she frets and frightens too easily. There are circles under her eyes. She was always a delicate slip of a girl who might be blown away into fading memory by the wind itself. Something plagues her, and I'll swear on the Holy Elbib of Balské that it's Gurthur."

"And I think you're full of horse-nettles, Elly," announced another maiden. "Gurthur is a Jacerin, and a very skilled healer. Besides, I find him very attractive. His eyes are like the pools of eternity. What could they have seen to become so wide and . . . and . . . and *knowing*?" She sighed, her own eyes far-away in a dream of handsome men with captivating eyes and strong limbs.

"They say a man's eyes become snake-like when they've played active witness to murder," said Elorani coldly. "But his trouble-making at court is enough."

"Is he still instructing the princess in demonology?" asked Masila. "I still want to know what her interest is in learning about witches and demons and spirits of the dead. Little good it will do her! Ghosts never set a crown on anyone's head, and that's a fact."

The handmaidens burst out giggling.

"At any rate," said Masila. "Princess Adenile has enough to deal with in her own home without learning of such wickedness. I think that the Lady Vestia ought to receive a medal of honor for saying NO to that spoiled brat."

"Hush yourself, you treasonous chit!" scolded Elorani. "Vestia is lucky she was not imprisoned and tortured to death. Had the argument gone any further, the charity-girl would not even now be alive. Let me not hear you speak of Adenile as a 'spoiled brat.' Opinions are like to get someone killed around here."

Another handmaiden sulked. "Vestia only got away with her opinion because she used to be Adenile's friend."

"And who came between them, eh?" Elorani glared at the speaker. "Gurthur, that's who. Those girls used to be inseparable. Vestia is only three years older than Adenile, but they loved each other like sisters. Shared and shared alike in everything they did. Neither could be above the other in knowledge or authority or anything else. In fact, Adenile used to demand that everyone call her friend 'Princess Vestia,' and that's how it was for a long time. Why, it was only a year ago that the two girls began having their petty differences. Adenile began to appreciate her title and future as queen, so her attitude began to frost slightly towards her friend, while Vestia abandoned her 'princess' title for that of a Jacerin. She is determined to join them, you know, and so part of her studies—given to her by the wizard Galdermyn, I might add—include demonology, so she can identify and fight her enemies properly. But Adenile! Lord strike me blind if that girl did not go green with envy. To her, it seemed that Vestia had a power, an authority over evil—which is quite ridiculous. Mortals have no authority over things so strong and ancient in their wickedness! But of course Adenile wanted this power, so she asked Vestia to teach her. And did the charity-girl grant Adenile her request? No, she did not! And of course the princess threw a fit and ran crying to Gurthur, who loves her dearly," Elorani's voice turned into a sneer. "And *he* said—"

One of the younger handmaidens made kissing noises and snorted into her hand as the rest of the young women giggled hysterically. The elder handmaiden glared at her sternly and continued.

"He said that he would teach Adenile all she wished to know if she would but arrange for a lover's meeting between himself and Vestia. Of course the princess granted *that* request—"

"Yes . . . ¿ And¿!"

"He grabbed Vestia and tried to kiss her—"

"*No*! He didn't!"

"Oh yes, he did! But Vestia caused such a fuss that he let her go and she ran away. The next morning, in she goes to the library to find Adenile, and such a scene! Name-calling every which way and curses thrown back and forth! Vestia was so worked up that she slapped the princess, and Adenile threw a book at her former friend. Their loathsome quarrel would have become a wrestling match if the guards hadn't rushed in and separated them! The King gave Adenile permission to study whatsoever she wanted, provided that it would aid in her preparation for the throne, and so now the princess smirks at Vestia, while *she* spies on the princess here and there, to see what her true motives are. Vestia believes no good of the princess because of Gurthur's influence, that I am sure!"

A sudden yawn made all the handmaidens jump. Unituriel was awake. She stretched herself luxuriously and then rose quietly, giving no hint that she had heard a single word. The handmaidens sobered immediately and rose with scarlet cheeks. Their mistress thoughtfully surveyed them each in turn, her soft eyes probing them gently. "Elanori, give me your hand. Pregnancy is a balancing act, and a kicking child doesn't make walking easy! The rest of you may go; I will not need you until we sit in court this afternoon."

The handmaidens solemnly departed, leaving only the elder handmaiden to help the queen down the corridor and into the parlor of the West Wing, where the queen could take her leisure time with her husband. The West Wing provided that privacy, with its own sun-room for light and warmth. Elorani knocked on the great oak door, announced the queen, and helped her inside. The king stood looking out of the window, his back to his wife. Behind him stood a small table set for two, with tea, cakes, milk, and ice.

Elorani assisted her mistress to a chair, bowed, and then melted back out of the room, as silent as she had come. The queen was left alone with her husband.

"How was your nap?" King Feromar Elthenburl turned. He was well into his fifties, but the strong nose and noble brow betrayed an almost immortal vitality that was quite handsome. Keen green eyes regarded his wife tenderly as he picked up her dainty white hand in his strong, weather-beaten ones. "Is it just me, or are you looking rather beautiful today?" he kissed her tenderly. "Would you like to help me call in sick this afternoon?"

She pulled away tiredly. "No."

"But the healers instructed you to take your leisure when you must. That means that I must certainly take hours off my own schedule to lounge and relax with you—maybe read you a book or two—or sing you exotic songs."

"Please don't. You'll only embarrass me."

"Who's here to care?"

"I'm not in a romantic mood right now, Feromar!"

He sighed and sat down, wishing that pregnancies did not cause women so many mood swings. His wife was mystery enough without those extra feminine puzzles. She had sufficient experience, wisdom, and beauty to be his equal in ruling. But talking to her was always difficult. Something about her made him feel shy and inadequate, both as a husband and a king. He sometimes felt as though she looked at him and saw a stranger. He wondered often if there had been a lover before him, and what he must have been like to command such devotion from a woman.

"You've been eavesdropping again." He gave her a secret smile.

"Why, I—I have not!"

"I know you, Uni. Pretending to sleep is your only way of catching up on all the court gossip. What have those boisterous maids spoken of today?"

"Nothing new. They told the story of The Argument again. I told you that you should never have allowed Adenile to study demonology under Gurthur! You didn't study it. You knew enough about the evils in the world. But I don't like my daughter learning about such wickedness. It makes me nervous."

"Now, Uni, you know that Adenile is a sponge for knowledge. I saw no reason to restrict her education. Give her a broad scope! She'll narrow her particular interests down. As for Vestia, she had to learn her place. A light whipping, I think, did her good."

"For heaven's sake, Feromar!" Unituriel said crossly. "It was their fight. You did not need to interfere and spoil Adenile. Gurthur spoils her enough as it is. You ought to banish the man. He uses his influence with Adenile to gain favors for himself, and—" The queen bit her lip and looked down at the white tablecloth.

King Feromar sighed again. "My dear, something about that man irritates you. You were violently opposed to his coming to Anthorwyn as a healer and counselor. But as far as I am concerned, Vestia can take care of herself. I am not about to banish Gurthur just because he has strong feelings towards the young lady. I gave him severe warning about attacking the girl, but I see no reason why he cannot court her. The match would be a suitable one. If she turns him down, that's that! I am not about to get in the way of her love life."

"I wish you would," the queen said dryly. "You certainly are not helping Adenile with hers."

"Adenile has the love life of a rock. She has a fierce, independent spirit. If she is so eager to rule Anthorwyn alone, why should we urge suitors on her? She takes her future responsibility very seriously. I have already put it into writing that she is my heir, unless you should give birth to a male before your fortieth birthday."

Unituriel looked sad as she replied. "I do not wish for her to rule Anthorwyn alone. It takes a man to do the ruling, like the father of a household. Adenile is too headstrong and spoiled. She has too many outlandish ideas for alliances and trade routes and businesses that will cause more problems than they would solve. At the moment she is too confident that I will not bear a son. She will suffer no rival, nor will she share her reign. Do you not worry? I do."

"Uni, you have thought all this over far too hard." Feromar picked up his wife's hand and stroked it. "I cannot understand you. All your life you have treated Adenile as an outsider. And why? I suppose it's because she takes after my side of the family. You never were fond of my father, if I remember correctly. He, too, was headstrong and independent."

"Not like this. Not like *her*." The queen buried her face in her hands. "She frightens me, my lord. It's as if Gurthur came and put a claim upon her, bestowing another kind of soul in her body. She was sweet once, my little Addy! Picking flowers every day and singing in the gardens. She was a golden, happy child. Now . . ." She shook her head and leaned back in her chair. The king leaned over her, anxious.

"Do not exert yourself, Uni. Think of your baby. Leave Adenile to me and concentrate on your own health. Giving birth has never been easy for you—my darling wife, you are so tiny, like a child yourself." Feromar clasped his wife's hands between his own and pressed them fervently to his lips before looking back up into her soft gray eyes. "I do love you, you know."

The Galtic Mountain range was small in comparison to the larger, more formidable ranges of the northern territories, but it was also uninhabited by man, and far from the shadow of the South. No trail or path had yet been forged through the Galtic range; it was a perfect place for a banished dragon. Tarragon had searched all day, and finally came across a slab of rock jutting out over a large cave-like dwelling. The young keldora had to first evict a grouchy bear, but the new cave proved to be warm and dry, and tunneled off in different directions through the mountain, leading to other magnificent underground caverns. Tarragon chose one that he liked, with a small, crystal pool at the bottom, and made himself at home. There, nestled in the heart of the Galtic range, he was hidden from the world, safe from the criticism of his elders, and far away from his home, friends, and everything he had ever known.

Chapter 6

Vestia Anthelion sat by a circular class window in the top of the tallest tower of the palace and observed the hustle and bustle of the people in the city. With her legs curled under her and her hair cascading down her back in rivulets the color of warm honey, she looked like a child, but her face had a familiar strength to it that gave away her wisdom despite her twenty-one years. Her mind was sharp as a double-bladed sword; she, too, was gifted with foresight. Lessons with healers and wizards had trained her in the ways of the Jacerin, the legendary group of men and women who fought during the Wizard Wars as witch-killers and demon-hunters. Her own father, she knew, had been one of these people, and had passed on to her his sparkling gray eyes and clever mind. Of her mother, however, she knew little, except that she had been a traveler in a gypsy caravan. Vestia was not ashamed of her heritage. She was serene and confident in her knowledge that she was destined for a great mission, though she was not at all sure what it was.

Idly, she breathed on the window and watched it fog. Her slim, white fingers traced the rune for happiness. There was not much to be happy about, lately. Despite the excitement of the Spring Festival, dark clouds loomed over Anthorwyn. The princess was still treating her like the mud on her shoe, and Gurthur . . . the man was impossible to get along with. For years Vestia had known of his infatuation with her, and she acknowledged him to be a handsome man, but his attitude towards dark magic was frightening. He knew more spells and incantations than seemed normal for one who claimed a past with the Jacerin, and when he spoke of Hebaruin, it was almost akin to hero-worship. His amber-hued eyes also haunted her. They were devil-eyes that followed her everywhere, and made her feel exposed and vulnerable. He was quiet, too, like the still night that hung low in a graveyard, or the chilly silence of a musty crypt. No, he did not exactly make her very happy!

In her lap she held a small, silver ball. She fondled it gently as she watched the activity below. Then she pressed her fingers to the glass panel and looked harder. A flicker of blue movement caught her eye, and she focused. No, now it was gone. A crowd was gathering about the marketplace, drawn by some attraction or amusement. Vestia sighed. The Spring Festival was a time of great chaos. Sometimes one just did not know how to deal with it!

In the city marketplace square, a commotion was taking place. Brightly-dressed people pressed against each other eagerly for a good glimpse of a fuzzy-blue dragon and his raven companion, trapped inside a metal cage, and guarded by two of the Anthorwyn soldiers. Standing nervously to one side was the fat shopkeeper who had found the trespassers in his gardening pots.

"You won't 'urt 'im, will yer, sire?" he begged. "'E's just a liddle 'un; can't 'urt no one no 'ow wid the tiny teeth 'e's got. Please, sire, let 'im go."

"You called us over, and now it's our job to stay posted until further notification," snapped the guard. "We won't let the crowd get at your precious prize, Lawro."

Umphy huddled in the middle of the cage, trying to pretend he was invisible. He heard every range of commentary, from the horrified to the very interested. Several times, children ran forward to press at the bars, making faces or throwing rocks. The guards shoved them backwards into arms of scolding mothers, and the men walked up to observe the legendary creature.

"It's alright, Umphy," muttered Arwos. "They're just curious. It's been years since dragons were actually seen in the North."

A wad of wet trash struck the raven, and he hopped backwards, swearing loudly.

"He'd make an excellent exhibit at the circus," remarked a tall, well-rounded man with a beard, indicating Umphy. He casually waved his plump, bejeweled fingers. "How much are you lads willing to take for him?"

"Nothing," snapped the guard. "He's under the protection of the royal family at the moment. If they want to sell him to your miserable show, they will—though I highly doubt it."

Umphy swallowed. Arwos nudged him. "That's a good sign, Umphy. Just hang in there a little longer. We'll get into the palace, yet!"

As they huddled there miserably, there was a shout, and the crowd parted to make way for a grand procession of armored guards, sixteen beautiful women, and ten powerfully-built men with bare, blackened chests. On their shoulders they bore an ivory litter with a golden roof, purple silk curtains and crystal ornaments. As the carriage stopped, a sharp voice cried out, and a man rode forward.

Umphy was immediately both impressed and frightened of him. The man reminded the little dragon strongly of his father: aloof and distant, yet with a confidant, dominant bearing. He sat erect in his saddle, with powerful shoulders and a proud, noble face. His head was bald, and his beard, though long and black, was shot through with silver. Crystal-clear, hypnotic eyes bored into Umphy without blinking. He was a man who commanded respect.

"What is the meaning of this?" he snapped. "My lady is not to be detained. Why are the streets so crowded that they do not give way for the Princess of Anthorwyn?"

Even as he spoke, a bejeweled hand pushed the curtain aside, and a woman poked her head out. Umphy's jaw dropped. He hadn't seen very many human females before, but this woman was stunningly beautiful. She had the flawless, porcelain skin of her Northern kin, and hair as dark as the Northern skies. Green eyes flashed like lightning.

"Gurthur, why have we stopped?" she grated. "What's in the cage over there?"

Another man, dressed in the gold and red silks, rode forward and then approached the princess. "'Tis but an imp of a dragon, my lady. I'll have these fools run off with their side-show."

Swish! Crack! The princess had a riding whip, and she struck the man violently on the side of the face. "Who are you to suggest anything, you son of a pig!" she raged. "I take no orders from you! Hold your tongue, or you'll find yourself a flayed feast for the crows outside the city gates! Captain, bring me closer! I want to see the dragon."

Arwos stood by Umphy. "That's the Princess Adenile," he whispered. "The only child of the king himself! Please behave, Umphy! They say she has a frightful temper!"

He didn't need to ask twice. Umphy swallowed as he found the princess staring down her regal nose at him. Nobody said anything. Then the beautiful, full red lips parted.

"Why is he caged like this?"

The guard trembled. "My lady, this dragon was found in the gardener's pots this morning. He alerted us, and we have captured him. Until the king can be notified, we are keeping him as safe as we may."

"Safe? What's all that junk inside the cage?" the princess pointed at the garbage and rocks. "If the people have been throwing things at your charge, you idiot, he's not being kept very safe!"

"I'm sure they do their duty well, your highness," muttered the young man, holding a hand to his smarting cheek. The princess swung her head around.

"Who asked you? You're dismissed from my sight and company, dog," she snarled. "You dare make comments to me about how the guards do their duty! You slime, you are not even born of this city! Get out! You should be thanking the king in sackcloth and ashes for the honor of even casting your unworthy eyes on my person! Now remove your worthless carcass from my sight before I have you arrested and thrown in the dungeons!"

The young man spat on the ground. "A plague take you and your kin!" he growled, before riding off in haste. "Enovan help the man who marries you, woman!"

The princess, with her nose in the air, turned back to the guards.

"As for you fools who call yourselves guards, get that dragon out of his cage. We'll see about this. You are taking orders from me now! You—captain—take the raven upon your shoulder and bear him hence. Gurthur, help the little dragon up here with me, in my litter. I wish to speak with him."

Umphy found himself enveloped in a stuffy, perfume-saturated atmosphere of silk curtains and satin pillows. The princess reclined luxuriously, swathed in sheers folds of violet and gold cloth. In one hand she held the riding whip, and in the other she held a large fan made of white peacock feathers. Dark hair tumbled like a cloud around her shoulders. A single white gem was bound around her forehead. Umphy thought he was looking at an angel.

"Are you hungry?" Adenile asked, reaching towards a golden dish heaped with fruits and sweets. "Help yourself. You must be dreadfully tired after your long journey. What an adorable little thing you are! Oh, I shall simply cry my heart out if my father does not let me have you as a companion. I shall be the most-envied princess in the entire land."

Umphy did not like to contradict her, but sat munching hungrily on a pomegranate. The bald-headed man rose close beside them, though the curtains prevented Umphy from getting a good view. The princess waved slim white fingers.

"You have nothing to fear from Gurthur. He is my tutor and confidant." Her eyes sparkled. "This must be your first time to the North, am I correct?"

"Yes, ma'am—I mean, yes, your highness."

"Are you here for the Festival?"

"No—I mean, yes—er . . ."

The princess laughed. "You must be genuinely overwhelmed. If this is your first time to the Northlands, I doubt you've seen a finer city. Would you like to look out and see the palace? Here, let me help you!" She pushed aside a curtain, and Umphy immediately stuck his head out of the window.

His jaw dropped.

The palace of Anthorwyn was rightly nicknamed "The Emerald." Built by skilled tradesmen and architects of Anthorwyn's classical age before the Wizard Wars, the palace shimmered with stone of white marble and green jade. Four spiraled towers surrounded the main building encircled by a twenty-foot stone wall with only one gate, which led to the palace doors. A tall staircase between fluted pillars of gold-studded jade rose up to the great iron doorways, carved with a dragon and a tree—the North's earlier recognition of the Guardians. The doors were faded with age, and the gold plating was flaking off, but the imprints of Umphy's heritage remained untampered with by time or weather. Above the doorway arched a magnificent beam set with diamonds, and a great golden dome crowned the palace roof. Umphy could not stop looking up. And as he continued looking up and up, his eyes caught sight of another building, built much higher and far bigger, up on the slopes of the mountain, almost directly above the palace.

"That is our temple to Enovan," Adenile said pleasantly. "It is where the monks tend to the sacred fires, and see to it that our Lord is properly praised. They have many fine works of literature in there, as well as ancient books on world customs, traditions, and historical knowledge. You should see their music library. Do you play music?" she indicated Umphy's flute. He had carried it with him in a little pouch made especially for him by the wizard in the forest.

"What? Oh . . . oh, yes! Yes, I do," the little dragon confessed. "I am rather talented."

"You must play something for the Festival. Even if my mother and father do not give their consent, you will play on my orders. Of course, you shan't be a disappointment, if your talent is real!"

As the procession made their way through the courtyard, people stopped to bow and stare. Nobles, dressed in expensive, perfumed robes made their reverences to the princess and stared in admiration at the young dragon sitting beside her. Sweet odors and rich fragrances wafted gently in the afternoon air. Music lingered in the corridors and behind walls. Umphy had never in his life experienced such beauty.

Suddenly, the entire group came to a halt, and the princess, aided by Gurthur, alighted from her carriage. A woman dressed in a light green gown studded with emeralds rushed forward, and Umphy nearly twisted his head off to get a good look. My, my, but nobles certainly were beautiful people!

"Your highness, you promised to help me give history lessons to the noblemen's sons."

"Oh, Vestia, I'm not interested!" Adenile sighed and looked to heaven as if seeking patience. "What have I to do with teaching a bunch of noblemen's brats about history? You know I despise teaching. Besides, it was not as if I *wanted* to go off with Prince Wynwith. Mother told me to."

"Was he as successful as the others?" Vestia asked dryly. Adenile snorted.

"It's none of your business, but if you really want to know, he's a peacock—" This was Adenile's word for a particularly odorous suitor. "—and I turned him away at once. Now mind your own business and keep your nosy nose on your own love life. I can always arrange for another midnight rendezvous if you wish."

The two young women stared at each other with unspoken threats, and the atmosphere was distinctly colder. Then Vestia noticed Umphy, and she spoke with alarm.

"A dragon! Adenile, where did you find him?"

"In a cage in the streets," Adenile tossed her head scornfully. "I'm bringing him to father. Naturally, a ruler must be aware of such guests in his kingdom."

Umphy blushed under Vestia's beautiful, star-struck stare. She looked genuinely interested. "May I come and witness?"

"And you with your studies?" teased Adenile, though her tone was not at all light. "Wouldn't you rather take that than watch the affairs of your future queen? You need all the practice you can get—seeing as how you'd like to be a killer like your father."

Vestia took a step forward, but her way was blocked by Gurthur, who stepped between the angry woman and the princess. Umphy clutched his tail anxiously, overwhelmed by the power and awe the dark man inspired. Vestia's chest heaved with indignation before she turned on her heel and stormed off in the opposite direction. Arwos, perched on the shoulder of the captain, let out a sigh of relief. Adenile laughed and turned to Umphy. "Pay no attention to her. She's only the charity-girl from an extinct city that was full of warriors—rash people who acted before thinking. She's as foolish as they were. Now come, let us go see my father."

Outside the palace gates, a beggar stood and watched the procession enter the courtyard. Then the gates slammed shut behind them. The ragged-looking man had long, straggly hair and a short, graying beard. A black kerchief was bound over his head, and he wore a patch over one eye, though the other, keen and clear, burned with a fierce hatred as he watched the princess' entourage go by. His one good eye alighted in particular upon the bald-headed man, and a low growl, like that of a mad dog, escaped his lips. He clenched his fists, and the muscles beneath the grimy tatters of his clothes bulged. He stood staring at the locked gates for some time. Then he turned and shuffled moodily away.

The royal guards followed the princess, leading Umphy and Arwos down through the corridors into a vast room with a high, vaulted ceiling, marble floors, and fluted, gem-encrusted pillars. Here swarmed the nobility in all their glory, wrapped in such finery that they almost looked edible. Enchanted candles hung from the ceiling in massive, golden chandeliers. The walls and ceiling were covered with colorful murals depicting the history of Anthorwyn: its discovery by the Northern explorer Taigate Wyntor; the foundations of the original six kingdoms by the six leaders of the pilgrims up from the interior; the building and construction of the city and its palace; the battle and victory of the Northlands against a Southern invasion, which was celebtrated every spring with a Festival; and, more recently, the coronation of the most important political figure of the North, Queen Yeviel (the present king's grandmother). Umphy could not take his eyes off of the grandeur. This was the court of the king, and a finer one in all the High Realms was not to be found.

The Princess Adenile strode loftily down the red carpet to where the king sat enthroned beside his wife. Gurthur walked two paces behind the princess, ensuring that people bowed to her. Behind him were the princess' guards, in the middle of which was Umphy. Arwos perched on his shoulder.

They stopped just at the foot of the throne, and Adenile made her mandatory courtesy, bowing her head and holding out both hands, palms up. She curtseyed slightly. "Good afternoon, my lord."

"Daughter." Feromar looked at his daughter kindly and extended his scepter, giving her leave to speak.

"I've found a dragon in the streets, father, watched by the royal guard. I thought it prudent to bring him to you, for he was in danger out there. People were spitting and throwing things, and he was very frightened. He's so little. And he plays the flute! May I have him? Say that I might."

The queen spoke gently. "Lady, for all your enthusiasm, you forget that a dragon is no mere animal, but a respected creature of power and wisdom far beyond what a human possesses. Perhaps we should hear what the little one has to say."

Adenile shot her mother a mean look, and the king frowned at his daughter. There was a chilly silence. Arwos hopped forward.

"Great King of Anthorwyn, my friend and I have come to—"

"Speak when you're spoken to!" snapped a guard, but the king raised his hand. He nodded at Arwos, and the raven nervously continued.

"Sire, I acknowledge you as my sovereign while I dwell here in the North. May you live long! I am Arwos Ebonfeather, a wanderer of the air. We've come seeking the aid of the wizard Galdermyn. My friend is ill, sire, and requires the attentions of the great wizard. But, er . . . if the princess would like him as a companion . . ."

Umphy looked over at Arwos in alarm. The raven shook his head at him. They could not put up a fuss. Too many tales had been told about the spoiled princess and her fierce temper. If Adenile wanted Umphy and she didn't get him, she would make sure that no one else did—including the much-needed Galdermyn. The king lifted his head. "Is it true that this little one can play the flute? Is he some sort of bard? Let us hear you play, and judge for ourselves whether your skills will befit our life here at the palace."

Umphy was placed on the spot. He put his flute up to his lips and concentrated hard, seeing the music in his mind and believing in it. The lullaby from his dreams resurfaced, and the little dragon began playing.

> *Let he who seeks find not*
> *And he who asks first knock.*
> *The mountain dark, the people dread*
> *Who live beneath the rocky ledge.*
> *They guard me, keep me safe from harm.*
> *Lest evil come and cast its charm.*
> *Find me, take me, if you can:*
> *I solve doors and puzzles, heart of man.*
> *Where to find me? The wise man knows.*
> *Find him where the blue stone grows.*
> *Use me well when thrice the sun*

Makes its turn on its fifth run.
Then let me lead thee, guide thee on
Behind the wall of silver-stone.
I'll take thee to three golden halls
And on beyond the valley falls.
There, silver bells are hung in rows
And brightly gleams the red-red rose.
The tree is tall; the dragon brown
Within that hall who lives deep down.
The empress white; her satin gown
Ripples eight beneath her crown!
The day on which I shall awake
Will be the day the foe's life I take.
And set me once again within the hand
That forever more will rule the land.

The sweet, haunting melody rose like a flower in spring, and blossomed just as beautifully. The court was silent, spellbound by the ancient tune. When Umphy finished, the king sat as if melded to his throne, his eyes faraway. Then he roused himself, descended the throne, and knelt in front of Umphy to look into his eyes.

"Answer me truthfully," he said quietly. "Are you of the lineage of the Guardians?"

"I am, sire."

"And do you bring tidings of hope for the North? Are you the sign that we have all been waiting for? Do you herald the return of the Guardians?"

Umphy was startled. He had not expected such a question and was in no position to answer it in the affirmative. He shook his head slowly.

"I don't think so, sire. I'm only here to see the wizard."

Feromar nodded. "I'm afraid Galdermyn is not here at the moment. He is traveling on an important errand. But I shall send him an invitation to come at the first possible convenience. And who shall I say is asking for him?"

"Umphy."

The entire court burst out laughing. This little dragon's name was amusing, and he looked like an Umphy—whatever an Umphy was. Nonetheless, the king laughed merrily, beaming from ear to ear. The ice was broken.

"Well, well!" he chuckled. "Welcome to Anthorwyn, Umphy. It's not every day we entertain dragons as guests. And you shall be a guest, for this is what I may decree. Your gift of music is a rare and beautiful one. If you will play for the Spring Festival a few weeks from now, you shall dwell here in the palace and given the benefits of a guest of royalty. Daughter, you shall have the care of him—not as a pet!" he said sternly. "It shall be your task to ensure that he is made comfortable and given whatever he needs."

Adenile bowed her head and curtseyed. "Thank you, father. Come, little one. I'll show you the place where you are to sleep." Umphy trailed after the princess somewhat hesitantly, looking back over his shoulder at his friend and wondering what exactly might happen now.

"One moment, sire," Arwos burst out. "If Umphy stays, then so do I. We're friends, he and I. You surely wouldn't part two good friends, would you? Of course not! Your kindness is famous and widespread across the Northlands. And if I could be of some use, I would be most honored."

"There's no harm in that," the queen said quickly. "Master Ebonfeather, you are a scholar, are you not?"

"I am, so please my lady!"

"Then you shall have the honor of assisting our master librarian in his studies." The queen spoke firmly. "I have assigned to him the project of tracing the family history. Perhaps you will be of some valuable help."

"It would be an honor, your majesty." Arwos bowed very low indeed.

Chapter 7

In the dark hours outside a village of the southeast, a small Green Dragon chuckled rebelliously as he tore ravenously into a deer he had hunted down in the forest. It was unusual for a dragon to be so far away from his home in the middle of the night, but he, bolder and more reckless, had decided to strike out on his own. His kill, a fine young buck, made a wonderful meal.

The vibrations in the air were so slight that only the dragon's sensitive tongue, flicking in and out, caught them. He stopped eating to look up and around. The vibrations were like a tingling buzz, heralding the presence of some animal. They stopped briefly, and the world went completely still. The dragon flicked his tongue in and out, trying to detect the vibrations again. But there was nothing. Possibly some small creature had rushed past, but nothing more. The dragon relaxed, lowering his guard. Again, he turned his head to his grisly meal, and began feasting.

The attack came from behind, so swiftly that the dragon had no time to cry out. Razor-sharp claws tore into the tendons of his wings, shredding them like paper. Jaws closed like a steel trap around the dragon's throat, severing the artery. In a matter of five seconds the violence was over. The Black Dragon raised its head and sniffed the air. Two twin-pronged tongues darted in and out, testing for vibrations and smells. The villagers were asleep, unaware of the danger standing right outside their gates. He ignored them. His business was not with the two-legged fools. He sniffed again. The unmistakable scent of the ocean lingered around the corpse.

Then, with the stealth of an assassin, the Black Dragon melted into the night, taking a course towards the East Coast.

Umphy was offered a bedroom in the palace, but he shyly declined in favor of sleeping outdoors. He was not used to a stuffy room full of incense and a fireplace, and the clean air of the North suited him much better. So Adenile led him out to the gardens instead.

Umphy knew he would love the palace life. His new home was a beautiful garden of winding, white pebbled paths and flowering bushes, with a large, intricately-carved stone fountain with fish. Around the garden was a tall iron gate, twined with creeping vines and flowers, and encircled by a hedge that wrapped a full extension across the menagerie. Tall fruiting trees grew here as well as rows and rows of dainty flowers, all arranged by color. The warm sun filtered down, bringing with it a balmy breeze that carried the delicate perfume of each flower. Umphy immediately crawled over to a shady hedge for a good doze.

It was interrupted by a growl. Umphy looked up with a start and gave a yelp of surprise and fear as a large, sandy-brown cat scowled at him. The little dragon had never seen a wild mountain lion before, and it scared him. Muscles rippled, claws unsheathed, and yellow eyes glinted fiercely at Umphy.

"Scram, pipsqueak. What do you think you're doing? This isn't a free-for-all! Get lost!"

Umphy had a hard time getting his voice. "Why?"

The cat snarled angrily, "Because you are lying underneath my bush. That's my bush, you know! Everyone here knows it's my bush, and nobody dares to lay under it. What are you, stupid?"

"I beg your pardon. I didn't know it was your bush. I just got here, and I—"

"Tenderfeet!" the cat roared. "When will they stop bringing in the tenderfeet? Green as new saplings they are, with no respect for anyone! Just you remember this: I am Kelhah, the mightiest of creatures here, and if you so much as put one toe across my territory again, I shall rip you into a thousand ribbons! You have until the count of three to disappear!"

Umphy didn't even wait for the cat to begin counting. He quickly scrambled away, and dove underneath the porch steps leading up to the back of the garden gatehouse. It was a tight squeeze, but Umphy made it. He was panting in relief and attempting to stretch his legs when he connected with fur and heard a yelp: "Oof!" Twisting his head around painfully, Umphy saw that his right foot had poked into the ribs of a small fox curled up in a ball behind him. The fox shied away from the young dragon, eyes wide.

"Holy Hemlock! Who're you?"

"My name is Umphy."

The fox stretched forward and sniffed him. "Well, the name is simple enough, but what are you? I've never smelt anything like you before."

Umphy felt a little uncomfortable. "I'm a dragon."

"A dragon! Gracious, I've heard of 'em, but certainly have never seen one. You're my first. Pleased to meet you. I'm Whirit. At least, that's what they call me. So you're the newcomer, eh? Welcome, welcome! Doubtless you've already received warmer greetings from Kelhah," the fox sniffed. "I heard him growling about something out there. What'd you do, spill his water?"

"I slept under his favorite bush."

"Oh, well, you're lucky you're new. If you had been someone else, Kelhah would have ground you into dust. That's him all over, sad to say. You'll have to forgive him. I don't think he ever had a mother."

Umphy liked the friendly manner of the fox right away. "That's alright. I didn't mean to invade his territory. I just wanted to sleep."

"That's understandable. But he's a pet to one of the royal family. Huh, if that doesn't let him think the universe revolves around his pea-brain! He's very territorial."

"Are there any others like him?"

"Well, there's me," Whirit grinned. "If you mean personal familiars. I belong to the Princess Adenile. But it's been a long time since she's spent any time with me," the fox added, a little sadly. "She's been so busy lately that she doesn't have time to visit me."

"Oh. Then she might not have time for me, either."

"Ah-ha, so you're the one she brought in today! I heard all the commotion. No, she probably won't have any time for you at all." Whirit lifted his nose slightly, and it occurred to Umphy that the fox might be a little jealous. He timidly backed down.

"I won't be staying here long," he said. "I only wanted to see the wizard Galdermyn and then leave. I suppose I'm playing my flute for the Spring Festival, too, but then I'd like to leave and travel around a little more." The thought of what he might do after his visit to Anthorwyn had not yet occurred to the little dragon, but the idea of traveling was certainly entertaining.

Whirit visibly relaxed. "Come, come, this is your new home for the moment! You'll get to know everyone in time. And this is the life to lead! Someone takes care of you, brings you food, smothers you with affection, and you almost never get in trouble for anything. Come on, I'll show you around."

Umphy quickly learned that there were three rules that the animals followed: Never go into the palace unless invited; stay out of the humans' business; and make them happy, no matter what. Umphy found these rules terribly restricting; he was used to exploring freely, asking questions, and serving his own emotions. But Whirit was a natural rebel in all his clever cunning. He boasted that he had been inside the palace several times without permission, and satisfied the little dragon's curiosity about what it looked like. "But seeing it for yourself if much nicer," he added. He also explained that humans had a natural tendency to involve animals in their problems, since they looked to them for comfort in times of hardship. Whirit had all kinds of gossip to chat about, and knew a great deal about almost every person in the palace. When Umphy timidly mentioned what the Stone Dragon Werso had said about the city, Whirit dismissed the rumor with a wave of his paw.

"Stone Dragons only come alive at night, which makes them extremely pessimistic creatures," he sniffed. "There's nothing evil in the palace. There was a huge disruption a couple months ago, but it's somewhat settled down." He proceeded to tell Umphy about The Argument between Vestia and Adenile. "Vestia's a nice girl but she's got a lot of puritanical beliefs about herself—nobody else should study demonology unless they're training to be Jacerin. But Adenile just wants to make a good queen someday. She has to learn how to protect her kingdom from enemies."

"But why does she need a teacher?"

"Because studying about dark magic is a dangerous thing to do. If not handled properly, it can suck you in, ensnare you, and never let you go. Weak-minded or overly-ambitious people—those who are blinded by one thing or another—are often targets of ghosts and spirits. Those who are possessed are almost never released from their tortures. So if you're going to study about dark magic, you need a solid reason and a strong teacher."

"I suppose that Gurdy—whatever his name is—is a strong teacher for Adenile?"

Whirit thought for a moment. "Personally, Gurthur gives me the shivers. He was once a Jacerin, but something happened to him. They say he came up from the South years ago—that he was imprisoned in Hebaruin for a time because his brother—also a Jacerin—betrayed him. Gurthur's a sort of jack-of-all trades: a healer, councilor, politician, sorcerer, and even a trained warrior. The king was excited to have him around, but the queen despises him. She never talks to him, never looks at him, and is never in the same room with him. The servants even say she's cursed him—they think it's because Gurthur took Adenile away from her. But the queen's never been close to her daughter—the whole palace knows it. They're like complete strangers."

"Poor Adenile!" Umphy could not imagine being at odds with his own mother. Mothers tucked you into the nest and told you stories. They nursed you when you were sick and cuddled you when you were hurt and needed comfort. Perhaps the princess had a bad temper because no one had ever cuddled her. The little dragon could not imagine anyone running to Gurthur for comfort. He was about as cuddly as a frozen icicle.

"You won't have to worry about Gurthur," Whirit said. "He won't bother you if you don't bother him. He's a strange man. But not likely to take an interest in you. Just keep out of his way and focus on pleasing the princess. The trick with any human is to make them happy. If you make them happy, they'll reward you for life. And that's the only thing that really matters in here: the rewards."

Chapter 8

The very next day, Umphy was comfortably sunbathing beneath a rosebush when the clink of chainmail woke him. Looking up, he saw one of Anthorwyn's guards peering down at him with a look of mild curiosity. The little dragon peered back up with a smile.

"What's up?" he asked.

"Come with me," the palace guard said stiffly. "I am to escort you to a luncheon with the princess."

Umphy scrambled to his feet immediately. After a week of waiting, he had not expected to be escorted anywhere inside the palace at all. Animals were strictly forbidden. But, then, dragons were not purely animal, either. He followed the guard through the gardens and up through the garden gate which led to the palace courtyard and up the steps to the back doors of the palace.

The guard led him through the gardens and though the back gate which led to the palace courtyard. Taking a flight of stairs to the back doors of the palace, the guard escorted Umphy into the servant's corridor and then through the lower kitchens.

"This is an awfully big place," he attempted conversation. "Are there lots of secret passages to explore?"

"The grounds of the palace are extensive," the guard replied. "And any secret passages you may find are used as shortcuts by the servants."

"I bet they'd be lots of fun for games of hide-and-go-seek," Umphy said cheerfully. The guard snorted, but said nothing. The little dragon tried again, this time more boldly. "Could we use one of the passages to get to the princess' room?"

"No," the guard snapped. He turned on Umphy and then, noticing the surprise in the little dragon's eyes, explained, "Her highness will not see you in her rooms. You are never to go there. The princess punishes any breach of privacy with torture."

"Why?" Umphy clutched at his tail anxiously. The guard shrugged.

"She has little patience for people who do not keep their noses out of other folks' business."

Umphy blushed with embarrassment. He and the guard now walked the terrace overlooking the Court of Women, where the queen's servants and personal friends lived. The little courtyard had no roof, and sun shone brightly down on a gem-studded floor. Plump silk cushions were scattered on the ground beside elegant displays of fruit and nut trees, floral arrangements, and stone fountains. A few women playfully splashed each other in a crystal-clear pool. Tables set with food, drink, and dishes of aromatic spices stood nearby. Umphy hoisted himself up onto the iron railing to get a better view. What a beautiful, luxurious place! The guard stood behind him in the shadows.

"It is forbidden for men other than the eunuchs to approach the Court of Women," he said quietly. "The princess awaits you down there. Remember to bow in the presence of the lady." The little dragon nodded and politely thanked the guard, who smiled briefly.

"My name is Daanan. Should you have any need for me, you have only to mention my name to anyone in the palace guard, and they will fetch me straight away." He bowed low, and left the little dragon to his own devices.

The gray-eyed Vestia was curious about the little blue dragon. She felt strangely drawn to him, interested in learning of him and the reason he had come to Anthorwyn—why he had come to *her*! She felt a bit of a connection with him that she could not explain, and she was eager to meet him face-to-face. She hurried out to the garden—and pulled up short.

The creature waiting for her was *not* the little blue dragon.

"Lady, 'tis an honor to find you here," Gurthur stood up from where he had been sitting. He stared at her without any emotion across his face. Vestia stood rooted to the ground, biting her lip in cold fury.

"You've been following me."

"Not at all. I came here to have a closer look at the little blue dragon—as you yourself have." A smile flickered over his thin lips. "Don't look so surprised. I knew you would want to look at him—seeing as how you are hell-bent on becoming a Jacerin."

She ignored his jibe. "Why do *you* want a close look at the dragon?" she asked.

"Dragons are so rare, and the Guardians have not been seen for over a thousand years. Why shouldn't I want to look? Come, come, child, you wrongly accuse me. Curiosity is my motive, nothing more. You, on the other hand, are anxious to see him because you feel that he is important to your *education*—" Gurthur sneered. "—and you see him only as a means to an ends."

"The Jacerin and the Guardians once worked together side by side. If I want to learn about a Guardian because of his kin's importance in the history of my forefathers, I think that's a damn sight better than ogling at him like an exhibit at a circus!"

"Ah, losing our temper, are we? You'll make a fine Jacerin, lady, a fine one indeed! Just like your miserable, pathetic father and all the rest of his colleagues—temperamental dogs, every one of them!"

"My father was an honorable man."

"You never knew your father," snapped Gurthur. "So you could not possibly know what sort of man he was. If he was a Jacerin he was no better than the rest of them—dirty traitors and renegade fools, every single one of them!"

Vestia wanted to cover her ears and run. "Why do you despise the Jacerin so much? They do nothing but good—"

Gurthur fixed her with an icy stare.

"You know it will never work, my lady. You aren't meant to become a warrior-healer like them. You are too much like your mother."

"You knew my mother?"

"Of course. In the days before I turned the age of thirty, I met your mother once, on the Northern Plains between Anthorwyn and Haeroné. She was laughing and beautiful then, but delicate like the morning dew which evaporates with the coming of the sun. You have all of her beauty, wit, and intelligence, but none of the delicacy she possessed. You have your father's strength," he spat. Vestia's eyes were wide. "You are young and beautiful, with skill and talents that need the proper appreciation. Galdermyn will only strangle your abilities, keep you in the dark, and assign you to a life of misery. He'll squander you as a gambling man squanders money. The Jacerin are bloodthirsty; they are merciless; they are like savage wolves who sneak, steal, spy, and murder for the sake of upholding their cherished 'code of honor.' What need have you to live a life of that kind of hypocrisy?"

"Those are not the ways of the Jacerin, and you know it," Vestia snapped. "You yourself are one of them."

"I forsook that path years ago. I swore an oath. My brother was a Jacerin, too. He betrayed me and gave me over to the Enemy! I vowed I would have nothing more to do with him or his colleagues. The Jacerin will deceive you, betray you, and murder you! I would not have that for *you*, Vestia." Gurthur stopped abruptly, as though he had said too much.

"And since when did you become concerned about my welfare?" The young woman looked at him skeptically. Gurthur did not answer. He stared at her silently, and Vestia felt her skin crawl. Gurthur was no normal man, for who could have the eyes of a snake without having been a prisoner of Hebaruin? She tried to speak scornfully, but her voice shook. "You don't frighten me! I have you to thank for Adenile's *welfare*," she said scornfully. "The king may tolerate you because of your utilitarian services, but they are slipping in favor of the princess' ruin. Someday your precious ward is going to make a very obvious mistake for the world to see, and not a soul will defend you. They'll say, 'He should have taught her better,' or 'What was the man thinking, to teach her such folly?' And then you will be exposed for what you really are: a destroyer of lives."

With that, Vestia turned on her heel and promptly marched back the way she had come, holding her head high. Gurthur remained silent, looking after her with his piercing eyes. Then he quietly left the garden in the opposite direction, pausing once to look at the rose bush that blossomed so fragrantly against one side of the castle. He reached out and caressed one of the buds, not yet in full bloom. For a moment, his touch was gentle. Then, suddenly, he viciously ripped the bud off its stalk and tore the rose to shreds, its ripped petals falling to the ground like drops of blood from a wounded heart.

The ragged beggar-man sat quietly between the bushes by the iron gate surrounding the gardens and watched the dark-robed man destroy the tender flower. He had overheard everything. Crawling back silently behind the bushes, his eyes gleamed . . . his heart pounded . . . and he waited.

Umphy felt like he was in heaven.

He sat beside the princess on her pile of white cushions surrounded by trays of food. The princess sipped blood-red wine from a gem-encrusted goblet. She wore a stunning gown of spun gold, while two servant girls fanned her with large bora leaves. Some of the other ladies attending the princess were looking over at the little blue dragon and whispering to each other, giggling behind their soft white hands.

"Pay no attention to them," Adenile said sweetly. "They're curious—as am I. Everyone is wondering about you. Who are you? Where do you come from? And why have you chosen this time to come to the North? We've not seen the Guardians for many years. Have you come to herald their return? And where have you been hiding all these years?" She sipped daintily at her wine. A servant placed a tray of food in front of Umphy: soft butter-bread scones with marmalade and sweet-green jam, cold meats and herbal cheeses, flavored cherry wines and ice, and crisp appleberry tarts. The little dragon set to with relish, pausing here and there to answer the princess' questions.

"I don't think I'm the one meant to herald the return of the Guardians," he said carefully. "I'm nobody important. I was born a runt, you know."

"That would explain your size. So why come here to the North just to look for a wizard to cure your illness? You don't look sick to me," Adenile observed.

"I have some kind of infection. My stomach hurts very often, especially when I'm dreaming." Umphy paused, worried. He hadn't meant to tell the princess about his dreams. But she laughed merrily.

"Dreams never caused anyone an infection," she said kindly.

"Mine do. I can't explain it. It's just something that happens."

"What sort of dreams do you have?"

Umphy recited his dream for the princess. "Dragons are not supposed to dream," he said. "We sacrificed night-thought for the sake of mental alertness even if our bodies sleep. Something is physically wrong with me if I have dreams!"

"Hm." Adenile quickly called for a quill and paper. "Dictate that lullaby again, Umphy!"

He repeated it slowly and carefully several times before she was satisfied. She stared long and hard at the paper and then jerked her head back up at Umphy, as if remembering something.

"I know a man who could help you. He is a healer and very learned in the arts of magic. Oh, he's no wizard, true, but I think you'll find him the equal of even the most powerful sorcerer in the world."

Umphy felt uncomfortable. He had a feeling that the princess was referring to the hypnotic man he had first seen riding alongside of her in the marketplace, and the thought was not a comforting one. "I think there's a difference between sorcerers and wizards, isn't there?" He remembered an early lesson from his father: *There is the Sweet Magic and the Dark Magic. The Sweet serves only the Illuminator. The Dark is the tool of the Enemy.*

"Differences are subjective," Adenile said loftily. "They are what you make them. Why, if you think about it, there is no difference between a sorcerer and a wizard. They both use magic. Where is the difference there? I see none."

Umphy did not reply. To him, the difference was clear as day, imbibed in his very being. A Guardian understood the light from the dark. But he did not want to hurt Adenile's feelings by rejecting her offer. After all, this was a woman who imprisoned and tortured anyone who set eyes on her private quarters. Something about the princess was secluded and secretive. Umphy, like all youngsters, burned with curiosity, but prudently held his peace. Instead, he asked, "Highness, are you in line for the throne?"

"I am." Adenile looked very smug. "If my mother does not give birth to a male child."

"And if she does?"

Adenile laughed again, but it was false and lacked merriment. "Let's not talk about it. You want to know if I am in line for the throne, and if I say that I am then nothing and no one else is!"

Umphy was about to say something else when a commotion on the terrace above caught his attention. The lady Vestia was struggling with two of the eunuch guards.

"LET ME GO, I WILL SPEAK TO HER!! LET ME GO, I'VE JUST AS MUCH RIGHT TO BE HERE AS YOU—"

"Guards!" Adenile shouted. "Release the charity-girl!"

There were some snickers from some of the girls. Vestia tore herself free of the guards and rushed down the steps. Her blue gown rustled as she marched over to the princess, fuming angrily. "I have to talk to you!" she snapped. Adenile chuckled and lay back against her cushions.

"Oh, Ves, go boil a potion. Can you not see that I'm in the middle of a conversation?"

"Please!" Vestia said urgently. "This is very important!"

"It's always important to you and boring as a blade of grass to me."

"No, but you don't understand; it's about Gurthur—"

"Oh for Enovan's sake, what's he done *now*?"

"He said—" Vestia stopped and looked over at Umphy. "Please dismiss the little one and your servants," she said coolly, ignoring the audible giggles from the other ladies. "I won't discuss anything in front of your entourage, just so you can have a good laugh with them later!"

The princess' eyes narrowed. "Do not dare to order me around, *charity-girl*. You forget that you address the Princess of Anthorwyn."

"Once upon a time, you were more than that," Vestia said bitterly. "We were friends, once, and titles meant nothing to you, then. Neither did power nor glory. We were as sisters before that man came between us and filled your head with ideas far above your understanding." Vestia gritted her teeth. "Now, either send your precious entourage away or come with me where we can discuss in *private*!"

Umphy secretly followed the two young women as they stormed through the palace and out to the gardens. Vestia had a power over Adenile that was intriguing; she strode in front of the princess, smoldering like a volcano, while Adenile followed behind her like a sulky child of five. There was no question of who was in command here. Vestia had the upper hand, and Umphy could not help but wonder what all this fuss was about. The two young women stood behind a bush in the palace gardens, snapping back and forth like a pair of eels. Umphy's heart pounded as he listened from behind a rock.

"—don't understand what that has to do with me!" Adenile said angrily. "You're getting worked up over nothing, Vestia!"

"It's not 'nothing,' and you know it! Does the king your father know about him? Is that why he took Gurthur into service? Because of—"

"Ves, for the love of Enovan, if this is another one of your little tricks to get me to banish Gurthur—"

"I'm not lying! That's what he told me! *He knew my parents!* Would I make something like that up?"

"You'd do anything to get rid of my tutor!" Adenile snapped. "You're only jealous because he will never impart to you the knowledge you *wish* you had! You're not the only one who can play with the supernatural, Vestia, so get off your cloud and tear that halo from your head."

Vestia said a word that no lady should ever say, and from his hiding spot, Umphy clapped a paw over his mouth in surprise. "This has nothing to do with your studies!" Vestia snapped. "I seriously think that Gurthur has an influence deeper here in the palace than you or I know. I think he is a spy for Hebaruin and he's getting you to meddle in things you don't understand!"

"Don't I?" Adenile's eyes flashed. "Of course you *wish* I did not understand it. You don't think I have a strong enough mind to study dark magic, and instead of telling me that to my face, you blame Gurthur. He's not an evil man. He's the only help I have in the world! Mother and father never spent so much as five comfortable minutes together with me, did you know that? Father is ashamed that I'm not his precious male heir, and mother is such a dainty, fearful thing; she's *afraid* of me! She hates being in the same room with me! I've had to lean on one man and learn to make a future for myself!"

Vestia stretched out a hand, and Adenile jerked away. "Leave me alone! You don't understand. You have *never* understood. I thought you were always on my side, the one friend I could ever rely on, and instead you started in with your 'holier-than-thou' attitude." The princess mimicked Vestia scornfully. "'I am fated with an important mission. I'm a *mystic*, so I know *everything*. I must practice with the men in the armory for a time of battle. I must study demonology in order to join the *Jacerin*!' You make me sick, Vestia. Don't come crying to me about Gurthur anymore. If you hate him so much, defend against him yourself! But do not involve me anymore, and do not speak to me ever again on this matter. Now go! Leave me alone!"

Umphy watched as Vestia ran out of the gardens, tears streaking down her cheeks. He could not see Adenile, still hidden behind the bush, but he could hear her crying, too. Bewildered, he turned around and gulped. Kelhah was standing directly in front of him, grinning wickedly.

"Well, well! What have we here?"

Kelhah was inches from the little dragon's snout. Umphy swallowed.

"What are you doing here?" the mountain lion asked pleasantly. "Have I interrupted a private moment?"

"No. I was just . . . just, er . . . enjoying the view."

"Oh, I see. I suppose that's what they call eavesdropping these days!"

Umphy glared. "Leave me alone. I'm not standing in your territory!"

"No, but you are on eggshells," Kelhah chuckled nastily. "Spying is a most unfortunate occupation. It doesn't pay well at all—especially if you get caught." Kelhah started stalking around Umphy in circles. Umphy pulled his tail close to his chest and watched the big cat move. Kelhah's wicked eyes gleamed. "But since you seem intent on information, I'll give you some. You may think it quite nice that the Princess of Anthorwyn showers you with attention. Sweets and roses every day with her, and not a single thing in the world to worry about, eh? I'd be wary, if I were you. She does not give favors. She takes them. She sees something in you worth noticing. That's why she's letting you look. Drawing you on. She's curious about you. And that might not be a good thing."

Chapter 9

"Don't listen to him," Whirit said after Umphy explained the incident. "He's just looking to get you into trouble."

"But why should he say those nasty things to me about Adenile? He's not her familiar."

"He is Vestia's familiar. He takes his mistress' side on *everything*. He thinks she's a goddess." Whirit rolled his eyes. "Like I said, he's also very territorial. He'd protect Vestia from the very demons in hell if he had to."

"Is she a part of the royal family?"

"No. Well, not a biological part, anyway. The king adopted her after the sixth Northern Kingdom fell into extinction. That was only about eighteen years ago; it was a huge affair. The people of that kingdom rebelled against their monarch and sought independence for themselves. That war lasted only a few months—Adenile hadn't even been born yet. Vestia was three years old, a mere child. They say her parents perished in the war. But she obviously inherited all of their passion. She's Adenile's rival in temperament, though the princess will never admit to that."

"And she's jealous of the relationship between Gurthur and Adenile?"

"Hardly." Whirit sniffed. "Vestia hates Gurthur. He could be the mud beneath her feet for all she cares. And for all his claims to be in love with her, I think he hates her, too. I don't know why, though. Probably because she keeps rejecting him for a life with the Jacerin. Gurthur was one, too, you know—but he never talks about it."

"Vestia said that Gurthur knew her parents."

"That's impossible. Vestia's parents were Northerners. Gurthur's lived closer to the Southlands all his life, until he made the trip North twenty years ago. He'd never been to the Sixth Kingdom. Came straight here to Anthorwyn. Vestia had not even begun to live at the palace. Why should he know about her parents?"

Umphy was confused. He did not feel that Vestia or Gurthur were the type of people who would lie barefaced to each other. He had many other questions on his mind, but he wisely refrained for the time being. After all, he was a guest, and prying into the affairs of his hosts was rude.

Over the course of the following week, Umphy forgot about the arguments between the people of court. The princess proved to be a dazzling hostess. She was extremely proud of her city, thinking it the best of the five, and spared no pains to convince Umphy of the same thing. He traveled with her wherever she went: to the city market, the forges and lumber-mills, the treasure-vaults, the gardens and parks, and, of course, the hunting grounds outside the city walls. The city was by far the largest kingdom of the North, and housed a population of over a million people, of which one-fourth composed the legendary City Militant. The others were wives and mothers, elderly retired, entertainers, artisans, tradesmen, noblemen and politicians, and naturalists. Umphy was astounded by the vast wealth of the city and the luxurious lifestyle of the aristocracy. Each enterprise and business had something to offer; Umphy had never before seen silk, smelled incense, or tasted cream pies (Arwos was right; the pastries *were* to die for). Adenile merely laughed at his insatiable curiosity, and showered the little dragon with gifts and amusements.

"My reign will be marked by the heights I will raise this city to!" she glowed, as Umphy munched happily on a strawberry-cream puff. The princess led a royal hunting party in the forests surrounding the city. She sat atop a milk-white horse; Umphy stretched his legs on the ground. "All this that

Anthorwyn has is not just for the inhabitants but for everyone around Balské. Think how much we could give and build in the ports of the East, or the mountains of the West! What do you think?"

"It's very nice," Umphy said politely, not knowing what else to say. Political matters were far above his head, but he didn't want to offend his hostess.

"Oh, it is!" Adenile beamed. "I have so many plans for the future! Plans that my father hasn't even dreamed of yet! When I become queen, we shall start mining in the Western Mountains. They are untapped. Would it not be a grand thing to find their riches, and to make paths through the mountains, so that travel will be easier? And we will establish peaceful links with the Elven Kingdom, so that we may have access to powerful allies! I've even talked with Gurthur about settling an alliance with the South—"

"The South?" Umphy sat up straight. "Your highness! Isn't that . . . well, isn't that where the evil Emperor lives?"

"He is a powerful monarch in a powerful realm. It would be wise to gain his trust and friendship. For too long have we, the North, been enemies with the South! It is foolish to continue such petty squabbling. Oh, I know, our ancient history teaches that there are demons and ghosts and other unpleasant things lurking there, but just think what I, as queen, could do! With my influence, we need not have use of such barbaric creatures. We will establish peace down there, and build up the South. In exchange, the Southern armies will come and help us against our enemies."

"But what enemies will be left when you gain Hebaruin's allegiance?" Umphy was puzzled.

"Oh, you never know who may be out there. A ruler will always have his rebels," Adenile smiled sweetly. "Uprisings would be suppressed and put down; rebels and enemy scum would be tortured and killed; and there would be no murderers or wicked men to hurt the innocent! And someday, I shall be Empress over all of Balské, the most powerful leader in the world!"

Umphy was completely lost. The princess had made sense up to the point when she spoke of an alliance with the South. Now she was hoping to be Empress? "It sounds like a big responsibility," he said timidly.

"Of course!" Adenile smiled happily. "But so exciting—don't you think?"

Umphy had never desired to rule over anything except beachside sandcastles, and he told Adenile so. The thought of one person ruling a real city, with so many people of different characters and temperaments, was overwhelming. "When the Guardians come back, you won't need to shoulder the rule all by yourself," he said hopefully. Adenile shrugged.

"Your kindred are dead or in hiding. It is men, now, who institute justice and peace. The time of the Guardians is over—it has been over, for many years now. You just haven't realized it yet. Here, Captain, is that a wild boar I hear? Frighten it out for me, will you?"

The captain of the guard urged his horse into the thicket. A moment later, there was a grunt and a sharp squeal as a huge boar darted out of the bushes. He was an ugly brute with twisted tusks and sharp spines along the ridge of his back. Upon seeing the hunting party, he snorted and charged, head lowered for battle, his hind feet kicking up leaves and dust. Umphy cried out and hid behind a tree, but the princess coolly raised her bow and let an arrow fly, neat and quick. It struck the boar through the heart, and he plowed headfirst into the soil, the momentum of his weight carrying his hindquarters over his head and smashing down lifeless upon the forest floor at Adenile's feet. She smiled sweetly.

"Dinner is served."

That night the royal family ate the roasted boar inside the palace and gave choice pickings to the dogs and animals in the gardens. Umphy was given a plate all his own, the strong red flesh served with fresh goat-cheese, slices of crisp apple and brown-sugar glaze. The little dragon licked the plate clean and then lay on his back to look up at the stars. The Northern lights shimmered overhead like banners of green and red, twisting through the sky and dancing with the celestial gems. The air was warm and sweet, and the little dragon had never felt better in all his life.

Suddenly, Umphy sat up, alert. His tongue sensed odd vibrations in the air—not wholly disturbing, but neither did they feel safe. He looked around and nearly jumped out of his skin.

A man crouched on the other side of the iron gate, staring at him. He was grizzled and gray, with a patch over his left eye, and bandages over his grimy, flint-like hands. Flanked on either side by shrubbery, and dressed from head to foot in tattered, grimy rags, the man almost looked like a part of the garden himself. He was silent and unmoving. His one good eye gleamed in the dark.

Umphy felt uncomfortable. That eye did not leave him. Finally, the little dragon got up and moved away back to his porch. Whirit was already asleep, gorged from leftovers, and snoring loudly. But for Umphy, sleep came slowly.

The man was watching him.

Chapter 10

Umphy did not mention the tattered man to the king. Since there were a good many people coming in for the Festival, the little dragon guessed that perhaps the man was a mere drunken beggar seeking out some kind of amusement. The incident fell from his mind.

The next morning, tidings were announced at breakfast that the wizard Galdermyn would be paying an afternoon visit. Whirit explained to the little dragon that Galdermyn was the head wizard of the Northlands. He made regular trips to each kingdom, giving advice and filling the kings in on news outside the High Realms. Galdermyn had many spy-chains and personal confidants around Balské, and they were his prime source of information unless he could personally get it himself. Galdermyn was a wizard who did not sit still.

Umphy liked Galdermyn the moment he saw him. Like all wizards, Galdermyn was a master at transformation, and arrived in the city in the shape of a great-horned owl. He landed directly in the palace courtyard and quickly changed back into his human appearance, just as the king came out to greet him. Umphy took a good, long look at him. He wore blue-green robes and a tall pointed cap, and his beard was long and white. In his hands he held a great staff of green bark, and his voice was merry as it rang through the great halls of the city.

"This place gets more crowded every year," Umphy heard him say, as he bowed before the king. "It's getting so that I think I may be claustrophobic after all. Nobody has any respect for private space anymore. Which is why I might as well invade yours, your majesty. Let us sit in the stateroom. What I must discuss with you is meant for your ears alone."

When they were safely behind closed doors, the wizard leaned towards the king. "First, let us speak of Adenile. I have here a letter from Prince Haramid, of the Iron Kingdom, requesting permission to seek her hand. He is away on business at the ports just west of here; otherwise, he might be here to talk with you himself."

Feromar took the letter and read it quietly. "Haramid is no fool. He knows his strengths, and he knows how to use them to his advantage. But why Adenile? He's never been interested in her before. I thought the man reserved all his emotion for battle. They do not call him Haramid 'Red-Sword' for nothing! The last time I laid eyes on Haramid, he was twelve years old, a lusty lad who enjoyed the armory and stateroom rather than the nursery. I couldn't ever see him as a father, much less a husband for any woman. But he would make a mighty ally indeed."

"I think, sire, that a mighty ally is what he looks for as well. That is not to say he is completely without feeling for your daughter. After all, Adenile is very beautiful, and Haramid is not a barbarian! He has the means to support a wife, and Adenile would become queen of a powerful kingdom."

"But would she be a fortuitous wife? That is what I fear. The match will mean nothing unless Adenile is willing to pull her weight in the marriage. She's become somewhat spoiled and independent. I'd rather leave Anthorwyn under her authority."

Galdermyn smiled. "Feromar, my old friend, I understand your anxiety to toss the reins to a younger, more eager person, particularly since she is like a wild horse that will be neither saddled nor bridled. The temptation to let her run wild and do as she pleases is strong. But you are still the king, and Adenile has much to learn before she can even be a fit wife for any man. How old is she?"

"Almost eighteen," Feromar said glumly.

"She's young and headstrong. In fact, she's very much like Haramid, come to think of it! Those two may get along well together—or they may destroy one another. My advice to you is to invite the prince to the Spring Festival. That is coming soon, is it not? Invite Haramid to come as an honored guest. Even if Adenile rejects him, you will need to make an impression upon him so that you may have him as an ally. You shall need such a one before long."

The king looked up at him. "You have information regarding Hebaruin?"

"Too much for my taste, I'll admit." Galdermyn spoke quietly. "A new threat has arisen, your majesty—quite literally, risen."

"Then the rumors outside of the North are true? The Black Dragon stirs?"

"I'm afraid it goes beyond that. I have fresh information on the movements of the South, and it is official: Morbane, at this very moment, walks the landscape of Balské. There was a killing just outside a southeastern village. My informant told me that Morbane heads now for the eastern shores of Balské." Galdermyn took out a map from his robes. He spread it on the table and used his quill-pen to mark the places where Morbane had been spotted. "He is after the dragon clans, your majesty. This is no time for secrets: the Guardians have made their nests on either side of the land, in the coves by the sea. Here is where Morbane made his first attack; you can see that he was hardly out of Hebaruin at all. He's about a two-week flight from Anthorwyn now, but he is not after human lives. His mission targets the Guardians."

"He's after the White Orb!" King Feromar gripped the edge of the table. Galdermyn shook his head.

"That's what puzzles me, your majesty. Based on the reports I've received, the Black Dragon is not hunting the way he normally does. Something has confused him. If he were after the Orb, he would have made one killing and gone directly back to Fordomt. However, you can see that he's made a killing here in order to sniff out the scent of the hiding place of the Guardians. Morbane isn't after the Orb."

The king's brow furrowed with concern. "I was led to believe that he had risen for the sake of retrieving it."

"So I thought, too. But why would Morbane *not* go after the Orb? The answer is simple: he can sense that it exists, but he does not know *where*. It is hidden in a manner that the Black Dragon cannot penetrate. Most unusual! So he runs like a man in a thick fog, slaying left and right, hoping to kill the right dragon."

"Could we not search for it ourselves?"

"With so few leads? If the Black Dragon is blind to its whereabouts, how shall we hope to make a search? Besides, the plot is deeper than this, my lord. While Morbane fumbles in the dark, Fordomt is aware of the prophecy. If the White Orb is out there, so is the dragon who will defeat Morbane in combat. That dragon will only be able to destroy him if the White Orb is placed in the Tree of Life. Time is *not* on Fordomt's side; he knows not when or how the prophecy may be fulfilled. Only the one who carries the Orb has that answer."

"What news of the Southerners' movements?"

"Troops of Southerners have been spotted as far north as the Yelme River. They have not yet crossed the Grindelid Mountain Range into the High Realm of the North, though I have no doubt they will try to push this way before long. But for now they have been stationed at every major village in the South, and they patrol the districts of Kalohmar, Visteria, Uperia, Wendowyn, and Sarharh. Once Fordomt knows about the dragon clans on the East and West Coasts, he will sent his troops in either direction to take their stations in the villages there. The major cities, thank Enovan, have not yet been touched, though I think Fordomt's first offensive move will be against the city of Curanon here in the southeast. It is a fair distance from Hebaruin, but it still offers resistance, and Fordomt knows that Curanon's ruler is a warlord who will put up a fight if his kingdom is threatened. Once Curanon falls—*if* it falls—there is nothing to prevent Fordomt from pushing his luck against the other important cities of the Inland."

King Feromar sighed, irritated. Galdermyn rolled up his map and sat down again. "I realize that the temptation to help your fellow kings is strong, my lord, but you have an entire city of your own to guide, and the entire Northern Realm must prepare for war, for I have no doubt that it will come. With the Black Dragon on the loose again, it is a surety that the Southerners will not fear to spread their sentries and devils ever northwards to make trouble. Sometimes the smaller hand is more perceptive than the large. If Morbane is blind to the whereabouts of the Orb, there are other means of finding it. And if it is found . . ." Galdermyn trailed off, muttering to himself. "The North is exposed and vulnerable. A border guard must be established once more, and the other kingdoms must be alerted to the dangers. If the North is threatened, the Five Kingdoms must unite or fall, one by one." Galdermyn paused. "To be extra careful, I suggest you hire the Jacerin."

"The Jacerin?" Feromar's lip curled. "I thought the line of the Healer died many years ago."

A smile crossed Galdermyn's lips. "Perhaps. And yet the Jacerin are not all composed of that line. Don't curl your lip at them, and don't think that it's a hope which is all hollow. They're good at their trade, and valuable allies to have." Galdermyn stood. "I impress upon you not to tell a soul of what has passed between us today. Trouble yourself little on the matter of your daughter. Do these things that I have suggested, but otherwise, carry on as usual. We must not release a panic on the city. Everything has its proper place and time, my lord. Let the sun rise but never let it set on a wasted day. You'll need strength for whatever lies ahead."

Umphy was sleeping beneath his porch when the shuffle of an old man's boots stopped directly in front of his nose. A cheerful voice hailed him, and the little dragon looked up to see Galdermyn beaming down at him, quite cheerfully. Umphy crawled out. "How do you know my name?" he demanded, sitting upon his haunches. Galdermyn chuckled.

"I've been talking to my brother in the forest of Poloran. He told me you'd be coming, and thought I'd want a look at you. How do y'do?" He swept off his hat in a grand gesture. "Afraid of me, Umphy? There is no reason to be. I am as harmless as my brother, and he's an old turtle. How are you enjoying Anthorwyn?"

"It's very pleasant." Umphy could think of nothing else to say.

Galdermyn chuckled. "A life of luxury is just what I dream about, so you're much better off than I am."

"Are you here to examine me?" Umphy asked. "Your brother said I had an infection."

"Hm, well, yes. May I?"

Umphy crawled out and sat before the wizard, who knelt down and prodded his belly with a few wrinkled fingers. The little dragon tried to hold still, but he giggled and squirmed.

"Tickles, eh? Does your little infection hurt at all?"

"Only when I have night-thoughts," Umphy said. Galdermyn looked sharply at him.

"Night-thoughts, eh? Unusual. Tell me about them." He listened patiently as Umphy described his dreams and the lullaby, but when the little dragon described the woman in white, the wizard stopped him.

"Have you ever seen her face?"

"No," Umphy admitted. "I don't ever recall anything about her, other than that she's enveloped in a white gown, with a white veil covering her head and face. She's very gentle. I'm never afraid of her at all."

"Hmm," Galdermyn nodded. "Does she shine?"

"Shine, sir?"

"Shine, glow, light up—"

"She seems to glow as if there were a light inside her," Umphy said.

"Ah!" Galdermyn nodded.

"Can you tell me what it means?"

"You're going to marry a princess," Galdermyn said off-handedly. Umphy stared at him, incredulous. "No, not really. In fact, I'm not even sure what your fate is. But *you* do. In fact, you have the very key in your hands."

"You mean the key to getting better again?"

"Something like that." The wizard reached into his robes and pulled out a little green vial. "I can give you a little anecdote for the pain. I can't cure what you have. Please use it sparingly—only one drop a day with a cup of cold water. And I would be extremely grateful if you told no one else about this. This infection is rare, Umphy, and rare maladies, as they say, should not be taken lightly. I think it might be best if we just see this through without any outside interference. After all, telling the wrong people might result in a lot of experimentation that would be quite uncomfortable for you. I don't want you falling into clumsy hands."

"I'll be careful, sir."

"Good. I might as well tell you, Umphy, that the lady in your dream is proposing a riddle to you. She wants to be discovered, and I'm afraid that you are the only one who can be the lucky finder. But in order to do this, you must solve the riddle. I wish I could stick around longer to help you, but I have business elsewhere. And speaking of business, have you seen the lady Vestia? I've come to check on her."

"Check on her, sir?"

"Yes, Vestia is my pupil, you know! Have you seen her? I have some news of great importance for her. Ah, well, I'll find her. Thank you and farewell . . . until we meet again, my fuzzy blue friend."

Umphy knew he shouldn't have done it. But he was wild with curiosity. Hiding behind the shrubbery, he peeked out to see Galdermyn approach the gray-eyed lady in a corner of the garden. She sat beneath a flowering apple tree, showers of the white petals falling with each breeze that came along.

Galdermyn sat beside her and spoke quietly. The beggar-man saw Vestia's eyes widen in shock, and her book fell to the ground. The wizard captured her hands between his own.

"You must be calm, my dear. Much shall be asked of you now that you know—"

"You are certain he escaped from—from—"

"My sources have spoken true. He will try with all his heart to make you his. But you must be calm and focus yourself. Do not throw yourself rashly into a situation that you know nothing of. He wants to remain secret! He must remain in secret, or his game is up. Act as though I have said nothing."

"I knew," Vestia shivered and then put her face in her hands, crying softly. "Somehow I always knew—"

"Hush, child. Do not fear. All will be well, I promise. You are now to be entrusted with a great mission."

"You mean—"

"Yes. The skills I have honed in you all these years will finally be put to the test. I must go now and round up what's left of his followers. That will take some time. When you need me, summon me with this." He touched her forehead. "You are the child of a mystic, Vestia. Remember that."

So it's true, Umphy thought with a shiver. *Gurthur escaped from Hebaruin and he has some sort of evil design against the princess and Vestia! But what could it be? What could he possibly want?*

Chapter 11

The sun sparkled and danced on the waters of the East Coast. Small dragons shrieked with laughter as they chased each other through the spray, picking up seashells and building sandcastles. A few older dragons sunned themselves on the rocky shores, basking in the heat of the beautiful autumn day. One drakona whistled at her mate from her cave, as she sat on her nest with five beautiful eggs. Her mate blew her a kiss, and went to hunt for fish. The Matriarch settled herself beneath the shade of a rock, her young protégé, Padina, skipping off to play air-tag with Jorgan. The day was pristine and beautiful and quite perfect for the Firespring Clan.

None of them realized the danger that lurked just above the clouds, honing in on the Green Dragons like a shark targeting the scent of fresh blood.

The Black Dragon moved swiftly.

The princess threw a fit when the king gently informed her that Prince Haramid of the Iron Kingdom was coming to visit for the Spring Festival.

"HE'S NOT A PRINCE; HE'S A FARMER'S BRAT WHO LIKES TO PLAY WITH ANVILS!!" Adenile screamed loudly, over and over. Nothing in the world would convince her that the prince was a dignified man ten years Adenile's senior, with a striking background as a warrior and politician. Anyone from another "inferior" kingdom was below contempt. Adenile threw things and screamed and beat her servants about like a madwoman, but nothing would change the king's mind. He was not about to put up barriers around the palace just because his daughter did not like the prince.

Umphy stayed out of Adenile's way and kept to the gardens with Whirit and Kelhah. The mountain lion was gradually coming out of his black mood in order to talk more directly to the young dragon, who delighted his friends with his tales of his family back home. Umphy had a natural talent for storytelling, and his words painted a vivid picture of the life he had once led.

"We had a richness of being together, cozy in our cave," he would say. "Mother and father encircled us with their wings so that we dragonets were sheltered beneath a warm tent heated by our breath and bodies. We ate the soft white meat of oysters and fish, but mother also gave us seaweed to chew, saying that it would strengthen our teeth and gums. Father told us stories of the fairies and gnomes and the creatures of Sweet Magic that walked abroad before the Black Dragons came, and mother played guessing games with us to train our minds and mental reflexes."

There was a familiar coziness between himself and his friends that reminded him strongly of his family. When they all gathered together beneath a tree to avoid the rages of the princess, they had something in common, and no topic was ever considered too delicate to indulge upon, including the recent actions of the king to station guards along the borders of the North. Three garrisons from each city were fully equipped to watch out for Southerners, and Anthorwyn had sent over a thousand soldiers in its effort to protect the borders. The king placed the organization of the Festival in the capable hands of his wife, and busied himself now with the soldiers and captains to outline defensive strategies and send letters of warning to the other kingdoms. So intense was his manner that many people stayed out of his way, coming into the gardens to relax and take their leisure, including servants and nobility alike.

It was also during this time, while Adenile was in her black mood, that Vestia came out often to the gardens. She was trying to escape Adenile as much as she was trying to escape Gurthur. Umphy liked watching her. She usually sat quietly in her favorite place beneath an apple tree, either reading or petting Kelhah, who lounged with his head in her lap and listened to her read out loud. She herself was an excellent storyteller, weaving tales of pirates and sunken treasure, mysterious crystal caves, magical flasks and bottles containing wishes, and islands inhabited by marvelous creatures. The animals were drawn to the strong, gentle sound of her voice, like chicks gathering at the side of their mother. Vestia was seen for days hanging around the garden; in fact, she did little else but sit and read and play with the animals.

"I am trying to become a Jacerin," she told Umphy shyly. "Your people and mine once fought alongside each other. I feel as though I've known you all my life."

She gave no indication that she and Adenile ever fought, and she never mentioned Adenile. Umphy thought that it was better not to take any particular side in the matter, or to wedge animosity deeper between the two girls. But he couldn't help but like Vestia. She reminded him strongly of his sister Possa, who had always looked after him like a second mother.

Nevertheless, he missed Arwos terribly. For days after the conversation with Galdermyn, Umphy tried desperately to think of how to solve his riddle, but nothing came to mind. He wished that he had Arwos to help him; he missed his friend, and needed someone to confide in, to help him with his new and complicated puzzle.

Then he remembered that Arwos was an assistant to the master librarian.

"Whirit," Umphy approached his little fox friend. "We aren't allowed in the palace unless we're invited, isn't that right?"

The fox yawned. "Right. What's up?"

"But you know how to get in, don't you?"

"I do." Whirit's eyes twinkled. "Why? Do you need to find someone in particular?"

"I need to get to the library." Umphy did not explain why. He felt that his desire should be enough. Whirit grinned.

"Say no more, my friend. We are now fellow rebels! Come with me."

Queen Unituriel of Anthorwyn was having nightmares.

She lay in the sun-soaked room of the West Wing, resting on her ivory divan and propped up by numerous soft cushions. Her mind, like those of her kin who had long ago inhabited the plains as fortune-tellers and seers, saw visions of past, present, and future. A small child with gray eyes and hair the color of ripe honey came running towards her with a bouquet of roses in her cherubic hand. But as the queen lifted the flowers from the little girl, she looked up and found herself standing upon a cliff overlooking the Eastern Sea. Smoke rose from the sand. She heard the screams and trumpeting of massive creatures below her, but she could not look down. The sea was stained with blood and white froth. Another scream split the air, bubbling up from the depths of nowhere in particular, and vibrated inside the woman's head until she awoke and realized it was herself, screaming in the pains of labor.

Whirit led Umphy to a corner of the garden that was secluded by the corner of fern-like shrubberies growing fast and thick along one side of the palace and the tall iron fence that wrapped around the entire garden. Pawing at some rubble heaped by the side of the palace, the fox uncovered a tiny door, hardly big enough for a grown human to even crawl through, but just right for a fox or little dragon.

"This was hollowed out long ago by gnomes," Whirit explained. "They used to be prominent visitors here in the North, until the wars made them run away towards the Heartland. The tunnel runs through all parts of the palace. Some of the doors might be blocked, but I believe the one to the dining hall is open. Once you get in there, take the nearest staircase. If you go up, the library is on the second level of the palace. But be careful. The royal family is not the only one to live in the palace. There are a good many noblemen and women visiting, as well as the politicians, councilors, and other important people. If you don't wish to be seen, take your time and be careful. Good luck!"

Umphy squeezed into the tunnel. It was dark and musty, but otherwise the visibility was not bad, and there was enough space to move forward and backwards, though he could not turn around.

As Whirit had pointed out, most of the doors were closed up and blocked. However, Umphy tried each one patiently, and finally discovered the door to the dining room. He poked his tongue out, trying to detect the vibrations. The room was deserted. Good! The little dragon squeezed out from the tunnel and looked around. The brass doors with their indented designs led to a corridor and a winding staircase. Umphy could not detect anyone in sight. In fact, the palace seemed silent and empty. Where was everyone?

Inside the palace, the queen's chamber was buzzing with frantic activity. Handmaids and nursing assistants fluttered about the ornate room like helpless, squawking chickens, giving orders to servants for wine, water, towels, more hot water, soap, napkins, more wine, and prayer-beads. Healers stood by the bed, monitoring the queen's slow, agonizing process, while the midwife, the best in the city, bathed the laboring woman's head, and spoke in low, reassuring, and confidant tones. The queen herself, in a white nightgown, gripped and twisted a wet rag as hard as she could, her screams vibrating off the walls. Sweat beaded her forehead, and her hair fell in heavy tangles around her pillows. Her face and lips were pale. Having children had never been an easy thing for her; she was like a butterfly with its slender, fragile form.

After an hour of watching the queen in labor, the midwife announced that the queen and her child would not survive. The midwife was a stout figure with strong limbs and a practical face. "Milady's hips are far too narrow," she said shortly. "And there is a blockage in her body from a previous birth. I don't know how long that's been there, but I'm amazed her majesty was even able to carry the babe this far without a miscarriage. At any rate, we must be prepared for the worst."

Princess Adenile, who stood in the room beside her mother, did not blanch or tremble, but her eyes were full of worry. Despite her differences with her mother, they had also shared moments of happiness together, and the young woman was timid of accepting the fact that her mother could die. She looked over at Gurthur. He, as Lead Healer of the palace, gave orders and directed the ointments, but otherwise stayed clear of the queen and sat in a corner on a chair, arms folded across his chest, his piercing, unblinking eyes staring at the agonized form on the bed. He did not meet Adenile's gaze at first. When he did, he gave her an odd sort of smile, one that did not offer any sort of comfort at all.

Umphy was helplessly lost.

The palace was enormous, and built like a labyrinth that spiraled upwards for seven floors. On top of that, there were a good deal of secret doors and passages that the little dragon kept stumbling upon, quite accidentally. Umphy turned this way and that, only to discover a new door or a new corridor. The palace, along with its state rooms and bedrooms, included a museum, a dining hall, gym, extensive kitchens, servants' quarters, training halls, lounge rooms, and a stage for theatrics. But Umphy could not find the library!

At last, he reached the top of the stairs to the east wing of the palace. Gasping for breath, he flopped down at the top and lay there, exhausted. Then his nose twitched. There was a funny smell coming from a crack in the wall. Umphy crawled over. The crack was small and slight, but for certain there was something on the other side—as the little dragon passed his paws over the wall he could feel a sort of small door there in the woodwork, cleverly crafted to look like a part of the wall. Another secret passage! Umphy pushed at the door but it would not open. Frustrated, he kicked at the wall, springing a hidden switch. The door pulled open, and Umphy crawled inside.

He was standing in a fireplace!

The little dragon squeaked and stumbled out, brushing soot and grease from his paws. He looked around. The room was unlike any other he had ever seen: octagonal in shape, all but three walls had full-length windows, giving a magnificent view of the Northern Plains. Besides the view, however, the room was sparsely furnished with elegant pieces: an ivory bed with a golden coverlet; and a wardrobe, bookshelf, and desk. The floor was covered with exotic rugs and cushions. But Umphy's attention was drawn to the desk. A large book was peeping off the corner. The little dragon drew closer.

"*Umphy*!"

He squeaked in alarm. Danaan, the guard who had once escorted him to luncheon with the princess, was peering around the door. "I thought I heard a noise up here! What in the name of Enovan do you think you're doing? This is the chamber of the princess! If she finds you here—"

"I'm lost!" Umphy cried. "I was looking for the library!"

Danaan tiptoed across the floor and gathered the little dragon in his arms. "You're not supposed to be inside the palace anyway. What are you thinking? The king will think you have overstayed your welcome, taking such liberties!"

"I have to see my friend; it's vitally important!" Umphy struggled and wriggled out of the guard's arms. He ran back to the desk. "There's something here!"

"*You* are *not* supposed to be here!" Danaan scolded. "What—"

Umphy smoothed out the pages of a large book. "What's an Elbib?" The original text was Icelic, the ancient tongue of the North, but Adenile had circled a word in red ink and printed "ELBIB" beside it very boldly.

Danaan could not resist being dragged into the little dragon's curiosity. "It is an ancient book of lore and spells, supposedly one that gives an account of the world and all its creations. There are only three in all the land, as far as I know."

"Why would Adenile be studying about Elbibs?" Umphy wondered aloud.

"I'm sure I do not know. You shouldn't be here! Come with me at once!"

"Wait!" Umphy pulled at a little note beneath the book. "My song! I remember; she wrote it down! And there's something else here . . . she's written at the bottom of the page . . . *temple*. What's the use of that?"

"The temple is where an Elbib might be kept," suggested Danaan. He immediately clapped a hand over his mouth. Umphy stared long and hard at him.

"But why would she write that piece of information down? What good would it do her? Unless she hoped to find the Elbib herself—why would she do that?"

"Time to go," Danaan said swiftly, plucking Umphy from the chair. "We've seen enough to have both our heads staked on poles for the crows."

Umphy was angry. "There's no need for that! She shouldn't be so sensitive! We weren't hurting anything. Besides, perhaps she is trying to help me solve my riddle!"

"Help you?" Danaan set Umphy down and locked the door behind them. "*Help you?* My little friend, the princess does not help anyone unless something's in it for her. Surely you must know that by now! You've seen the way she scrabbles after power. Do you think anyone would even dare contemplate an alliance with Hebaruin, for example, unless something was in it for them? If the princess is taking an interest in your riddle—whatever that is—it can mean nothing good. You'd best never go poking around there again! Come, I'll escort you to the library. We'll keep this incident between ourselves."

The queen gasped for air. The vision in her mind was clouded by a massive dark shape that blotted out the sun and caused smoke and fire to rise from the ground. Her eyes burned. She was waist-deep in a foaming sea of blood and the sky was filled with fire. She cried out in desperation, willing herself to connect with someone or something. Mystic that she was, the queen found herself staring out from the eyes of a gigantic creature laying upon the rocky shores of the eastern shores, and pain sliced through her stomach as she screamed again and again, begging for help.

As Umphy and Danaan descended the stairs, the little dragon paused and flicked his tongue out. Something did not feel right. The vibrations in the air were violent and unnatural. They pulsated through the roots of his tongue down his throat and into his heart.

"Umphy? What's wrong?" Danaan looked back at him. Umphy seemed to have frozen solid. He blinked a few times and then, with lightning speed, rushed past the guard, who gave a *"whoop!"* and landed flat on his back. "Umphy! Come back! Where are you going? You little nuisance, get back here!"

The little dragon did not stop or pause. Someone, or something, needed his help. He did not know how to help or where he was going. The vibrations guided him. As they grew stronger and stronger, Umphy suddenly realized what was wrong: a dragon was in pain! A dragon had been hurt! He raced through the corridors frantically, trying to find the injured creature.

Adenile flew across the floor to Gurthur's side and clutched his shoulders. "Do something!" she cried. "Don't just sit there!"

"She is dying," Gurthur said quietly. "There is nothing anyone can do."

"But you're powerful!" Adenile commanded. "Summon a bansith!"

Those in the room who heard Adenile went very still. A bansith, also known as the highlander's ghost, was usually the spirit of a woman who had died in childbirth or had been murdered in the days of her pregnancy and so haunted lonely hills and plains screaming shrilly. Those who invoked her aid for a safe delivery were bound to give her something by way of compensation—usually a child or another loved one. They were then taken by the bansith and never seen again. Adenile's request for such a spirit was borderline treason. But the princess grabbed onto Gurthur's robes.

"I don't care what she wants; she can have it! Now summon her!" The princess struck her tutor violently across the face, her nails drawing blood. "*You son of a dog; summon the bansith!*"

Gurthur's eyes blazed.

Suddenly, and without warning, the tall oak doors burst open, and little Umphy sped into the room. There was a gasp at his presence, but the little dragon heard nothing. He halted, flicking his tongue out to test the vibrations. Yes, here they were! They pounded inside his head like a hammer. The injured creature was here, lying upon the bed, although she looked nothing like a dragon. It did not matter. Umphy dodged the astonished, angry hands that reached out to grab him and slipped nimbly up beside the suffering queen.

He did not fully know why he did what he did. He took her hand and placed it on his forehead. Nobody made a move to stop him. They were spellbound by what happened next.

Umphy began to glow. The light came from within, illuminating the little dragon's entire body and lighting up everything within a radius of five feet. Umphy's eyes were closed as he held the queen's hand secure to his forehead, his body recognizing the ancient heritage deep inside his soul. Again, his mind saw the Tree of Life.

Enovan Illuminator gave unto me the first gift of Guardianship, to heal and protect and bring the Sweet Magic to the land. Welcome to thy legacy, Chosen One. Thou art one part of me. Thy brother is my other. Thou art my Heirs.

Color flooded back into the queen's cheeks. The ocean in her mind became unfrozen, and the wall of fire vanished. She was carried out of the dragon's body and back to the state her mind was usually in: the vision of the plains, filled with wildflowers, and a child running towards her with a bouquet of roses. The child's eyes were gray and smiling.

"Daughter," Unituriel groaned. "My daughter."

Adenile rushed forward and clasped her mother's hand.

"Nay . . . not . . . not you! Not . . . you! You . . . you would have summoned—" The queen's body contracted with pain, and she screamed again. The midwife caught the babe as it was forced out into the world, crying loudly.

"Another little princess, majesty!" she declared proudly.

Adenile backed up against the wall. Her face was white. At the rejection from her mother, all color had drained from her face, and she stared at the queen like a lost child who has been left in the dark without a guiding hand. Her lip trembled.

Umphy had stopped glowing. The queen's hand fell from his forehead limply, and he shook himself nervously. The vibrations in the air were not so harsh anymore, and the vision of the dragon was gone. Umphy didn't know where he was. People were staring at him. The little dragon felt very uneasy. What had he done?

"Umphy!" Danaan finally rushed in on the scene and gathered the dragon up into his arms. He began stammering his apologies at the lords and ladies and healers, and tried to back out of the room. His way was blocked by the king, who was coming through the door at the same time.

"OUT OF MY WAY, YOU IDIOTS!" King Feromar almost took the door off its hinges as he burst into the room, looking haggard and eager all at once. He strode across to the queen and midwife, roaring. "GET OUT, YOU RAGGED LOT OF HEALERS, OUT, OUT, OUT! What is the meaning of this?" He glowered at Danaan. "WHAT IS THE DRAGON DOING INSIDE THE PALACE? I THOUGHT I GAVE STRICT INSTRUCTIONS THAT HE WAS TO BE KEPT OUTSIDE!! THIS IS NO PLACE FOR HIM; GET HIM OUT!! DO YOU HEAR ME? GET HIM OUT AT ONCE!"

"NO!" Adenile burst out. She placed herself between her father and Danaan. "YOU LEAVE HIM *ALONE*!!"

The king paused. Umphy peered out fearfully from between Danaan's arms. Nobody spoke. Then Gurthur approached the king and bowed low.

"Your majesty," he said gently. "You forget that the Guardian is a guest in your home. Milady was on the verge of losing her child when he came to her and healed her with a single touch. It is a very special dragon you have in your palace, my lord. Were it not for him, your wife might have died, and the babe along with her."

Adenile choked and ran from the room, tears streaming down her cheeks. The king made as if to follow her, but the nurse tugged on his sleeve boldly, and placed the newborn child in his arms. The king's eyes shone. Then he looked back down at Umphy, who felt as though he had awoken from a strange and unsettling dream.

"Tell me everything," the king demanded.

Jorgan, the young keldora who had stood beside Tarragon at the Recognition ceremony, lay inert on the rocky shores of his home on the East Coast. His ears were ringing with the attack that had come so swiftly, and without warning. But he was still alive. Gasping for breath, he tested the air weakly with his tongue. The scent of death lay all around him; smoke and an unsavory odor of burning flesh filled his nostrils.

His body was a mass of sharp pains; almost every bone had been broken, and to move even one muscle sent lances of agony shooting from head to tail. He could barely recall what had happened. One minute he had been soaring through the air, trying to spot fish, and the next minute something had struck him like a thunderbolt, slamming him down into the earth and knocking him unconscious. When next he woke, there were screams of terror, the ground quaked as with a life of its own, and a fearsome roar, more terrible than any he had ever heard before, shattered the very rocks around him. One eye, caked with blood, saw a huge, dark form, rising out of the smoke, like some kind of nightmare. Then Jorgan had blacked out completely.

Now he could feel something pecking at his nose. He opened one eye—his only good eye left. A seagull was scavenging him! Fury and a determination to live bubbled up inside Jorgan. He growled loudly, and the seagull squawked, hopping back a pace.

"Hm! Now there's one that barely made it!" it chuckled. "You, sir, are as good as dead. You look like a beached whale!"

"'m nah . . . nah deh . . . not d-d-dead yet!" Jorgan spat out blood. His head swam with pain and nausea. He could hardly speak properly.

"Well, if you aren't now, you will be in a few hours. You won't last long, not in your condition! Dear me, what happened here, anyway? I've never seen such a wreck in all my life. The very rocks are too hot to stand on, and there's blood every—"

"Shu' . . . up!" Jorgan did not want the details. His mind, though foggy, was reaching out and seeking aid. There was only one creature he could think of who could help him.

"Co-co-come . . . h-h-here," he croaked. "M-m-mu-mu-must f-f-fin . . . find T-T-Tarahh . . ."

"You have a message for Tara?" the seagull squawked. "Who's that?"

"M-m-mout'ns . . . b-b-ban'shed. Tara . . . Tara . . . Tarragon!" Jorgan was exhausted. The seagull cocked its head.

"A friend of yours was banished to the mountains, and his name is Tarragon? Do you want me to bring him? Do you know which mountain range he's at? Hey, don't follow that light yet! Come on, I need more information! Don't start the journey down that tunnel! Which mountain range?"

But Jorgan, exhausted and greatly wounded, had slipped back into unconsciousness. The seagull thought for a moment, shrugged, and then flew up into the air. He was not a brave bird, nor was he interested in helping others unless it served his own purposes, but this dragon intrigued him. He wondered who Tarragon was, and if he would be able to help his friend . . . all that remained alive after the attack of the Black Dragon.

Chapter 12

Umphy was a hero. News of the little dragon who had rescued the queen raged like wildfire across the city and throughout the North. Umphy became an overnight sensation, the toast of the city. Never had anyone been given so many honors as he. The king named him an official citizen of Anthorwyn, and granted every kind of freedom and right for him. He was to be treated like royalty at all times and wherever he went. Forgiveness for entering the palace unwarranted was granted quickly, and the king gave Umphy further permission to come and go as he pleased. He showered the little dragon with presents and tributes. Most importantly, the king granted Umphy permission to visit Arwos in the library, even going so far as to extend similar liberties to the raven as well.

The library was not as big as Umphy had expected. It was rather small, with shelves packed from wall to wall with books and scrolls. A dusty old librarian, wrinkled with age and wisdom, snored behind his desk, his head face-down on an open book. With every snore, dust flew up into the air. Umphy peered around cautiously.

"Arwos?"

"HA-HA!! I KNEW YOU WOULDN'T FORGET ME IN YOUR HOUR OF FAME, MY FINE FELLOW!!"

The old librarian managed to sleep through the ruckus as the large, noisy raven scattered books and scrolls in his attempt to reach his friend. He settled down on a copy of *Gnome History* and jerked his head in the direction of the librarian.

"I can't possibly tell you how ridiculously boring it is in here. Have you come to let me out for a bit? I think if I spend one more day researching how the Praedic line of the family differs from the Draelin line, I'll go insane. D'you know, that crazy queen—cheers and good health and long life to her newborn infant, by the way—wanted me to research into the entire family history? For what? Aside from a few familial black sheep, there's nothing to mar the family name of Elthenburl. They're direct descendants of the Praedic people who were first nomads of the Northlands in the ancient days of—"

"Arwos," Umphy interrupted. "I need your help."

The large raven ruffled his feathers. "Anything to oblige! Particularly if it gets me out of the library. Tell you what, why don't you tell me about it at the Baccinian Bar on the west side of the city? I've had the pleasure of visiting there once before on another of my travels. Their Darkdrake brew is so strong it'll melt your tail off. Er . . . but don't add any of the spices to it. You're still a young 'un, yet."

For safety's sake Umphy accepted an escort of five guards, who brought the little dragon and his raven friend to the bar and then promptly indulged in the best beer in the land. Umphy and Arwos sat by themselves at a booth. The sight of the famous little dragon and a raven in a bar drew different reactions. The barmaids came around and offered different foods and drinks. One rowdy man called for a song, and another wanted to know whether or not Umphy could prove that ale was flammable. A traveling, drunken bard sat on the table and began singing verses of *The Gypsy Fairy* while Arwos squawked at Umphy to cover his ears. The guards kept pushing the eager customers back, going so far as to draw their swords, but no harm was done, and Umphy and Arwos were finally left in peace.

"Whew!" Arwos gasped.

"Maybe we should have stayed in the palace," Umphy fretted.

"Keep your horns on. A bar is the perfect place to talk. There's so much conversation that it's impossible to single out just one. We look less suspicious. Besides, the palace has got enough eavesdroppers as it is. I don't trust a single person in there. Now, what's the trouble?"

Umphy poked his tongue into his Darkdrake brew and sneezed. Wilderoot pepper-juice! That's what made it so spicy and dark! Nursing his tongue, the little dragon explained in detail first his encounter with Galdermyn and the diagnosis the wizard had made concerning his "infection" and dreams. Arwos hopped from one foot to the other. "I say, a riddle! How exciting! Well, you've come to the right raven! Riddles are my forte! But you'll find nothing that will help you in the library. The only things in here are family records of Northern history."

Umphy shook his head. "I don't think the thing we've got to find is in there anyway. I think it might be inside an Elbib in the temple!"

Arwos squawked and fell over. Picking himself upright again, he peered into Umphy's face as though checking for mental anxiety. "An Elbib, eh? How do you know there's one in the temple?"

The little dragon related his experience in Adenile's room and the words of Danaan the guard. "She wrote my words down and everything. I think she believes that there's a chance the answer to my riddle is in the Elbib in the temple!"

Arwos looked around and then lowered his voice. "Umphy, I think it's odd that Adenile should have such a strong interest in helping you out. If what the guard says is true, what could possibly be in it for her?"

"That's what I'd like to find out."

"I don't trust her one bit. Going to her for answers isn't going to solve anything. She'll either scream or curse us right out of the city and we'll be right back at square one again: trying to find out what the heck is wrong with you. If solving a riddle is going to do it, we might as well go up to the temple and have a look around before Adenile gets to it." He looked around and then lowered his voice. "I say, do you ever have the feeling that you're being watched?"

Umphy craned his head around.

The one-eyed, ragged man in the tattered black cloak stared back at him! He sat in a corner booth with a mug of ale and a plate of half-eaten food. Umphy looked back at Arwos.

"I know him—I've seen him before. He's just a beggar who hangs around outside the garden gates."

"Are you sure? He could be—" Arwos lowered his voice. "He could be a spy of Hebaruin!"

"I thought you said the Southerners haven't come this far north!"

"I said nothing about spies. They go where they will. I don't like the looks of that one. You say he hangs around the palace gardens? Are you sure he's not watching you?"

"Well . . . lots of people have come in for the Festival," Umphy argued. "He could just be another amusement-seeker." His theory was weak and he knew it. "But anyway, what sort of harm could such a tattered old man do to me?"

Arwos said nothing.

Inside the palace, Adenile sat sullenly upon a couch, propped up by large, silk pillows. A maid, deaf, dumb, and blind, stood behind her with a large Iyip-palm, fanning her mistress. The princess looked particularly stunning in a scarlet gown with gold trimming, but her red lips pouted in genuine irritation. Gurthur stood before the princess. His clear eyes burned hypnotically.

"Your highness has not been sleeping."

"SHUT UP!!" Adenile hurled a golden goblet at her advisor. It struck him on his bald, bowed head, splashing wine all over him. "What's it to you if I sleep or not? What do you care? Why don't you go off to meditate in a corner, or slobber after Vestia? You disgust me, you . . . you . . . FOOL!!"

Gurthur said nothing. His cheek bore the scars of her nails where she had struck him. He let the princess rage. Her temper would die down soon, as it always did. He watched as she sobbed brokenly. Then she grabbed a glass fruit bowl and hurled it. He sidestepped, and it shattered against the far wall.

"Lady, if you had summoned the bansith, the payment for your mother's life would have been the infant's—or another's. The bansith collects the souls of children to compensate for the child she lost in childbirth when she was flesh-and-blood. In return, a curse should have fallen upon the palace. Everyone in that room heard you demand the incantation of me. If I had made such a one the curse would have fallen upon both you and I, and your position for the throne would have been in jeopardy."

"You were afraid!" Adenile taunted.

"If you care to put it that way."

"I DO CARE!!" She spat at him. "I am the future ruler of Anthorwyn; you will do as I say! Perhaps you have forgotten your vow to help me gain power! If that is true, you'd best put your thinking cap on again because otherwise I think a trip to the torture-rack will *make* you remember!"

Gurthur touched his scarred cheek and smiled thinly. "Fear not, my lady; I have not yet forgotten my vow. For me to forget is to be struck down by the devil himself. Your rage, I think, springs more from the fact that your mother rejected you at a time when you stretched out your hand to comfort her. Is this not so? You have been crying for days. You are angry because you feel that so many have deserted you and let you down. First it was Vestia. Then your mother. And now, you believe, me as well. But I have always been here for you when you needed me, highness. I have withheld nothing from you, and I will not do so now."

Adenile burst into tears again. Gurthur slid into the empty place beside her on the couch, and Adenile threw herself into his lap, sobbing. The hypnotic man stroked her thick black hair tenderly. "There, there, my pet. No need for apologies. Your mentor understands and knows you unlike any other, and that transcends all heartache, does it not? You are my future queen, are you not? How could I ever let you down? I was thinking of you, my sweet princess, when I refused to summon the bansith. There will come a time, perhaps, when we will need her aid, yes, and the aid of many other spirits like her. I can build you up as the most powerful woman in the world so that even Fordomt himself will grovel at your feet. You will have the command of ghosts and demons, great and terrible armies, dragons and the fairy-people, kingdoms and provinces near and far. You will be fairer than the day and more terrible than a horde of men with banners and spears. Your rule will be long-lasting unto the ends of the earth, and you will be loved and feared by all who see you!"

Her eyes flashed. "Tell me what I must do."

"You must go into an alliance with Hebaruin. Only the Emperor can give you what you seek."

"An alliance needs something of value offered. I have nothing to offer the Emperor!" Adenile growled. "Nothing! I doubt he would be interested in my person—what could I possibly give to him that is worth anything?"

"The White Orb of the Guardians."

Adenile jerked her head up. "What did you say?"

"The prophecy is coming into its fulfillment, lady. I have foreseen it. And of all miracles, the one that you seek is within your very grasp! Your little blue dragon bears the White Orb."

Adenile snickered. "That's a very handsome joke, Gurthur. Now be serious with me."

"I would never lie to you. He turned back the icy hand of death that gripped your mother; only an Orb-bearer could be so powerful! And why should he seek the most powerful wizard for an illness? You told me once that his illnesses were affected by dreams he had—dreams that no dragon should ever have. He is the Bearer of the Orb, I am quite certain. And if you placed the White Orb in the hands of the Emperor, your rewards would be well beyond those of, say, an Empress . . ."

Adenile sat up straight. "How may we attain this Orb?"

Gurthur was silent.

"Do you mean—"

"There is but one way, your highness. You know what it is."

Adenile wrung her hands. "You're mad. Umphy—how can you ask me to kill him? He's—he's just a baby! And he's—well, he's a good friend," she stammered. "He listens to me—not like you or Vestia ever did, but—he's so innocent. Naïve. And he trusts me so! I couldn't kill him. I just couldn't!"

"Then your aim at ultimate power is forfeit."

"Oh no, no!" Adenile leapt to her feet. "There must be some way of attaining the Orb without—without killing *him*!"

"I assure you, there is no other way, unless he coughed it up. But he will not do so until the Orb itself is ready to be released. Who can tell when that will be? You must make a choice, your highness. Ultimate power, or the little dragon's life? Would you sacrifice everything you have worked so hard to attain, only to be defeated by a silly little dragon you only met two weeks ago? Surely your heart cannot be so touched that he means that much to you. If you would like me to do the work, you have only to say the word, and your precious white hands will remain unsullied by the deed. But you must make your choice. And you must make it soon, or else the Black Dragon will come here to the North and destroy it in search of the Orb—then no one, not even you, shall have the crown. Well? What is it to be?"

Chapter 13

Razot of the Firespring Clan was running away.

It was the first time he had ever run from a battle, much less a single foe. But this was no ordinary foe that had assailed the clan. The Black Dragon of Hebaruin was a monster from hell, and not even Razot could face him without trembling in fear. At the first sign of the attack he had fled his cave and deserted the other dragons. What were they to him, anyway? They had worked hard to build up their families, and where were they now? Dead and rotting in the sand because the majority of them stood by their stupid codes of honor and tried to fight back and protect each other! Razot snickered to himself. What a bunch of fools. The Guardians were nothing but peace-loving simpletons. He could not imagine how they could have ever been powerful. Morbane, now he had the real power and strength to rule over Balské better than those sappy do-gooders ever did—

A blow from behind felled Razot. He lifted his head, spitting out dirt. *What the—*

"Kin of mine . . ."

The voice was low and harsh, the breath poisonously foul. Razot broke out into a cold sweat as a set of jaws lowered beside his face. Thick saliva dripped and hissed like acid from teeth the size of double-bladed swords. The low growl was inches from Razot's face.

"Thou hast black blood in thee . . . kin of my intermarried species. Ye have lived among Guardians. I smell their stinking scent in thy veins." The sharp, huge claws pressed between

Razot's shoulder-blades, pinning his wings down. "I have work for thee."

Razot nodded furiously.

"Ye shall help me in my work. Take control of the villages. Search the forests, mountains, streams, and high valleys. Kill anyone who opposes thee. Bring me news of the Guardians and thou wilt have a share in the triumph that is to be Fordomt's when the White Orb is settled in the Iron Crown and the Tree of Life is destroyed."

The pressure lifted off Razot's back and he picked himself up. Ruthless amber eyes held him captive.

"Do not fail me!"

The week before the Spring Festival was a busy one. The entire palace was ordered to be cleaned. The cooks were given special instructions for meals, and they began to cook the food: golden-white loaves of bread with honey-butter, cheese-rolls with apple-cinnamon spread, jelly trifle, grouse and wood-pigeon roast, almond cakes and flans, venison roast with goose and peacock meat, creamy strawberry tarts, pies, dips and sauces of all kinds, spicy soups, and vegetable pastries. Men rolled up the wine casks and set aside only the very best. Musicians began rehearsing their music. The ladies and gentlemen of the court began picking out their most splendid attire, and the tailors were all kept very busy with the demands for new ribbons, silk, silver and gold buttons, and ivory chains or pearl hoops. Gardeners brought in flowers from all over the land and began making their arrangements in court. The entire palace was brought to surpassing excellence.

Umphy, as one of the entertainers, knew he should have been practicing his flute, but he was too excited to think about music. A few days after their conversation in the bar, the little dragon and Arwos decided to visit the temple.

"And let's keep this hush-hush, shall we?" Arwos said. "We're not about to let anyone on to our little plans, especially that princess of yours. She's got enough to keep her busy; besides, it looks like she's coming down with something."

It was true. Adenile had not yelled or raged for several days since the birth of her new sister, whom she did not even try to see. The queen, upon hearing what she had spoken out loud to Adenile, tried her best to placate her daughter, but Adenile seemed deaf. There were dark circles under her eyes from a lack of sleep, and she avoided everyone, keeping to her room and taking her meals alone. Umphy felt very bad for her and wrote her a get-well note of praise and thanks for the princess' excellent entertainment. When he presented it to her, however, she burst into tears and ran away. Later, Umphy found a pretty little drawing of himself and the princess, holding hands and the words "Friends Forever" printed across the top. Umphy thought her behavior very strange, but Arwos brushed it off as "stress" and told his little friend not to worry so much.

The trip to the temple was a good two hours long. Arwos had suggested flying, but Umphy was excited about using the path for the first time. It ran from the back gate of the palace gardens and through the surrounding forests up through the rocky slopes of the mountain until it broke the tree-line and continued on upwards to the temple, built into the mountain itself. The way was difficult, and people were even discouraged from visiting because outside influence was reportedly destructive for the meditation of the monks who lived inside the temple housing. The temple itself was massive, known for its impressive stone pillars which reached over a thousand feet high, the eternally-burning lamps, and gold plating. Here was the chief place of worship for those dedicated to Enovan; they lived and breathed the incense-filled air, took apprentices every five years, and carried on the sacred traditions of worship and artistry. Some of the best wines came from the temple, as well as beautifully-illuminated manuscripts and ornate musical scores.

"We'll need permission to look inside the library archives," Arwos said when they reached the top. "But not a word about looking for an Elbib. It's so rare; the monks will probably hoard it up and say they don't have one!"

The monks were not hard to find. Umphy had never seen holy men before, but Arwos pointed them out as figures garbed in simple, white linen tunics and voluminous trousers of deep blue. A group of them hurried towards the little dragon and his friend, but one monk with a long black beard and kind brown eyes knelt and received them graciously with the traditional sign of welcome: hands out, palm up. Umphy returned the greeting.

"And what brings you to the temple? I am Brother Multook. Your name is Umphy, isn't it? From Anthorwyn? We've heard of you. It is an honor to receive a Guardian and his friend as well. Do you wish to speak to the High Priest?"

"Thank you, but we've come to see your library," Umphy said politely.

Brother Multook was more than happy to escort the little dragon and his friend. The great temple was much larger than the palace but very dark and difficult to see without the aid of torchlight. Sometimes they passed rooms full of candles and incense, and other times they passed by great stone pillars beyond which lay an uncertain darkness. As they went deeper and deeper into the temple, Brother Multook explained that the extensive architecture was due to the builders tunneling far back into the mountains. Some of the rooms were natural caves of glittering splendor, with crystal-clear pools for bathing and pristine beauty for contemplation. "If you look carefully at a map," Brother Multook added. "You will see that we truly are located in the heart of the Evuinari Mountain Range. Mortals who dedicate their lives to Enovan come here for instruction. Some of them never leave because they make it their home. Others leave and gather followers elsewhere, or they become hermits in the forests. Some of our order have gone on to become Jacerin, though we abhor violence of any kind. Yet each man is free to follow his path as he sees fit. It is Enovan, and not man, who has the Plan."

When they finally came to the library, Arwos sneezed.

"It is a little dusty," Brother Multook apologized as he fiddled with the massive iron lock. He hurled all his weight upon the doors, and they slowly opened with a protesting groan. Umphy coughed. The air was very musty. Cobwebs hung from the rafters. Dust lay in thick layers upon the shelves and rows of books and scrolls. The entire musical library had never been opened for over a thousand years, and it showed.

"Whew," Arwos remarked. "You sure this is the library? Looks more like a museum to me." He sneezed.

Umphy was scandalized. He ran from corner to corner, picking up the ancient lyrics and texts, scanning them frantically.

"Why has nobody come in here?" he demanded. "I thought that monks were scholars of art and history!"

"Alas, so we are supposed to be," said Brother Multook sadly. "The neglect has been recent within the past fifty years or so. Our last High Priest was a man who admired the wizards and old warriors, and he came from a long line of men who had believed in and trusted in the Guardians. But when the Guardians did not return after their first defeat, the old laws changed. Men, without the spiritual guidance of the Guardians, needed a light in the dark. So that is when our order emerged. We followed in the footsteps of the Guardians as far as spiritual matters went. Once, we were scholars, artisans, healers, and guides on the road to spiritual happiness. But we could not do it all. So we now direct ourselves to prayer and spiritual guidance, while the academic part of our order has somewhat fallen into disrepair."

"That's for sure." Arwos shook his head and sneezed again. "Id's dusdy."

"Again, I apologize. I will leave you two alone now to do your research. But when you finish, you have only to strike the gong out here and another brother will show you the way out." Brother Multook bowed and was gone.

Umphy began shifting through the piles. "There's too much," he murmured. "How on earth can I find anything in here?"

"Check the index," Arwos hopped over to a cabinet full of the different files titled alphabetically. "And look under 'ancient texts' or 'Elbib.'"

"Oh Arwos—"

"Umphy, just do it; we haven't got all day to spend in a dusty ol' library!"

The two of them began searching, but even after a whole hour, they had discovered nothing. The library was thrown into disarray and everything was out of order. Arwos angrily shredded the nearest scroll.

"This is complete nonsense! Come on, let's just ask the monks if they have the book in a special glass case, or something. I'm allergic to all this stupid dust." The force of his next sneeze bowled him over backwards into the open texts of another dusty manual.

"Hey, look at this!" The raven suddenly flapped up and down. Umphy trotted over and helped Arwos off the pages of the open book. The raven flipped through carefully. "This is a very old book. Must have belonged to the wizards at some point. See the headings? Those runes? This is a book about the ancient lore—yes, by heaven—I think we found it! This is an Elbib!"

Umphy had never seen such a large book in all his life. It contained stories, prophecies, lessons, and great secrets from the dawn of time. It recorded the entire history of Balské and spoke of the Guardians up to the time of the death of the Brown Dragon. There were scores of musical texts, poems, and stories in their original tongue, and also sayings of great wisdom. Numerous, beautiful drawings of color illuminated each page. As the two friends looked through carefully, Umphy squealed and pointed out: "Look, look! It's the Tale of the Brown Dragon! His tale, Arwos! The one we hear about so often!"

Arwos began reading.

THE TALE OF THE BROWN DRAGON

When the Earth was newly formed, Enovan the Almighty formed upon the land and sea and sky the creatures that would inhabit these three realms, and formed from the clay of the ground a creature who would be master of all three: the Brown Dragon. And He gave to all creatures gifts: to the fox he gave great cunning, and to the bear he gave great strength, and to birds he gave flight. But the Brown Dragon, looking around, saw the Angels that the Lord had made, and he admired them, and wished to be like them in some way. Then the Lord asked the Brown Dragon, "What gift wouldst thou ask of me, O my child?" And the Dragon replied, "Sire, you have created all these things wonderful and good, and for my life I am grateful. You ask me to name my gift, and so I will be bold and ask to be like the Angels which You have created so wonderfully!"

The Lord smiled and replied, "That cannot be done, for they are immortal spirits, and it is written that they should be what they are, and that dragons be what they are!"

Then the Brown Dragon's head drooped, and he felt ashamed. But the Lord said, "For thy asking, though, I praise thee. For ye have not asked after wealth or riches, but for the virtue which these Angels embody. Therefore I say that ye shall have, as thy gift, an Angel Virtue which shall pass down through thy descendants for generations to come: ye shall be a Guardian, and of thee will be born those who will help keep peace and justice upon my earth. Ye shall serve me and bring a Sweet Magic to the world, such as it has never known, and help it to bloom for my glory."

The Brown Dragon was overwhelmed with gratitude, and bowed low. And it was as the Lord spoke: for years and generations afterwards, the dragons multiplied and became known throughout the land as the Guardians, for they established a fair reign of justice, peace, and healthy prosperity everywhere they went. With mankind the dragons formed bonds of trust and friendship. They brought gifts of wisdom, lore, healing, and kindness. Thus the land blossomed.

When at last the Brown Dragon had lived out his days, he found the burial site which the Lord had made for him, and he buried himself deep in the earth. Then he said: "O Lord, the time has come for me to give myself back into Your hands, so that You may give my spirit back to the three elements which You have set upon the earth: rock, air, and water!"

But the Lord said, "Nay, there is yet more to the story." And he granted the Brown Dragon one last gift, that of foresight. And the Brown Dragon cried:

"Lord, I see dragons fighting dragons, and men turning on women, and women turning on their children, and children turning on their parents. I see the earth burned and blackened, and a great smoke and flame! I see the blood of a thousand souls that scream out to me! I see war and horrible things that You did not create. I see terrible violence!"

The Lord ended the vision and said, "It is written that soon there will come a time of great trial of the Guardians. My Enemy will strike at my creation and try to destroy the Guardians, to discover their Secret. But thy Secret is thy Angel Virtue, which is my mark upon each dragon's spirit. It cannot be discovered nor destroyed. But it will waver and fall, and hide itself in shame and fear, for the foe that will arise shall be powerful, and he will threaten to wipe out the Guardians.

"But fear not! For I will not leave thee alone in the bitter darkness. Behold, this is my sign of hope for thy people:

> *My Sacred Tree shall sprout from thy body*
> *Of thy death will come the Tree of Life*
> *The crown of My Tree will hold eight jewels:*
> *Eight Orbs to be the fruit of eight dragons*
> *Seven will be lost and found again.*
> *The eighth shall be the sign of hope.*
> *When they are placed within the crown*
> *Thy spirit will be renewed upon the earth*
> *The weak will shine forth to aid the mighty.*
> *The mighty will rise to guard again.*
> *The twain will slay the Evil Worm;*
> *Evil will fall, his people will scatter,*
> *And peace will walk abroad once more.*
> *And a New Spring will come to Balské.*

"The Guardians will rise again."

"Look," Arwos pointed in awe. "After the story comes the prophecies of the Orbs!"

The open book displayed eight small poems in Original Icelic. Interspersed between the poems were depictions of eight beautiful women holding different objects. The border of the two pages was a golden vine which curled at the side as an enormous tree. Sitting at the base of the tree was a fair young woman—very young, with large brown eyes set within a delicate face.

"Arwos, that's her!" Umphy gasped. "That's the lady I see in my dreams!"

"Look at the poem," Arwos urged. "She's standing right by the eighth poem."

VNA ROSVM
IM TUTANIA BEL HENGVN DWS
GLIMT SHINVN ROSVM NI-RVDNI-NAE
TRE ALTAE; ORM BRVNAE
VNSI IDNI-'ALLA VN-DWVL OT DEPNAE
INES-VNDAE EVUINAE; IDA SATINWN
RIPVN SENE VNDVN IDA VNGLIS . . .

"I don't understand." Umphy scratched his head. "What is it?"

"Umphy, that's your song! In its original language, *that is your song!*"

"But what does it mean?"

Arwos stared at him. "Umphy. How thick can you be? Look! Eight Orbs, eight lovely women, and one of them belongs to you. You're an Orb-Bearer! *You've got an Orb growing inside you!*"

Umphy froze. Then he chuckled nervously. "Arwos, no more Darkdrake brew for you."

"I'm serious! Look, this can't be a coincidence. You have dreams—that's not normal for a dragon; you told me so yourself. You heal the queen and her child when she's on the brink of death—how many other Guardians can do that? And now we discover that the lady of your dreams is the same one in this Elbib beside the prophecy of the White Orb!" Arwos stared at his little friend as though seeing him for the first time. "Holy Bola-Trees!" he whispered.

"Arwos, it can't be me!" Umphy said furiously. "It's nonsense. I'm a runt. I'm only four years old! For me to have an Orb inside me—that's not possible! Only adult dragons can carry Orbs; you know that. They're the only ones who could possibly handle them and spit them out, too. If I tried that, I'd kill myself. I haven't got the strength to carry an Orb around, much less cough it up!"

"There's only one way to be sure," Arwos said mysteriously. "Yuna Rose is proposing a riddle for us to solve here. If you're not one of the Chosen Two Dragons of the prophecy, then maybe there's a clue here that will lead us to him. If and when we find him, we should probably alert Galdermyn to his whereabouts. After all, there is a Black Dragon on the loose!"

"What?" Umphy clutched his tail.

"I heard Galdermyn speaking to the king about it. Morbane has officially been set loose but he's having difficulties finding the Orb. Nobody knows why. So he's attacking the Green Dragon clans to find the Bearer."

Umphy trembled. For the first time in a long time he remembered his home by the Western Sea. "Momma . . . papa! Possa—Arwos, my family is in danger!"

The raven pushed the Elbib into Umphy's open paws. "Then all the more need for speed, my fuzzy blue friend. We'll take this and try to make heads or tails of it. Come on, let's go."

They left the library, locking it securely. Umphy was hopping up and down in his anxiety to go, so Arwos struck the gong with his beak. The vast ringing noise echoed up and around the cavern-like corridor in which they stood, but no monks came shuffling to attention. After a few minutes of waiting, Arwos rolled his eyes.

"Come on, Umphy. We'll just have to navigate out of here ourselves."

They started down the long corridor, their way guided by the occasional torch. The monks must have been called away to prayer or daily meditation because the temple was completely silent except for the dripping of water in some of the natural caverns and pools. Arwos, riding on Umphy's shoulder, suddenly halted his friend.

"Listen—d'you hear that?"

Umphy stopped and perked his ears. He heard nothing.

"Must be my imagination," Arwos grumbled. "The sooner we get out of here, the better. This place gives me the shivers."

Umphy carried on, but now the raven's fretting was beginning to worry him, too. He stopped again and tested the air with his tongue.

Something was wrong.

"Umphy¿ What is it¿" Arwos felt the shoulder beneath him suddenly go cold as ice, and the little dragon shook with fear. Umphy clutched the Elbib tightly, willing himself to stay as calm as possible. He could sense danger in the air. The vibrations had been almost nonexistent before, but now they flowed in and out like waves. Every nerve in the little Guardian's body was tense and alert. His eyes instinctively moved upwards towards the void of blackness above their heads. Arwos hushed. He had never seen Umphy so frightened or so on guard. The little dragon spoke as quietly as he could.

"There's something up there, and it's hunting us."

"Keep going," Arwos whispered nervously. "I'll watch the ceiling; you concentrate on getting us out of here."

Umphy moved with hesitancy. The vibrations followed, stalking ruthlessly. What was it¿ Umphy had never before smelled anything like it. *Not human. A creature. Not even an animal. Something else.*

Suddenly, both dragon and raven heard the heavy thud of a thick body as it dropped to the floor behind them. Umphy half-turned in terror, but Arwos launched himself off his friend's shoulder with a scream.

"RUN FOR IT, UMPHY—I'LL SAVE YOU!!" Arwos cawed loudly and scratched at the spectral figure. Umphy heard a demonic hiss and then he was running, running faster than he ever had in his life, his heart pounding against his chest in terror. Arwos flew beside him, his talons bloody. Umphy could heaer the swift, deadly movements of the creature. His tongue picked up evil, horrible vibrations; something deadly slithered from pillar to pillar, much bigger than any creature he had set eyes on yet. Arwos was right behind him; the little dragon could feel the racing heartbeat of his friend. Arwos had never been so frightened before. "UMPHY, RUN FOR YOUR LIFE, AND FOR GOD'S SAKE, DON'T LOOK BACK!"

Umphy put on an extra burst of speed. But just as they rounded the corner, something dropped from the ceiling and coiled upwards before them, blocking the exit into sunlight and freedom.

The massive serpent was sixteen feet long from snout to tail, and colored a deep red hue, like the color of a bloody sunset. Amber eyes glinted dangerously. The giant maw opened wide, revealing two sharp fangs that dripped venom, and the passageway to death and beyond. Umphy was frozen solid in terror. Arwos was helpless to give him any advice.

Suddenly, and without warning, a man leapt out from between the pillars and placed himself between the little dragon and the serpent. Umphy caught a glimpse of the bandaged hands and the eyepatch, but this beggar-man held a sword in his hand and he wielded it expertly. The serpent seemed afraid of him, hissing loudly. Then it struck, full-force. The beggar dodged to the left; Umphy and Arwos dodged to the right; and the serpent missed all three targets completely. The beggar stabbed down into the soft flesh at the back of the creature's head, shouting, at the same time, "Go!"

Umphy grabbed Arwos and ran for the exit. They did not stop running—or flying—until they were safe inside the palace again.

Part Three

The Quest Begins

Chapter 14

The knight rode up the steep slope of the Galtic Mountain Range, his silver armor flashing in the sun, and his blade of steel unsheathed, and ready for battle. He was one of the many who was riding out to challenge The Dragon.

The only village beside the Galtic Mountain had been, for the past few weeks, plagued by a nighttime menace: a dragon raided their cattle. Since there was no way for the terrified people to spread the word and get help, their own men rode to challenge the dragon. So far, none have been killed, so it was well-known that the dragon was not looking for a fight. Nonetheless, he was still a nuisance.

This tragic hero trod up to the doorstep of the slumbering beast, and there he dismounted, noted with distaste the scattering of cattle's bones, and shouted a challenge. Annoyed, the dragon pretended only to sleep on and turned in his sleep, sending a few rocks off the top of the cliff. This angered the hero, and he rushed, full throttle, at the posterior angle of the unknowing creature, blade pointed directly outward. The result was ultimate catastrophe because for one, it is very painful to be stabbed between the plates of the hindquarters; and secondly, it is extremely humiliating. Within five seconds of this major injury, the dragon leapt up, expelled a harsh bit of flame and a good deal of noise, and then, turning upon the luckless hero, creamed him with one swipe of his mighty paw, which sent him flying out of the cave and tumbling down the mountainside—not dead, but carted home with a broken leg and a few crushed ribs.

This episode ended any high hopes the man had for glory.

Tarragon growled deep in his throat and buried himself deeper inside his cave to go back to sleep. He was irritated by the occasional knight in shining armor, but his code of honor would not allow him to kill a human. Besides his run-ins with humans, however, Tarragon's life was extremely boring. He hated being restricted to a cave that only allowed so much exploration. He missed his home and friends and games. He wanted to fly again and grow up with the other keldoras.

He was, however, destined for another fate.

One evening, Tarragon was sleeping peacefully in his cavern, his mind devoid of dreams or visions, as was proper for a dragon. But something nagged at him. For the past two weeks he had felt strange, as though he were really and totally alone in the world, without anyone else to know of his existence. He owed this troubling feeling to his exile; after all, he really was, in a way, cut off from everyone and everything, except for random squirrels that happened to tumble down into his lair. Aside from them, however, he had no one to talk to. The feeling of complete isolation bothered him.

It had grown stronger and stronger as the days passed. Tarragon had almost left his cave to check back on his friends on the East Coast, but fear of his elders and stricter punishment always made him hesitate. But he felt that something was wrong. He just couldn't figure out what it was.

He rolled over anxiously in his sleep, and fell into a pool of ice-cold water. Sputtering, the Green Dragon shook himself off and blinked rapidly, panting for breath.

"Nightmares?"

Tarragon looked up. A large seagull was perched on a piece of dead wood close beside the pool, staring at him quite oddly. Tarragon shook his head.

"Dragons don't dream. I merely felt . . . anxious."

"You'll excuse me for dropping in like this and being forward," the seagull remarked. "But are you Tarragon?"

The large dragon's head shot up like lightning. "I am! That's me! Who sent you? Are you from the East Coast?"

"Well, what's left of it, anyway. I've come on behalf of . . . well, dash it all, I didn't even get his name. But he knew you, alright. Managed to wheeze your name before conking out completely. I'll be surprised if he's still alive when you go back."

Tarragon felt icy fear grip his spine. "What do you mean . . . what's left of the East Coast? He conked out? Still alive . . . ? When I go back? What's going on?"

"Of course, I don't expect you to know. You were banished, right? Well, here I am to un-banish you! Some dragon on the throes of death told me to go get you, though he blacked out before he could tell me which mountain range you were in. I didn't know where to start, and it's been mortal hard asking anyone about dragons these days, particularly since all of Hebaruin's looking for 'em, and Morbane himself is one the loose, according to popular rumor. I finally got a clue from a few of the local forest-dwellers here . . . by Envoan, I can see why that dragon asked for you. You look as though you could pound the tar out of whoever destroyed that poor fellow's home."

Tarragon had not received such praise in a long time. He had only been gone for a month, but in that short time he had grown slightly bigger and stronger. Standing on his hind feet he was from foot to snout a full twenty-five feet. He was almost as big as a full-grown male dragon, powerful in every limb and muscle. The seagull regarded him reverently. "I'd hate to be the fool who made you mad."

Tarragon got to his feet. "Explain what happened."

"I told you. I've been sent here—"

"I know, I know. But what happened to the coast? Did you see?"

The seagull swallowed. "I saw the results of . . . of . . . of whatever came through there. It wasn't a hurricane or a water-spout, that's sure enough. No force of nature could have done this. The air was filled with thick, black smoke, and the sands were soaked through with blood. You don't want to know anything more—it might make you sick."

"My—my clan . . . ¿"

"That was your clan¿" the seagull groaned. "Oh Enovan preserve us! A Green Dragon clan, wiped out—and you're the only survivor!"

Tarragon fell heavily against the side of the cavern, causing the earth to tremble. He was numb with horror. His clan! Jorgan, Padina, the Matriarch, his family . . . all of them, dead¿ Tarragon felt like throwing up. Not since the death of his parents had he felt so lost and terrified.

The seagull assessed the situation quickly. "You have to leave here and see for yourself," he said. "It isn't pretty, but perhaps you could find some clue as to who or what did this. Then you can avenge your clan."

Vengeance was far from Tarragon's mind. He could only see Padina's face in his mind, the sweet young drakona who was successor to the Matriarch. It was impossible that she was dead. And Jorgan! That thick-headed nincompoop could fly faster than storms could whip up lightning bolts. Surely they were not dead! Surely the whole clan was not all lost! Tarragon got to his feet again, shakily.

"I must go," he croaked. "I have to go see, they can't all be dead, and there must be some survivors—I have to find them!"

The seagull watched as Tarragon made his ascent out of the cave and into the light above. He decided not to say anything, nor to accompany the large dragon back to the graveyard he had left behind. Sometimes, it was best, though hard, if some people discovered the truth on their own. At the same time, the seagull did not want to be around that creature when he did discover the truth. Something told him that Tarragon was no mere Green Dragon, and that whoever had destroyed his home, family, and friends would pay dearly for its crime, though it was even a demon of hell.

Tarragon's wings, fueled by his desperation, took him quickly across the slight distance between the coast and his mountains. It was a day's journey, and he flew through the night, but as Tarragon neared the cliffs he called home, the sun was just rising, and the familiar smell of the beach reached his nose.

He landed on the cliff overlooking his cove and steadied himself, preparing for a gruesome sight. But when he looked down, nothing could be seen but rocks, sand, and bleached driftwood. Not a dragon was in sight.

Puzzled, Tarragon swooped down and landed on the shore to observe the crags of rock dotted with empty caves.

"Hulloooo-o-o-ooo!" he called, cupping his paws about his snout. "Hullooooo-o-ooo-ooo! Padina! Jorgan! Assista, Marmy! Anyone! Can you hear me? Hulloooo-oo-oo-o-o!"

There was no reply. Tarragon tried giving a familiar honk of distress, like a flare signal. But nobody came out. The entire cove was deserted.

Tarragon decided to search closer to see what he could find. The caves were empty and almost untouched, except for scorch-marks and traces of soot around the walls, and one cave had a nest full of broken, blackened egg shells. Along the rocks, he overturned bits of bone and a skull. He sniffed at this frantically, trying to detect traces of a familiar loved one. It was no one he knew. He turned this way and that, seeking anything that would lead him to the whereabouts of his clan. He was angry, frustrated, and confused. If there had been such a massive slaughter, where were all the remains? No one would disturb bones, surely, even after the birds of prey and crabs had picked them over! So where had they all gone? Tarragon slammed his body furiously against the cliff and roared as loud as he could.

"AAAAAAAAAARRRRRRRRRRRGGGHHHH!"

Then, there was nothing else to do except to pitch camp and think.

An hour passed when Tarragon's musing were suddenly interrupted by the rumbling sound of a thousand, heavy feet stampeding across the ground above the cove.

"Behemoths!" the dragon thought. "What are *they* doing so far from the inland?" He ducked as chunks of his ceiling came crashing down around him. He scrambled wildly out of the cave and pulled up short as the body of a massive creature toppled over the cliff and landed with a heavy thud at his feet. The behemoth, who was many times larger than Tarragon, scraped at the ground feebly with its thick feet, and gave a dying moan. The dragon gingerly stepped around the body and flew skywards and looked down. He gasped at the sight.

Hundreds of behemoths were stampeding across the plains above the Eastern coves. They trumpeted loudly as they rushed along, stumbling into each other, pushing violently to the edge above the cove. Swooping lower, Tarragon could see the cause of the panic: a pack of very large wolves. They ran behind and between the trunk-like legs of the behemoths, snapping and growling fiercely.

As Tarragon watched with horrified interest, one of the wolves, slightly smaller than his companions, ducked between the massive legs and was kicked violently backwards. The wolf howled in pain and rolled this way and that to avoid the stampede. Tarragon flew closer, but the herd moved on, with the pack closely behind. The lone wolf was left in a heap of fur on the ground, a cloud of dust settling around him.

The dragon landed gently beside the wolf and looked him over. His eyes were closed, though barely breathing, and he was badly bruised. Tarragon nudged him gently with his snout, and the wolf's eyes flickered.

Suddenly, the wolf leapt to its feet, bared its teeth, and snarled!

"Back off; I'll puncture holes in your slimy nostrils if you try anything, see!"

Tarragon bared his own teeth. "See? I'd like to see you try, you sniveling bag of fur and bones!"

The wolf gaped and crumpled to the ground like wet paper. "Oh, please don't! If only you knew, you wouldn't be so cruel!

It's a hard life for us wolves. We must put up a vicious façade, or else we'll never survive!"

"And you think that chasing behemoths across the coast is trying to survive?" Tarragon snorted. "That's the stupidest thing I ever saw in my life."

"Aw, admit it—it was grand. Little ol' us, chasin' those big ol' monsters! Brave, wot?"

"Suicidal. You could have been killed!"

"Granted. But the thrill would have been worth it, don't you think? It's the best thrill in the world, bar jumping off cliffs into the ocean. Have you ever done that? I love it. There's nothing like the adrenaline rush. It makes one realize that life truly is worth living. Hey, what's your name anyway?"

"I'm Tarragon."

"Pleased to meet you. I'm Tworgar Sundance. That was my pack that just went by—hm, and they're not going to turn around and fetch me back anytime soon. Stragglers get left behind, and last week, we lost Fondot in another stampede." Tworgar winced. "I guess I came close to going that way myself."

"You did." Tarragon watched the wolf carefully. "Well, what are you going to do now?"

"I don't know. What's to do around here, anyway? Got a place to live? I could use some water. Positively parched, I am."

"Well, ah, there's some back at my cave—here, let me help you." Tarragon hoisted the wolf over his shoulder and returned to his cave. Tworgar's eyes widened.

"Holy hemlock . . . I know this place!"

"You do?" Tarragon set his burden down, and Tworgar trotted around like he owned the place.

"Sure, I do! My pack crossed this place about a week and a half ago while hunting. Egads, it wasn't pretty."

"You saw what happened? You were there?" Tarragon asked quickly.

"Saw what happened, no I didn't see that. But there were three live dragons milling around like crazy-creatures, wailing and hooting and making quite a commotion over the dead. They took away the remains just over that cliff yonder. Then they left."

"Left!" Tarragon grabbed the wolf. "Where did they go? Did you see which way they went? Was there a young male and female among them?"

"Urk . . . lemme go! I couldn't tell how old they were—and I couldn't tell the males from the females. We didn't get a close-up view; we figured it was too dangerous. They went northwest, I'd say."

"Northwest . . . of course, they're going to warn the dragons of the West Coast!"

"I don't think they'd do that," Tworgar said.

"Why not?"

"Because every mother's son is out looking for a dragon or two. The mainland is swarming with Southerners, and they're using their methods of persuasion to recruit spies. If your friends tried crossing from coast to coast, they're in for trouble. My guess is that they could be in hiding again."

"I've got to find them," Tarragon said wildly. "They're all I have left. This was my home, and I just came back yesterday, after a month of being banished. I have to go find my friends immediately!"

"Good idea," Tworgar barked. "When do we leave?"

"Who's 'we'?" Tarragon asked. "You're wounded; you're not going anywhere. Besides, this is my business, not yours. I can accomplish this on my own, thanks."

"Oh really! Hoity-toity, an' all that, huh? Listen here, Mister Independence, you don't know what you're getting into. You don't know, for instance, where they've gone; in fact, you wouldn't even know where to start looking. What's more, you aren't even aware of how much trouble you could be getting into. You may not have heard this, but the Black Dragon of Hebaruin has risen and is stalking the East right now—in fact, I wouldn't be surprised if your home was obliterated by him! If you leave now, you make yourself vulnerable."

"If I stay here, I'm vulnerable, too" Tarragon growled. "What exactly do you suggest?"

"You need a good guide. I can show you along roads and through forests that haven't been taken over yet by the Southerners. But you can't just rush off willy-nilly into the wild and honk your calls of distress and expect a reply. You've lived all your life by the coves—well, except for this last month—and you don't know the lay of the land like I do. I may be young, but my pack's traveled just about everywhere in the six years of my life, and I know Balské like the back of my paw. So, how about it? Can I come?"

Tarragon sighed. "Alright, alright! You're right; I don't know what I'm doing. I'll need help, and I suppose you'll have to do."

"Oh, thank you, your royal majesty," Tworgar rolled his eyes. "I feel so honored by your choice."

"Where do we go first from here?"

"The Galtic Mountains aren't far from here. Beyond that is the Wild Realm, where the Southerners have not crossed into yet. There's an old spirit there—not dangerous, I promise!—who might be able to tell you where to start looking."

Tarragon groaned. "I just came from the Galtic Mountains."

"Oh, so this shouldn't be a problem for you, then!" the young wolf barked happily. "Let's fly, shall we? I've always wanted to fly. This is going to be so much fun. There's so much to see—hey, maybe we can go raid a few villages on the way, eh? Steal a few beautiful women? We can always ransom them off to rich kings later. Or maybe we can go chase behemoths. I'll show you how to do it. All you do is . . ."

"I hope he shuts up for most of the trip," thought Tarragon moodily, as the wolf continued to yap. "Other than that, I have to admit, I wouldn't want to be alone."

Chapter 15

King Feromar was shocked and upset when Umphy and Arwos told their tale. A host of guards were sent to the temple. When they returned that evening, they reported that a large and venomous serpent, stabbed to death, now lay burning outside of the temple in a dung-heap, while the monks cleansed the corridors with holy water. No sign of the beggar-man could be seen. Since no motive could be found for the attack, the king stations guards at the temple and then asked Umphy to remain in the palace.

"Why did you go to the temple without your escort?" he asked. Umphy exchanged a glance with Arwos, and the king's eyes hardened. "I will not have this kept secret," he said sternly. "You say your purpose at the temple was to do some research. Research into what, might I ask? Master Ebonfeather, your research is here, where the queen commanded you to stay. And as for you, Umphy, I cannot even think what you would have to research."

"Arwos thought there might be more information about your majesty's kin in the temple," Umphy blurted. He had hid the Elbib beneath his porch. "I came along to help him, that's all."

"Well, well, and so I hope your efforts were not in vain. But it was foolish to walk about without an escort. You were lucky to have escaped. But I think it would be better for you to stay in the palace from now on. Guards will be posted at your door."

The queen, sitting at his side with her infant daughter, looked at the little Guardian who had saved her life and nodded quietly. Her eyes had filled with tears as she listened to the account of the attack and seemed disappointed to hear that the beggar-man had not lingered to receive his thanks. She also seemed very insistent on having a full description of the man, which Umphy thought very odd. The queen took a mighty big interest in him! "Had you seen the man before?"

"Never," Umphy lied. Suppose he said yes—what else would the king ask? Where had he seen him, and what was he doing following Umphy around? They would set a trap for the man or hunt him down and perhaps throw him into prison for spying on the palace grounds. Umphy could not wish a fate like that on anyone—particularly harmless beggar-men who saved little blue dragons from large demon-serpents in temples.

"I can't understand it," Arwos said later, as they retrieved the Elbib from beneath the porch in the gardens. "He *must* have been sent to protect you, like a secret bodyguard. But who would do that? Someone who knows you carry the White Orb—"

"Who *thinks* I carry the White Orb—"

"You're going to deny that to the grave, aren't you?"

"Let's not talk about graves," Umphy shivered. "We were nearly sent to ours."

"Hey—look!"

By the iron gate stood Vestia. Her hands clutched the bars tightly as she pressed her face forward. The ragged man stood on the other side, his bandaged hands covering the girl's. He was speaking rapidly, his eyes never leaving her face. Vestia's eyes were red from crying, and her face was twisted painfully. The beggar kissed her forehead, and was gone in a moment. Arwos and Umphy crouched low, watching in fascination. Vestia rubbed at her eyes and then left, still sniffling. Arwos turned huge eyes onto Umphy.

"Did you see *that*? He must be some sort of long-lost lover! Oh how *romantic*!"

"Don't be ridiculous," Umphy snapped, suddenly protective. "Vestia hasn't got a lover. Kelhah told me so. But I think they may be friends," he said. "Perhaps they're working together!

Galdermyn spoke to Vestia on the same day that he came to see me. He told her that Gurthur had actually escaped from Hebaruin and had some sort of plan up his sleeve, and that now she must be entrusted with a valuable mission and secret! Do you think if that man was sent by Galdermyn to protect me, Vestia must also be working with him?"

"I'm not sure," Arwos murmured. "They looked mighty happy to see each other. They could be more than working partners. But there's a grain of truth in what you say. We could go and ask Vestia what's going on. *She* won't throw a fit if we poke into her private affairs!"

"Oh no—we mustn't!" Umphy grabbed onto his friend's tail-feathers. "Galdermyn himself told Vestia that everything must be a *dead secret*! If we go asking her who the beggar-man is and what he has to do with us, Vestia might spill important information that Galdermyn did not want her to tell! It's enough for me that we can trust her, Arwos."

"Alright—well, if you're so sure—"

They recovered the Elbib from under the porch and brought it with them into the palace. The king had given Umphy one of the palace bedrooms for the night before the Spring Festival and stationed guards outside. Arwos and Umphy were free to discuss in secret, although Arwos had to stop Umphy once or twice from gleefully bouncing on the bed.

"We're here to study," he scolded. "So let's study.

> *Let he who seeks find not*
> *And he who asks first knock.*

"A seeker who does not find . . . hm, that sounds like someone who looks after something with greed or lust. And if you want something, you ask first, right?"

"But they say to knock before you ask. Knocking is polite."

"Doors, Umphy, doors! Seeking . . . a door . . . knocking on the door to find . . . Umphy, this riddle is a map to the Tree of Life, I'm sure of it!"

"What makes you think that? Nobody knows the way to the Tree of Life. It's guarded and kept hidden from all eyes. A map has never been designed." Umphy sighed. Arwos danced in frustration.

"There are three parts to your dream, Umphy. The first part reads like a riddle. The second part gives verbal directions to the Tree of Life. The third part details what you have to do: place the White Orb in the Tree. You have to do it, Umphy; no one else can!"

"I've told you before; the idea is just plain silly!"

"And I'm telling you again: you have an Orb growing inside of you. That's no mere infection you have, and you ought not to brush it aside so modestly. Do you know how much danger you might be in? Morbane is out right now looking for the Orb, and if we're not careful, a witch or a demon might snap you up! Now look:

> *The mountain dark, the people dread*
> *Who live beneath the rocky ledge.*
> *They guard me, keep me safe from harm.*
> *Lest evil come and cast its charm.*

"Who are the people dread, and what is it that they guard?"

> *Find me, take me, if you can:*
> *I solve doors and puzzles, heart of man.*
> *Where to find me? The wise man knows.*
> *Find him where the blue stone grows.*

"They guard a key," Arwos said excitedly. A key unlocks doors, and of course you've heard of the 'key to someone's heart' and a 'key to a puzzle." The dread people guard a key, and the wise man who lives where the blue stone grows knows where to find that key!"

"Why on earth would I need a key? Ouch!"

Arwos pecked Umphy between his ears. "You ninny, obviously there is a doorway to the realm that protects the Tree of Life. If it's locked and guarded, you need a key to get in!"

"I might as well ask for a well-armored army and a sword of my own, too" Umphy grumbled. "The 'locked' part doesn't worry me so much as the 'guarded' part. How are we going to fight our way past 'dread people' to get a key and then, on top of that, get through a mountain pass guarded by who-knows-what just to get the key in the lock?"

Arwos thought for a moment. "You've got me there. But we obviously can't stay here and sit on our behinds. If we don't get that key, you'll never make it to the Tree of Life."

"Could we hire a Jacerin?" suggested Umphy.

"How many Jacerin do you know?" Arwos demanded.

"How many do *you* know?"

"I asked you first, and anyway, nobody knows how to identify a Jacerin. They look like very ordinary people nowadays—after the Wars, they wore nothing to distinguish them from others. They used to have a uniform and a tattoo, but they keep such things secret now."

"Would it be possible to contact Galdermyn?" Umphy asked. Arwos shook his head.

"Sending a message would be too risky. Besides, we don't even know where he's at these days, and we can't ask the king about him again; his majesty will start to think we're up to something. We have to follow your dream by ourselves, Umphy. You are the Bearer of the Orb, and you are meant to go questing to put the White Orb in the Tree of Life!"

The little dragon hesitated and then looked at the riddle again. He stroked the picture of Yuna Rose and remembered when he had told his sister Possa—it seemed ages ago!—that he would go adventuring and find the lady in white. Something about it frightened him; perhaps it was the uncertainty of how everything would turn out. He had never in all his born days dreamed that something so wonderful could happen to him, that the most precious of all treasures should be embedded safely within him. It explained his stomachaches and dreams and somehow encompassed his life with all its peculiarities. Seven dragons before him had carried and coughed up the Orbs. Had they led similar lives? Umphy suddenly felt part of an elite group. He smiled, and Arwos cheered.

"Yes! That's the stuff! We'll go a-questing, just like heroes! But Umphy, we can't let anyone else know about this. Something attacked us, and I am sure it was no coincidence. Giant snakes just don't live in the sacred temple and attack innocent bystanders without a purpose. We've got to find a way out of here as soon as we possibly can. To find the key we have to look for the wizard who lives where the blue stone grows—that's what the riddle says."

"But who could that be?"

"I'm not sure. For some reason it sounds familiar, but I just can't place it. The thing to do is perhaps travel to the Evantyri and ask for help there."

Umphy pricked up his ears. The Evantyri was the sacred home of the Elves and fairies. Nothing evil crossed its borders, for not only was it protected by the most powerful of enchantments, but the Elves were also skilled with blow-darts, crossbows and longbows, and daggers. They were a shorter race than mankind, and knew the subtler arts of warfare. But they were also an extremely wise race, gifted with long life and far-seeing eyes and minds. A majority of Elves were scholars, and others simply knew all about Balské because of the many experiences of exploration in the land. They were physical, mystical beings that were the very stuff of legends and folklore. Umphy was excited. "You know the way?"

"I most certainly do! Told you I was a wanderer of the air, didn't I? I wouldn't be much good if I didn't know my way to the Evantyri!" Arwos cackled in delight.

As Umphy drifted to sleep that night, his lady in white came and visited him again. But instead of singing the song of the riddle, she smiled tenderly at him and leaned down to kiss his fuzzy forehead, her hands tenderly stroking his face. Her smile was full and real.

Arwos, however, could not sleep.

It was too exciting! His friend, his little dragon friend, had the Orb of Orbs inside him! The prophecy was coming into fulfillment! The raven nested at the foot of the bed, his beady eyes wide awake and staring around. After a while, he decided that a good stretch of the legs would perhaps calm him down. After all, he needed his sleep. There was much to do!

The door was locked, but the window was slightly cracked, and Arwos wriggled out. He flew across the darkened courtyard and the silent corridors. Stopping down in the garden, the raven dipped his beak into a forgotten pitcher of water and began drinking. But as he gulped his drink, a shadow fell across the floor, and he quickly hopped backwards, hiding himself behind a bora-tree. He heard voices, and then two cloaked figures stepped out of an open doorway, keeping still by the trellis of roses that grew beside them. Arwos recognized Gurthur. But the cloaked figure was a stranger.

"Lady, if what you must say is private, we are hardly in a private place for matters of serious discussion." Gurthur's eyes were like a cat's in the night: strange and luminous.

"I will say what I choose when and where I like," said a woman's voice.

Vestia! Arwos thought. *What's she doing out here confronting Gurthur like this?* The hypnotic man smiled thinly.

"I hinder you not. Speak, beloved."

"*I am not that!*" The woman's voice was sharp and carried a threat.

"You were ever such to me."

"You should know by now that you will never have me. It matters not what you do to me. But Adenile—why have you chosen to attack her? What has she done that you should cause her such bitterness?"

"We've discussed this before."

"Yes," the woman snapped bitterly. "We've discussed how your influence works. I know full-well how you cunningly wrap yourself around a victim like a snake and squeeze until the breath is gone, the bones are broken, and the internal organs are but a pulp within a fleshy sac. You would swallow me alive in your victimizing!"

"Yes, and you rejected me!" Gurthur grabbed onto the woman's hands; they gleamed soft and white between the black-gloved hands that squeezed tightly. "I swore I would ruin you."

"By punishing Adenile!" The woman ripped her hands away. "By hurting and twisting that beautiful young woman into a witch for your own personal satisfaction—"

"Adenile bores me these days," Gurthur purred. "Let's talk about you, my sweet. You have something I want. You and I both know what it is. It is a secret within these walls."

"That thing which you desire you shall never have. I swore to protect—"

"Your vows will do you little good. I have the upper hand, and you will do nothing because you fear that I will tell the king—"

"You will tell him nothing!"

"Would I not? Ah! But, you see, he does not know about you. And I have every intention of telling him the truth. In fact, I have intentions to tell him more than that."

"You ask me for something I have no rights to give!"

"Find a way, my darling. Find a way." Gurthur reached out and stroked the ivory-skinned cheek beneath the hood. "You are no fool. I think you would rather die than see your precious Adenile go to Hebaruin, am I correct? Or . . . is there someone else you care for more? Someone, I think, who holds a greater power over you? You must choose between them."

The was a long silence. Arwos wondered if his pounding heart could possibly he heard. Gurthur continued to speak quietly, threateningly.

"If you choose to send Adenile to her fate, well, perhaps you will have rid yourself of a very annoying, spoiled brat, after all. And then perhaps you think that Anthorwyn will be left in peace! But that is not my intention at all. I will not stop until you are in ruins, until your name is run lower than the mud you tread upon, until you are no better than a flea-bitten, rabid dog in the gutter! I hold the ace. Refuse me my desire, and not only will Adenile be thrown to the wolves, but your very world will be destroyed. I will summon Morbane hence—I can do it, you know!—and he will not only kill the little dragon but demolish the entire realm of the North without further ado. What do you think of that?"

Arwos remembered the snake in the temple. *So that's his mission! Gurthur wants the Orb! He knows that Vestia is helping to protect Umphy because of the Orb! And if she doesn't give it to him, one way or another, Gurthur will send for Morbane—we've got to get out of here! I've got to warn Umphy!*

The raven flew back to his room in the palace. Umphy was sleeping peacefully on his cushion, oblivious to the impending danger. The raven shook him with one foot.

"Umphy!"

The little dragon snored and rolled over. Arwos flapped his wings.

"Umphy, wake up!"

"Unnhh . . . wha . . . ?"

"Get up. Where's your flute?"

"What are you talking about?" Umphy rubbed at his eyes. "It's midnight, Arwos."

"I don't give two figs for midnight. Get up, and get your flute. We're getting out of here."

Umphy sat up and blinked owlishly in the darkness. He yawned. "Why? What for?"

"There's no time to explain. Just get your flute and come with me!"

The little dragon sat there for a moment, tired and irritated by his friend's yapping. He yawned again and scratched his shoulder. "I'm not going anywhere. It's too late at night, Arwos. Can't it wait?"

"No! It can't! Get up! You don't understand! We're in danger. *You're* in danger. Gurthur's trying to kill you!"

Umphy's eyes widened and he clutched at his tail. "What! Why? How do you know?"

"He's in cahoots with the devil. I heard him talking just now to Vestia. He knows she's protecting you. And he told her that if she didn't give you over to him, he would send for Morbane! Do you understand? He's a madman! The entire Realm of the North is in peril!"

"Vestia would never hurt me—"

"How do you know that? She may be a sweet girl, but if she doesn't do as she's told, the Princess Adenile will go straight to Hebaruin and the rest of the North is history. That's quite a threat, and I wouldn't snub my nose at it, just because you happen to like a sweet, gray-eyed girl!"

"But how would Gurthur have even guessed that Vestia is protecting me?" Umphy asked, bewildered. "How would he know?"

"He's got dark magic coming out of his ears," Arwos snapped. "Everyone knows it. The man led Adenile straight into a bonfire; *that's* no secret around court! Now come on, let's get out of here."

"But how? The doors are guarded. Oh Arwos, I wish we hadn't come here!" Umphy put his paws over his eyes and started to cry. "We won't be let out until tomorrow, when it's time to play my flute for the Festival! Gurthur could make a move at any time! What are we going to do?"

Chapter 16

"HEY!!"

Customers at the bar looked over in the direction of the yelling. The bartender, a small man with a rather large nose and huge dark eyes was shaking his fist at the intruder in the doorway.

"I said you no come back here! What you think you do? Get me outta my business? Dis no first time, demon-slayer! I say we no have demons, and you come back and say yah, you got demons, and then my business goes bad!"

"Oh, shut up," the sullen intruder snapped, plopping himself down at the bar and resting his elbows on the counter. "I don't want your bottled ghosts. Father found out what I did and beat me raw with that damned cane of his."

The bardenter giggled like a naughty child and held up a small glass bottle. Inside swirled a tiny cloud that gave a mournful wail and beat against the walls with miniature fists. Two eyes glared malevolently out at the young man, who stuck his tongue out at it. "Those things are illegal, Lucca, and if the governor hears what you're keeping in here besides Darkdrake brew and willow-wine, it'll be you with the whip across your back, not me!"

"My bottle-ghosts are not demons. What you want, eh, Erastil? What you want here?"

"A drink," the young man grumbled. "Strongest Darkdrake brew you've got, and add about a pound of wilderoot-pepper juice. I need something to forget the day."

"Aw, you poor little man—Veeva! Allisandi! Fetch the brew, an' make it strong, d'ye hear? Now, Erastil, my friend, you tell Lucca all about it, eh?"

"I'm sick and tired of it all, Lucca!" Erastil put his head in his hands and gripped his fair hair. "I can't stand being a shopkeeper's boy when the governor needs able-bodied men to help resist the Southerners that are coming through the village, day after day! They're a bunch of bullying beefcakes, and I hate seeing my home bend under the pressure of Hebaruin's forces. I want to fight!"

"Eh, you are no different than the many others who want to beat back oppression," Lucca sighed. "But you are only a lad. The Southerners are strong, they are vicious, they will kill you. When you gonna settle down, eh?"

"Whenever I marry a woman rich enough to provide for a life of ease," Erastil laughed. "Because I am as poor as all get out. What do you think, Lucca? Will one of your pretty daughters marry me?"

Behind the counter, six plump young women with dark brown hair and colorful scarves giggled into their hands, blushing like roses.

"Eh, they not rich, they go marry farmers," said the gloomy bartender. "Impossible to keep all of them around forever. An' the way you speak, it not long before we lose you, too. The Southerners, they kill you, Erastil! They take you, beat you, throw you in dark holes with demon-dogs!"

Erastil chuckled. "I'm not afraid! It took four of them to hold me down and beat me up last week. They're not so vicious against real warriors, one-on-one! I bet if I had a sword—and a couple of daggers—and a mace—I could—"

"You could get yourself into some serious trouble," growled a voice behind the young man. Erastil turned and looked into the face of a Southern-bred man, standing over six feet tall. His lower lip was pierced with a five-inch nail, and his amber eyes flashed menacingly. Erastil stood up.

"I don't recall asking your opinion, slime-nose!"

"You should heed the words of the wise little drink-seller," the Southerner purred in a low, gravelly voice. "Fresh little upstarts like you are well-liked by the razor-teeth in Hebaruin, where doubtless you'll go if you—wait a minute, I recognize you. Erastil, isn't it? The little shop-boy?"

There was loud laughter behind him. More Southerners filled the bar, their skin gleaming with golden bracelets and tattooes. They surrounded Erastil in a ring. The young man stood his ground.

"I thought you might remember me, seeing as how you were the pansy who had to call for assistance in beating me up!"

The Southerner growled and pushed his face close. "Think you're so tough, don't you, little boy? Well, mark my words, you won't be able to lift one finger by the time Fordomt's finished with you! He settles with rebels the same way he settles with all his enemies: death and torture."

Erastil spat. "I think Fordomt is a slime-tailed, flame-boiled, half-baked excuse for an emperor who thinks that burning up the land makes him all-powerful. Tell him to go climb a tree, and tell him Erastil Anthelion sent you!"

The Southerner hissed from between his teeth. "You've started fights in the past with my people. It would be wise not to begin one now."

"Why not?" the roguish young man taunted. "Afraid you might have to call for more assistance? Wouldn't want to lose face with your men, would you?"

"Soon we'll have no need of wasting our time with snot-nosed brats like yourself. Fordomt has followers besides ourselves, yes, good followers, strong followers. Be they monster, demon, or ghost, your precious little town is in for a bit of a rought time with the followers of Fordomt!"

"Oh, I get it. The pig-headed fool of the South is too afraid of farmers and shopkeepers with their torches and pitchforks, yes?"

The Southerner grabbed Erastil and shook him.

"You are a coward for speaking lies and slander against the Emperor, and no curse would ever make me regret crushing your skull between my hands!"

"Please don't; it will make a horrible mess," Erastil said dryly. "As for being an arrogant fool, well, I'm not insulted. There's no insult where the truth is clear as day, and I'll say it again: Fordomt is no emperor; he's a spineless, slug-bottomed, bird-brained, lily-livered, yellow-gutted, fish-eyed son of a pig who feeds on rats and should have been spanked by his mother!"

There was another horrified silence, and then everyone ducked for cover as the Southerner bellowed like an injured bull and brought his fist around to slam into Erastil's head. The young man neatly slipped under the Southerner's arm and dodged to the left, coming up with a right hook and catching his opponent off-guard. The devilman staggered backwards into the arms of his friends, who propelled him forward. He came at Erastil, shrieking and raising his deadly blade. Erastil ducked and bobbed, trying to stay out of the reach of the sword. Leaning back over the bar, he quickly grabbed a bottle—the one containing the ghost—and smashed it into the Southerner's face. He let out a strangled yell of pain as the glass cut into his skin, and the ghost did war-whoops, dive-bombing everyone in the tavern and dropping bottles on people's heads. Now the one-on-one fight turned into a rowdy brawl, the little ghost shrieking with glee and whipping back and forth between people to either spray them with beer or pelt them with candied walnuts. Kegs of beer went flying and the men let out a surging yell.

Erastil still held on to his end of the broken bottle. He was pounding for all he was worth on the Southerner he'd insulted when another devilman rushed up and grabbed his arms, pinning them behind his back. Another Southerner got hold of the young man's struggling legs. Erastil kicked out, smashing his foot against the Southerner's face; he staggered backwards, and Erastil pushed back until the adversary behind him smashed his spine against the sharp bar counter. The Southerner released him with a scream, and Erastil picked up his broken bottle.

"ALRIGHT, YOU SOUTHERN DEVILMEN, WHO WANTS SOME MORE!?"

That's when someone broke a chair over his head, leaving the young man unconscious on the floor.

Tarragon was getting very tired of listening to his new friend. Tworgar sat on the dragon's back as they flew through the air in the direction that the young wolf led them. He spoke fervently of his studies and his pack and the different hobbies he had. Tarragon was getting very annoyed. The wolf, however, didn't seem to care.

"Yes," he yapped on. "I'm no good with most studies, although I love stories, and I can sing. But I've always been a bit of a scamp. My friends and I love chasing behemoths. Can't say as we'd ever dare chasing you, though. A whole flock of dragons is really playing with fire, or running with knives, or whatever the phrase is! No, we'd probably leave you alone. Did you know that your species is the most powerful in the world? You surpass even wizards in wisdom. No, nobody would mess with the likes of you!"

"You don't have to worry about me," Tarragon said. "I'm not a violent dragon by nature. The most harm I've ever done is break a few legs or arms when attacked by the knights."

"Hah! That's nothing compared to the worst you could do. I daresay you could rip one of those behemoths into shredded wheat for breakfast."

Tarragon looked down at himself. "Hardly."

"Hardly? Heck, you've got biceps on top of biceps. The females must be all of a swoon over you. Got a lady? Goodness, I can see you do. What's her name?"

"Her name is Padina, and she's not my lady. She said once that she'll never marry," Tarragon said briefly. "But that—that seemed so long ago."

"Women have fickle minds, my friend, and once she sees you, she won't even think about staying single! Is that what you were banished for? Stealing all the good-looking ladies? Or did you get into a fight? I'll bet the low-down skunk never raised a paw against you ever again! Did you win?"

"No," Tarragon snapped. "I didn't."

"Ah," Tworgar was quiet.

By the end of the first two days, Tarragon was grateful for a companion. He was unaccustomed to the vast expanse of wilderness that surrounded him on all sides, and the odd cries at night disturbed him. Tworgar knew his way around the plains and forests, and soothed the dragon's anxieties. When they came back to the Galtic mountains, Tarragon found the shelter of his old cave and permitted Tworgar to spend the night with him there. Tworgar outlined the next few days for his friend.

"When we reach the cave of the spirit, she'll give us our course for sure. Be extra polite, though—she's not anything to mess with. I mean, I know you're a Guardian and all that, but spirits can be downright nasty and they'll take no nonsense from anyone. She's only a couple days' flight from here, if we stay on the east side of the Galtic and make our way north and then there's a small break in the mountains that leads to a hidden valley. We'll take the passage through there and wind up in the Wild Realm. The spirit lives among the monoliths. Now we'd best get some sleep. There's a long day ahead of us, after all!"

Chapter 17

The day of the Festival dawned fair and bright, and the city rose early to prepare for the evening. The streets were packed tightly with vendors and craftsmen from all over the North, and the marketplace plaza was filled with the tents of the thousands who crammed into the city for the festival. Great kings, princes, and noblemen from the North, middlelands, and other, distant lands thronged to the palace. Banners and flowers were hung. Lights were prepared in the windows. The entire city shut down its trade and marketing for one day. Women laid out their very finest of gowns; men polished their swords and boots. Children laughed and clapped their hands in anticipation of the evening festivities. The food would be beyond description, and the games would exceed all expectations. Everyone was in a high-spirited, joyous mood—except for Umphy and Arwos.

The little dragon had cried himself to sleep, despite having his best friend near him for comfort. Arwos, on the other hand, had been too frightened to sleep. When the guard finally let them out in the morning, he could not help remarking on the haggard appearance of both creatures.

"And you must be in your best shape to play tonight, Sir Dragon," he encouraged Umphy. "The Festival lasts until the morning hours, you know! Take naps throughout the day, now, rest up, and get some snacks to sustain you! You will need all your strength for this evening!"

"He's right, Umphy," Arwos snapped out of his horror-stricken mood and immediately led his friend downstairs to the kitchens. "We have to make plans. Let's take some food here and then go out to the gardens. We'll relax and figure out a strategy or two."

Umphy bravely agreed. The kindly kitchen maid supplied the two friends with a picnic basket filled with soft, warm bread; creamy honey-butter; spiced sausage-links; blueberry tarts; and small white cakes. They proceeded to take their fare out to the sunny gardens, and sat in the sun, eating and drinking, and talking.

"You'll be expected to play your flute before midnight," said Arwos. "Once you do that, we'll excuse ourselves from the party and make our way back here. We'll fly out from the gardens and head west to the Evantyri. Don't worry; I'll be with you every step of the way. But we can't just sit on our tails after the music, do you hear me? We've got to bolt, the two of us!"

"Shouldn't we tell the king about what's happened?" Umphy asked. "Perhaps he could help!"

"I'm not relying on anyone but myself and my plans. The king has Galdermyn to aid him if he needs it; let him handle his own problems when they come along, but nobody is going to interfere with my plans for saving my own skin—and yours, of course," Arwos added. "No offense to the king, but he would only try to keep you safe under lock and key, when what you really need is your freedom to run. And we're going to do just that. No, we won't tell the king a thing. Stick by me, and we'll see this through, young fellow!"

The Spring Festival always began when the flowers of the North started to bloom, heralding not only spring, but the dawn of a new year for the North, and all its cities. On that night, nothing could have been more beautiful. Pillars, tables, chairs, and balconies were draped with garlands of flowers and silk banners. The tables groaned under the weight of the amount of food set out: delicate-flaked pastries with sweet-cream filling; cheeses of all shapes, sizes and flavors; simmering meats of every variety; rich wine and cordials; hot, fluffy bread, and fresh fruits and vegetables from the valley. Music was provided;

lights in colored lanterns were strung from every window in every street. People flocked to the palace as the time drew near for the festival. In the streets, vendors sold their wares: colorful pots, pans and jugs; elaborately-carved statues and vases; bottles of the finest wines with gift baskets of fruit, meat, cheese, and vegetable spreads; knives, toys, clothing, and bolts of the finest cloth to be had in the land. Entertainers pushed forward with their acts: gymnasts twirled around on poles and ropes and mats; comedians and buffoons worked together in skits and plays; grand performances were held by the circus; and there were exotic dancers with serpents, bears, and other animals. A traveling gypsy caravan told fortunes and gave out candy and flowers to the young people who showered them with gold coins. There was laughter and light around the entire city.

In the evening, when sunset fell over the mountains, the noble people gathered in the king's court where the feast had been laid, tables spread, and the dance floor prepared. Everyone was dressed in their finest. The array of women's gowns was like a rainbow of color moving gracefully through the courtroom. The men wore dark velvet greens, blues, and reds, accompanying the ladies at their sides. At the head of the room, the king sat in his throne, robed in his majestic finery; his wife, dressed in a purple gown with silver trimming, sat beside him, holding her infant daughter. Adenile and the Lady Vestia stood nearby, dressed in their own special attire. It was clear that Adenile was not feeling in the best of spirits; she looked radiant in a gown of pale green, but her eyes held none of their original life and charm. They looked dead and hollow now as she stared out silently at the throng of people amassing in the great dining hall. Vestia timidly ventured to reach out and touch her friend's hand. Adenile looked up at her quickly and then pulled her hand away.

Umphy and Arwos were given seats of honor by the throne. The raven fussed about his friend.

"Try and look happy, Umphy. We can't let the bad guys know we're onto them."

"But how are we going to escape through all that?" Umphy gestured at the crowd. "There's too many of them."

"We'll think of something. You're a dragon, after all. Maybe if you squirted a ball of fire—"

Umphy looked horrified. "I am *not* supposed to use my fire for such destructive purposes! Mother always said that if a dragon uses his flame against humans, he breaks a code of honor!"

"You wouldn't be hurting anyone. Just puff some flames to get the masses shuffling out of your way!"

"I can't do that," Umphy protested. "It's an improper use of flame."

Arwos sighed. "Then you're going to have to think of something else because otherwise we're never going to get out of here."

At that moment, the doors swung open, and the trumpeters announced the arrival of Prince Haramid of the Iron Kingdom. Everyone, even the princess, looked up.

Haramid was twenty-eight years of age, a valiant man from head to foot. He was tall and muscular, with fiery red hair and snapping black eyes. His dashing, red-and-black velvet cape was thrown roguishly over one shoulder. He strode into the courtroom with confidence and grace, flanked by six guards in gold and black armor, with steel-spiked wrist cuffs, and spears of silver and trailing red flags. Haramid did not smile, but walked forward, bowed to the king, who rose.

"My lord Haramid, we are honored by your presence here this evening."

"An invitation from the lord of Anthorwyn is never to be refused," Haramid bowed low again, and then made a particular gesture of respect to the queen. "My lady, accept the congratulations of my entire kingdom on the successful birth of your daughter. I have brought a token of my goodwill for the little princess."

He waved his hand, and a servant stepped forward, bearing a chest. Haramid opened the gilt lid to reveal a set of twin daggers, crafted from the finest steel, and elaborately set with rubies. "These daggers were given to me as a present on the day of my anointing when I was but a child," he said. "But when I grew older, I chose a sword for my weapon, and no other will serve me better. I hope, however, that your daughter may find a use for these beauties, as they were crafted by our men with Elven-metal, and set with gems mined and cut straight from the mountains of the North!"

"Beautiful!" Feromar exclaimed. "What an—er, interesting gift for the little princess. I am sure she will make good use of them when she is older. I thank you on her behalf, and indeed, on behalf of our entire city. You are most welcome, Prince of the Iron Kingdom! Come sit beside me, and tell me all the news of your father and his city!"

There was so much to see that night. Umphy could not take his eyes off of the musicians, and Arwos could not take his eyes off the blushing young ladies standing in a row waiting for someone to ask them to dance. Food was served: spicy meats, sparkling wines, fresh fruits, sweetmeats and breads, sugared candies, and pastries so dainty that they melted in your mouth. The tables were laden with spiced fruit, stuffed peacock, sauces of cream and honey, decorative tubs of rare jewels and ropes of pearls, and a magnificent ice statue of a dragon. Dancing and music lit the hall, and rocked with laughter. There was singing, juggling, acting, dancing, storytelling, and many a good laugh. For many years it was to be the greatest night anyone had ever remembered in the North.

"Quite a lovely evening!" Umphy remarked to Arwos, who grinned and nodded.

"Oh, I'll say it is, young fellow, I'll say it is! Just don't forget to be on your guard. Have you got the music ready?"

"Yes, I've memorized it very well." Umphy replied, talking normally to Arwos. They kept up a stream of steady talk, trying desperately to act normal.

"Did you ever see anything quite so odd!" remarked one of the ladies, not far away. "A raven and a dragon, here in Anthorwyn . . . in the court of the king himself!"

"Aye, lady, but look at the eyes of the bald man there, on the throne. His eyes follow like a hawk's! They haven't left the little dragon all evening!"

"Oh, never mind him! Goodness, but we're not here to observe old men in long black robes! Of what use is he to us? Only look at that fur the queen is wearing! Must be quite the latest fashion!"

When the waltz had ended, Haramid suddenly rose and held out his hand to Adenile.

"My lady, will you dance?"

His voice was firm, but tender, and almost a little shy. Adenile had never looked lovelier; the pale green gown highlighted her sparkling green eyes, and her red lips looked soft as rosepetals. Her hair fell in dark ringlets about her face. She felt too weak to dance and yet too exhausted to say no or put up a fight against the man she had thrown a fit about a week in advance! Now she accepted his hand politely, grateful for the strength it provided as Haramid led her from the throne and onto the dance floor. Everyone else stepped back, and the king signaled to Umphy.

The little dragon raised his flute and began to play. He had prepared nothing, of course, but instead of the usual lullaby, a new melody, haunting and sweet, welled up in his heart and played out naturally through the tips of his paws and the pipe of the flute, distilling the most enchanting sound anyone had ever heard.

The guests were utterly spellbound. To them the music was foreign and mysterious, with undertones of strength and power that filled each man and woman with a sense of fulfillment. It was beyond anything they had ever experienced before. Umphy did not know, and could not have known, that he was playing music that was inside of him, as it was in each Guardian. His music, though he did not know it, now bespoke of the mysterious love between dragons: the power and strength of the male, and the devotion and grace of the female; the ritual courtship of touched noses, entwined necks, gifts of love and trust, and a traditional fight or two to win the heart of a chosen loved one; the secret wedding, apart from all others; the mating, an affair so private and sacred that nobody but the earth and sky knew of it; and the family afterwards, and the bond of loyalty, trust, friendship, and love that could never be severed.

"My father used to be a demanding teacher," Haramid said softly as he danced with the princess. "He had me studying the Elven script and the Icelic tongue at the age of three. By the time I was six or seven we were speaking at least three or four different speeches fluently. Father used to say that poly-linguists were the diplomats of the times. Scholars, he believed, made the best politicians. He counted them more important than warriors, for they spilled blood by the sword, while scholars made peace with mere words." Haramid seemed thoughtful. "But as soon as I was old enough, I spent every minute in the guard-room and armory, learning about weapons, tactics, maps, strategies, battle-plans, and war stories. In my time and experiences, peace is not bought with the words and pleadings of men and their books and ideas. They exist in theory. Peace comes with a price, and that is, unfortunately, the price of a man's blood. I was thirteen when I killed my first foe."

"Who was it?"

Haramid looked down at the princess; she looked genuinely interested.

"My father's counselor."

"Oh!"

"Don't look so damned shocked," Haramid snapped suddenly. "I understand you're not exactly Madam Petite-and-Proper, if I may be so bold."

"Well, you *are* being bold—a perfect beast. Who the devil told you to come in here and whisk me off my feet just to tell me stupid stories about your past? I really don't give a hoot anyway!"

He chuckled. "Now look at you. There's the spark back in your eyes. You looked very sad and faraway before I asked you to dance."

"What's it to you what I look like? It's my own business what I look like and what I think about, and none of yours at all!" But Adenile stayed in his arms. "You're a bit of a bold prince, aren't you? Why did you kill your father's counselor?"

"The man was a traitor," said Haramid calmly. "He cursed my father and brought him down into ruin—he made him what he is today. So I challenged the old dog to a duel."

"And did he accept?"

"Of course. I challenged him in public; he had to accept, or else lose face. He was no great swordsman, but he was forty-two and I was thirteen. I cut him down clean enough, and he had the courage to die like a man."

"And he did not curse you?"

"On the contrary, he blessed me for doing what I needed to do. He said the kingdom would profit from a man of action, rather than a man who spent more time thinking and giving orders. I'm no fantastic politician, lady; I've seen battle and torture and faced countless adversaries of different natures. I am a man of strategies, plans, motivation, and inspiration. My victories come from hard work, not meditation."

"Admirable," Adenile said, struggling to keep the fascination out of her words.

"And women, I like to say, are won by hard work, too."

"You are an impious dog to say so."

"I think I speak truth. You were only a little girl when I first met you, but I remember you screamed loudly for cake. I felt very sorry for your father."

"My father is *proud* of me. I am his heir."

"And I'd like to be his son," said Haramid pleasantly.

"You dare . . . ! You hardly know me!" Adenile hissed.

"On the contrary, I think I know you very well. I had the good fortune to meet your grandfather when he was still alive. No man could be more of a mule—or have such a temper. They say you are his spitting image. Is that true?"

"You are a boor," Adenile said loftily. But her stern countenance soon fell, and she giggled—why, it seemed like years since she had last giggled like a girl of twelve with her first love! "My grandfather!" she chuckled. "I have but one memory of him, and it was before he died. He was in his bed, wasting away—and clobbering the nurses and healers about the head with anything within arm's reach because he was tired of porridge!" She giggled again, and was profoundly pleased when Haramid joined her in a good chuckle. He had a rich, deep laugh and a rare, beautiful smile that few had ever seen. His arm tightened about her waist, and she looked up at him, feeling in that moment that nothing could ever compare to dancing with a handsome man—Prince Haramid wasn't so bad after all.

The music ended, and so did the dance. Haramid bowed to the princess, and she curtseyed, as the entire court burst into thunderous applause. The king was beaming from ear to ear, and his wife smiled happily. Adenile herself took Haramid's arm and looked up at him like a child wanting to be led by the hand. The prince escorted her back to her seat, and the festivities resumed.

"Umphy, let's go!" hissed Arwos. "Exit stage right! Come on, make tracks!"

"Did you see that?" the little dragon squealed excitedly. "I think I made them fall in love, Arwos!"

"You idiot, who cares about those two lovebirds—Gurthur's the one we have to worry about! Morbane is still out there! Come on, move yourself!"

"Umphy!" the king cried. "Come over here and meet Prince Haramid. He's all in wonderment over you!"

Arwos rolled his eyes in despair. "You and your fame . . . hurry up, will you?"

The little dragon sat down beside Adenile and Haramid. The princess gave him a hug and kissed his cheek with genuine affection. The prince reached out and took Umphy's paw.

"Delighted to meet you at last, my friend. Word of you has spread throughout the North, and I wondered if I should ever meet you. You've gained quite a reputation!"

"Thank you, sir," Umphy said brightly. "I was honored to play for your dance with the princess. She and I are very good friends."

"He is the best friend anyone could ever have," Adenile said softly.

The little dragon had no choice but to make conversation. He was aware that Arwos was getting very impatient, but there was nothing he could do without being unceremoniously rude. He noticed, out of the corner of his eye, that the queen was talking gently to Vestia. The two women sat side-by-side, and it suddenly occurred to Umphy that Vestia looked very much like Queen Unituriel. The young woman was stone-faced and silent, a frown on her face and tears glittering in the corners of her eyes, but then she swallowed hard and nodded. The queen patted her cheek and then leaned over to speak to the king.

A few short moments later, the king stood up, a golden goblet in his hands. All activity ceased.

"Lords and Ladies of the High Realm of the North, it is my good pleasure this evening to welcome you again and offer a toast in memory of the victory won many years ago in liberation of the Northlands and the founding of the five kingdoms. This night I am proud to say that we not only celebrate that triumph but also a union of hearts."

Haramid and Adenile whipped their heads up at once and then at each other in bewilderment. The king looked very pleased indeed. Umphy looked from the king to Vestia. Why, the girl was about to cry! What was going on? Arwos was making frantic gestures, but the little dragon did not budge.

"It is my joy and delight that I present to you the Lady Vestia Anthelion and the Lord Gurthur Nowyn, who shall plight their troth before you all. He has asked for her hand and she has granted it with all her heart."

"LIAR!!"

The voice screamed out from the crowd! The king turned in confusion as people were shoved left and right. Umphy almost leapt from his seat in surprise; the mysterious beggar-man strode boldly through the sea of people and stood before the throne. His one good eye fixed upon Gurthur, who cried out in dismay and turned pale.

"ARREST THAT MAN!!" he screamed. "HE IS A DISTURBER OF THE PEACE!!"

Guards filtered out of nowhere and surrounded the beggar-man. Whipping back his tattered cloak, the man revealed a leather scabbard from which he drew a sword. The king held up his hand. "Wait! Guards, escort that man here."

The beggar-man was brought before the throne. He did not bow, kneel, or give the proper greeting with his hands. He stood proudly with his head held high.

"Who are you, and why do you interrupt our ceremonies?" Feromar asked quietly. The ragged man lifted a finger and pointed it, like a lance, at Gurthur.

"You wish to know my name, sire, and I will give it to you in good time. But first, I wish to tell you why I interrupt your ceremony. The man sitting at your left, sire, is not the man you think he is. I have battled my way through hellfire and pits of tar and oil to come North for my revenge—a revenge that has been twenty years late in coming—Boranthion!" he spat at Gurthur, who stood silently, white with rage. The queen had also gone white in the face, and her fingers slowly crept to her lips as her eyes widened in horror, looking from Gurthur to the beggar-man.

"My name is Novanthelion Gwynide, Jacerin!"

The queen gave a piercing shriek and fell to the floor in a dead faint. The crowd burst into a buzz of excitement as the king dropped to his knees beside his wife. Gurthur screamed again.

"ARREST THAT MAN!! HE IS AN IMPOSTER AND A LIAR AND A DISTURBER OF THE PEACE!! WHAT THE DEVIL ARE YOU FOOLS WAITING FOR—*ARREST HIM*!!"

For an elderly man with one eye, the beggar moved with the speed of a youthful athlete, his sword flashing in the light. The crowd screamed to get out of his way. Adenile stood up as Haramid leapt over the table to join the guards in their attempt to subdue the man. Vestia kept screaming, "Don't hurt him! Please, don't hurt him!" before leaping into the fray to try and stop the guards. Arwos grabbed hold of Umphy, and the two friends looked around for escape, but the crowd was too tight about them.

"HOLD!"

In two strides, Gurthur had taken the Princess Adenile and twisted her arm, holding her close with one hand and pressing a sharp dagger against her throat with the other. Everyone froze.

"Gurthur, what in Enovan's name do you think you're doing?" the king got to his feet and glared at his healer and counselor.

"I am doing precisely what I should have done earlier," Gurthur said venomously, his hypnotic eyes flashing with cold-blooded malice. His grip tightened on Adenile, and she gave a little wail.

"Father!"

"*Shut up, you little witch*!" Gurthur hissed. "And you, lord Haramid, stay where you are. If you take one step closer, I'll have this wench's blood."

"Leave her alone, Boranthion!" the beggar spat. "Your battle is with me."

"STAY OUT OF IT, FOOL, OR I'LL SLIT HER THROAT!!" Gurthur screamed like a madman. He looked back at the king. "Go on, sire. Perform the rites. I will have Vestia, or I will send your daughter straight to Hebaruin, and the Black Dragon will have the North."

"*Blackmail!*" Feromar spat. "I will have none of that, lord Gurthur! You have overstepped your boundaries; now release my daughter and explain yourself!"

"Release her? I think not. She is *my* pawn, sire, not yours. If you wish for your daughter's safety, you will perform the rites and give me my due. Vestia has accepted me as a husband—"

"BECAUSE YOU FORCED HER HAND, YOU MISERABLE COWARD!!" The beggar strained against the guards. Gurthur ignored him.

"True. Once Vestia saw that her beloved Northland was in danger, she accepted me willingly. And I say again if you don't perform the rites, sire, Adenile will go to Hebaruin, and the North will go to hell. Take your pick. Vestia the charity-girl? Or Adenile, your beloved little child and heir to the throne?"

Vestia looked at Umphy and mouthed *Run!*

The king folded his arms. "You're bluffing, lord Gurthur. What have you to threaten the North with?"

Gurthur smiled. "Why, the Black Dragon of course."

A gasp rose from the crowd. Haramid leapt forward. "You lie!"

"I do not lie. I can summon Morbane just as any Southern can."

"And what is your purpose for such a deed? Why should the Black Dragon, the most powerful creature in the world, listen to a two-legged human fool?"

"Because," Gurthur said calmly. "I know where the White Orb is!" Adenile struggled, and Gurthur stabbed the dagger slightly into her skin. "Do not worry, my princess. I have always looked after you, and I always will!" He spoke loud enough for all the people to hear. "Did I not tell you the little blue dragon possessed a powerful treasure, one that could make you Empress, just as you always wanted? Didn't I tell you that all you needed to do was kill the dragon and place the Orb in Fordomt's hands? It was so simple, but you were too weak. And now we must make a terribly long and boring complication out of the affair!" His voice rose louder as he spoke to the crowd.

"If you wish to save the North, there is one thing I ask for. I wish for Vestia's hand."

There was another silence. Nobody moved to save Vestia. Instead, they all turned to look at Umphy in wonder and surprise. He was here? The Bearer of the White Orb was in their very presence? It was absurd, that they should place the hand of a lady in that of a madman, but for the safety of the North? For the protection of their princess? They murmured quietly between themselves. Gurthur smiled and relaxed his hold on Adenile. He could feel the scales tipping in his favor.

Suddenly, Adenile pushed his arm away and twisted out of his grasp. Before Gurthur had time to react, the princess grabbed a goblet of spiced wine and threw it directly into her tutor's face. Gurthur screamed and clawed at his face.

"RUN, VESTIA!" Adenile screamed. "GET UMPHY OUT OF HERE!!"

Umphy was swept off his feet as Vestia swooped down on him and ran for the back door. Gurthur wiped the stinging liquid from his face just as Vestia disappeared out of sight. Screaming insanely, Gurthur leapt from the throne and grabbed Adenile, shaking her like a rag doll. His hold was broken by the beggar, who held his sword at his throat.

"It's over, Boranthion," he said. "Give up now, or be slain!"

"You think you always had the best of me," Gurthur sneered. "You were always the better Jacerin, weren't you, Novan? But which of us studied our dark magic more closely?" He laughed. He still held onto the princess' hand. "*Gorgovo!*"

There was a flash of light, and the beggar stood holding his sword at empty air.

Chapter 18

The village of Hadrake in which Erastil lived was built in the southeast, just on the other side of the Galtic mountains, in a valley known for its fertile ground and rolling hills. The main road leading north cut directly through the village, so the people were quite used to seeing Southern soldiers march through their district. They were not prepared, however, for the creature that took possession of the village the same day that the North commenced its festivities. While the city of Anthorwyn celebrated a victorious heritage, the southeast village mourned the loss of their freedom as a huge dragon bullied and frightened its citizens into submission. Southerners within the village rounded up each person regardless of age or gender, and held a village square meeting. New rules were posted: outgoing mail, trade, and travel were forbidden; meetings could not take place unless a Southern official was present; all homes and businesses were subject to daily inspection; and a license was needed to keep a particular trade open. If the regulations were not kept, or the rules broken, fines were paid, taxes doubled, people whipped and beaten, or else tortured and killed. The first day that the new laws were posted, Erastil's guardian, the shopkeeper, refused to show his license—because he did not have one. Erastil watched, horrified, as his guardian was dragged from the shop and beaten in the streets. When he rushed out to intervene, a dark shadow fell over them, and Razot snorted violently. Erastil was forced to watch, helplessly.

"Don't worry about me," the shopkeeper spat later, as Erastil ministered to his wounds. "Those lousy—" he said a word that he usually only said when he was drunk. "—think they can get away with this garbage, eh? We'll fix them right enough—"

"Father, there is a dragon right outside the gates," the young man said dryly. "It could burn down the village if we rise up in rebellion. We have to wait—perhaps it will go away—"

"Huh, not likely," the man spat blood from his mouth. "Gaw, those soldier-boys did a piece of work on me, didn't they? And since when have you ever decided to wait? Those are strange words from your mouth, Erastil. Usually I have to tell *you* to wait."

"That was when we could have given the soldiers the licking they deserve," said the young man. "We didn't have the constrictions of rules. Now they're enforcing them with the threat of dragons! That creature outside wasn't put there to guard us, that's sure."

"Do you really think it will go away?" the shopkeeper winced as Erastil applied a stinging salve.

"Perhaps. This is a wide territory. I have no doubt that it will move on before long. It isn't every day that Fordomt can come up with Black Dragon's spawn, and he has other towns and cities to bully into submission."

The shopkeeper was quiet for a moment. "I trust your words, son," he said quietly. "I'm sore frightened, though. They'll tear down my little shop and force me to pay double my taxes if I don't find some kind of work and get my papers in order. Worse yet, they might send me to the brimstone mines in Hebaruin."

"They'll do not such thing, not as long as I'm around," Erastil grated. "We'll get you some papers and you'll open shop tomorrow like the rest of the vendors, do you hear me? They won't take away your livelihood, not while they've got me to contend with. I'll make those dirty swine pay for what they've done to you, aye, and I'll protest on Hebaruin's doorstep if I must."

The shopkeeper sat up gingerly and tested his arm. He looked keenly at Erastil. "You're not a little lad anymore, son," he said. "Even when you were a wee bit of a boy I couldn't keep you from playing with wooden swords and chasing around imaginary enemies. You were meant to follow the life of a warrior, and I see that now with each passing day." He winced in pain. "Aye, and you've got healing hands, though this nasty bit will take some time to fully recover." Then he smiled. "You could be a Jacerin."

"It's what I've dreamed of since I was a little lad," Erastil gripped the table edge hard, a shadow crossing his face. "But I have not got the proper training or the connections."

"Connections, aha! Listen, lad, it's time you realized—" the shopkeeper bit his lip and looked at Erastil's eager young face. "Well, never mind. But hark, son, if you've a mind to join that elite group of demon-slayers, I'd not say no. You weren't meant to stay bound to the soil like a farmer, or tied to a shop or a village like me. No, your path is free. You're of age to choose to be anything you've a mind to be. And if you want to join the Jacerin, then you take the back gate and seek out your fortune, lad!"

"I can't leave you here." Erastil gripped the man's shoulders. "I won't leave you here by yourself. We've got to get those papers drawn up, and—"

"Listen to me, Erastil." The shopkeeper gripped the young man by the shoulders. "Your duty to me right now is to do as I say, and I'm telling you to get out of here and find success in freedom. I've almost lived out my days, but you have long ones ahead of you, and you're meant to do wild and wonderful things! You must promise me that you will find the Jacerin and fight in the war against the South. Give them a good drubbing for me. Listen, here's what you must do! Go into the chest beneath my bed. Here's the key. Open it and you will find a simple glass vial."

The chest beneath the bed supposedly held all the shopkeeper's worldly treasures: a picture of his late wife, a lock of her hair, her jewels, a few books, rare herbs and powders, and a tiny, brown glass vial. Erastil picked it up. Something was inside.

"Father, is this a ghost?"

The shopkeeper cracked a smile. "Bottle-ghosts are not demons, as well you ought to know, son. They have the power to grant one small gift of transportation per person, with the promise of freedom. The ghost's name is Leili. She's a bit temperamental—I've had her for years because I wasn't going anywhere. But you are. Listen! Take Leili and wish to be transported to the Galtic Mountains. There is a spirit there who will give you aid. Ask her where you shall find the Jacerin and any other questions you may have about your future. But be extremely polite. The spirit is not an enemy, but she is powerful enough to curse you if you anger her. She can either guide you to good fortune or have you run down into wickedness. Now, pack what you need and go. Make me proud of you, Erastil."

Erastil pressed his father's gnarled hands to his lips in gratitude. He could say nothing for the tears that choked him, but the shopkeeper understood everything.

Vestia sat with Umphy out in the gardens. The palace was in turmoil, but the mystic hid herself well in the bushes behind the iron gate. Umphy clung to her as a couple of guards rushed past, and then the trees rustled, and the beggar leapt down to join them. Arwos was perched on his shoulder. They huddled together close to the stone wall, hidden well by the shrubbery. They spoke in low voices.

"That was close. They nearly had us both," Vestia gave a weak smile to Umphy.

"And they *will* have you if we do not act swiftly," the beggar said. He looked at Umphy. "You found the Elbib, I noticed. Have you solved the riddle to your dream?"

"I—I only know that I have the White Orb—and that I must take it to the Tree of Life," Umphy stammered.

"Excellent," said the beggar, but Arows fluttered down from his shoulder and faced him.

"One moment, sir. I think you owe us an explanation for all the spying you've been doing. You've been following us around and watching Umphy, and then you saved him in the temple. Besides that, we saw you talking with Vestia here yesterday afternoon. What's your business with us, and who are you to a lady of the court?"

The beggar sighed. "We are in a great hurry, and my tale is too long to tell here."

"I'm not budging until you give us the essentials," Arwos hissed. "For all we know, you could be working for Hebaruin, and pulling the wool over everyone's eyes. You just made quite a scene back in the palace. What's your game?"

The beggar looked irritated for a moment. Then he sighed again and slumped against the wall. "My name is Novanthelion Gwynide, a Jacerin of the Original Healer's line. I came to Anthorwyn only a few weeks ago, like yourself, to search for my daughter. Galdermyn told me that she was in the palace, and that I was to look for a gray-eyed girl with hair the color of honey and a strong, proud face. That young woman is Vestia."

Umphy looked in wonderment at her. "Vestia! This is your father? But Whirit the fox told me your parents were slain in the downfall of the Sixth Northern Kingdom!"

"My foster parents were slain," Vestia said gently. "Galdermyn has spoken many times to me that I am the daughter of a Jacerin who was imprisoned in Hebaruin. He warned me never to tell anyone of him, for my safety's sake. The line was supposed to be dead. If anyone from Hebaruin knew that Novanthelion Gwynide's children walked the earth, they would target them and destroy them. When my brother and I were born—"

"You have a brother?"

"We were separated at birth. I went to the Sixth Kingdom, and my brother was taken in by a shopkeeper in a southeastern village."

"But why were you in Hebaruin?" Arwos asked Novanthelion. "Why were you imprisoned? You are a Jacerin, and your line was the greatest of all of those who joined your fellowship!"

"Ah," Novanthelion's eyes burned. "But there was another who was as great as I in the skills of defense against the dark magic, although much more knowledgeable about such black sorcery than I ever was. It interested him very much. It offered him amusement. Such wickedness fascinated him, caught him up in its web until he was consumed by it. He was much more cunning than I." Novanthelion bit his lip and put his head into his hands. He was trembling. When he raised his head again, Umphy saw a tear in his eye. Vestia reached over and clasped her father's hand. Novanthelion seemed unable to get the words out.

"That man was my brother. In those days he was known as Boranthion Gwynide. But people today know him as Gurthur Nowyn."

"Gurthur!" cried Vestia. "But he said—he told me it was *he* who had been betrayed by the Jacerin and thrown into Hebaruin. He hated them! He did not want me to join them because of what they did to him!"

"He told you a half-truth," Novanthelion growled. "If he was betrayed by the Jacerin, it is only because he chose to see it that way. My *brother* was the one who betrayed *me*. And he did it because—because of a woman." He looked softly at Vestia and tenderly caressed her cheek. "Your mother."

Umphy and Arwos exchanged quick glances. Novanthelion spoke quietly. "Boranthion and I were both in our thirties when it happened. We patrolled the North in those days, and we happened to be riding across the Northern Plains between the kingdoms of Haeroné and Anthorwyn when we saw a gypsy caravan being attacked by goblins. We drove them off and the grateful gypsies explained that they were delivering incognito a very special guest to the palace for her betrothal to the king." He paused. "Favia was her name, and she was the most beautiful woman I had ever set eyes upon."

"The queen!" Arwos gasped. "You mean—do you mean to say—that Queen Favia Unituriel is Vestia's mother? Well—but—then that makes Adenile Vestia's half-sister!"

Umphy remembered what Whirit had told him about the two girls having similar interests, spirits, and tempers. The news was not quite as much a shock to him as he supposed it should have been.

"Are you—er—married?" he asked Novanthelion. The Jacerin smiled and shook his head.

"I wanted to marry her. I begged her to come with me, to elope, to go far away to a place where it would be just the two of us and our children. She adored me, loved me with a passion that seemed too great for her tiny form to handle. But her duty was even greater. She was a gift from her father to the king of Anthorwyn; she was to bring peace between the kingdoms. She was so frightened of disobeying her father, but torn between doing her duty to him and following her heart. In the end, she chose to do her father's will, but she told me that I would always hold her heart. I believed in that—and trusted it. Her last words were my one strength in Hebaruin."

"And Gurthur betrayed you because he was in love with Fa—the queen?" Arwos shook his head in disbelief. Novanthelion clenched his hands.

"He was wild with jealousy when she spurned him. He did not see the great difference between the two of us."

"Differences are subjective," Umphy said softly as all eyes turned to him in surprise. "They are what you make them."

"Ah, so he passed on his words of wisdom to the princess, did he?" Novanthelion said bitterly. "Envy festered sorely within his heart. My brother had always been very proud, and the blow to his pride was not easily healed. He was quiet and did not rage outwardly. It was only when he led me into a village full of demons that I realized in a flash just how much he hated me.

"I had been informed by Galdermyn earlier that month of the birth of my twins—a boy and a girl. My brother did not know, for I suspected that telling him might reopen the wound. I did not know at the time that the wound still festered. Well, Boranthion told my colleagues and I—eighteen men total—that there was a village full of demons—minor ones—and that our services were required. I led my men into the village, but before we knew it, we were surrounded by full-grown brimstone-demons—and they are not minor enemies. We were inadequately prepared to fight them. Five men were killed, and the rest—including my brother and me—were taken to Hebaruin. He was set free after a year with the promise that he would work for Fordomt. I and my companions slaved in the brimstone-crystal mines of Hebaruin. For every curse they uttered against Boranthion, a sickness or death would grip them instead. It is forbidden for a Jacerin to utter any kind of curse, for it will only backfire upon him. I kept my lips sealed and dreamed of Favia.

"I only managed to escape a few months ago. I went first to the village in the southeast to spy upon my son, and was content with my findings. But it was my daughter that I truly wanted to see, for Galdermyn told me that she was as beautiful as her mother and a mystic like herself. I also wanted to see Favia and make sure that she was happy in her life. I did not want to come and disrupt anything. I only wanted to see them. Well, imagine my surprise when I followed *you* two in—" he nodded at Umphy and Arwos. "—and who should I see but Boranthion in the entourage of the princess herself! Before that time I had no thoughts of vengeance. A lack of uttering curses made me forget of my brother's evil deed. But when I saw him there—all I could think of was the danger my daughter might be in. I could not get into the palace. But I could sit by the garden gates and spy. And I must admit, you fascinated me, Umphy. I had never seen a dragon before, and you do have that infantile attraction going for you, I must say." He paused.

"It did not take me long to figure out how matters stood. Boranthion was in the center of it all: the fight between Vestia and Adenile, the disruption between the princess and her own parents, and the hatred she felt for so many people. And why? I asked myself that question over and over. What did he hope to gain by attacking the princess? I found out only last night."

"You were there?" Arwos whispered. "You saw Gurthur talking to Vestia—you saw that she protects Umphy, and he wanted his White Orb—"

"No," Novanthelion chuckled. "No, that was not Vestia. I could see the lady's face from where I sat, but her back was turned to you. It was Favia to whom Boranthion spoke. He knew she was protecting Vestia from him, and he wanted her—" Novanthelion broke off and ground his teeth angrily, nostrils flaring with heated, inner rage. "Well, it was Vestia or the North's obliteration. A tough choice. He knew that Umphy has the Orb, and he knows what he looks like, too. Such descriptions are precisely what Morbane needs in order to go looking for his quarry. Favia was caught. Boranthion meant to ruin her because she rejected him. I think he suspected that Vestia was Favia's daughter, but he was willing to overlook her relationship to him for the sake of destroying poor Favia's little heart. Naturally he would have told her that I was dead, otherwise my appearance tonight would not have caused such a shock to her majesty."

Arwos grinned good-naturedly. "She was out cold, sir."

"I did not mean to make such a vile disruption. But I knew that Favia would put her duty above her own personal love. And she did. She gave Vestia's hand to her own uncle! But I could not bear that. Anything—the torture of the South, the heartache of giving my love to another man—anything but watching my daughter wed the man who would have killed me and destroyed the life of the woman who rejected him!"

Vestia was crying softly, her face in her hands. "But he's taken away Adenile—she's in Hebaruin by now. I heard him shout the transportation spell. It's a very powerful incantation. What will he do to her? And what will the king do to you, father? When he discovers the truth—"

"The truth must be made clear. I was content to let the deception live so long as it did not hurt anyone, but there are lives at stake now—not only the princess', but Umphy's as well, and all the innocent of the North—and indeed, everyone in Balské is now vulnerable."

"So if you hadn't said anything tonight, none of us would be in danger!" Arwos accused. Novanthelion shook his head.

"Boranthion works for Hebaruin. Even if he did get Vestia, he would have continued to ruin the life of the princess and her mother. He would have gone back on his word—you do not know Boranthion as I do! You may have noticed his eyes—they were not always amber-hued and snakelike. They were once blue, as mine are—one is, anyway."

Umphy noticed for the first time that the man did indeed have a clear blue eye, sweet and refreshing as a pool of water in the summer sun. But it was filled with pain and a lifetime of experience. He put a paw over the man's bandaged hand.

"Sir," he said. "I think we can trust you. You saved our lives in the temple—"

"I followed you up because I had a feeling that you would be attacked. A Guardian with fame is an open target for one such as my brother."

"We must get to the Evantyri," Umphy said. "It's a place of safety until we can get information and direction on where to go next."

"I agree; you cannot stay here in the city. But you need someone besides you little raven friend to go with you," Novanthelion said quietly. "He is a brave friend; I know it for a fact. But you face dangers out in the wilderness that even a raven cannot stand against."

"Will you come with us?" Arwos asked.

"I wish I could. It would be just like the old days," the Jacerin smiled. "But I must remain here and give aid to the king. He will need every bit of guidance that he can get, now that the Northern Realm is a target for the Black Dragon. No, I think I will send another with you." He smiled at his daughter.

"Vestia?" Arwos asked skeptically. "Are you sure she's—well, I don't like to seem rude or doubtful, but how good are her skills?"

"I am a mystic," Vestia said. "As Galdermyn's pupil, I have learned to use my mind as well as my body in the defense of others against the forces of evil. My abilities as a warrior will speak for themselves, but I may boast that they surpass all of Galdermyn's expectations. If you wait here, I will change my clothes and pack. It will take me all of ten minutes, I promise!"

"There's just one thing I want to know," Umphy said as Vestia ran to collect her things. "You said, sir, that Gurthur had attacked me in the temple. But why would he do that? What was his motivation?"

"It was his action to prove to the lady Adenile that he still worked for her," said Novanthelion. "I knew enough from the gossip and conversations in the gardens to know that the princess wanted power. From your conversation with Galdermyn, I knew at once that you carried an Orb. If Adenile got her hands on it, she would either have long life and power from keeping it, or she could trade it in to Fordomt for a chance at greater glory. But she did not have the ability to attack you. She loves you too much—in fact, I believe you are the solitary creature she loves without a thought to herself. You gave her what no one else did: unconditional love. You have your youthful innocence, Umphy, but you also have something else playing into your favor: your inbred need to give unselfishly of yourself for the sake of doing good to another person. All Guardians instinctually protect people, but your extra virtue is charity, and that made a huge difference in the life of a spoiled young lady who needed someone to love her."

Arwos sniffed. "Seems to me a good spanking might have had the same effect—or not," he wilted underneath the stern glare of the Jacerin. "Umphy does have some interesting qualities about him—for being a castaway runt, young fellow, you're certainly a very underestimated creature!"

"Let us hope that all the wrong people continue to underestimate him," Novanthelion stood as Vestia returned. She was dressed in a simple walking tunic and trousers, a belted skirt covering her legs modestly. Her hair was twisted back into a braid, and she wore a sword at her side. As she wrapped a cloak around her shoulders, Novanthelion reached into his pocket and brought out a silver locket. He fastened it around his daughter's neck.

"Your mother gave this to me as a token of her love," he said. "I think you should have it now. Inside is a special herb that will heal any illness or mend any wound, and a lock of her hair. Take the sewers beneath the city. They were useful passages during times of war, and they will lead you to the ruins of the old temple in the mountains. There is an enchanted portal there. I've used it before, and few others know about it. From there you can make your way to the Evantyri. Make me proud of you, dearest one!" He took his daughter's face in both hands and kissed her forehead. Then he shook Umphy's paw. "Good luck, young man. I'm extremely jealous that I can't share in the adventure, but my daughter will look after you with the skill of her ancestors, and Arwos will be an equally fine companion. I hope that when we next meet it will be on the field of victory. Farewell, now, and good fortune go with you all!"

Chapter 19

Arwos perched on Umphy's shoulder as the little dragon followed Vestia through the gardens and around the palace walls. They stopped in an alleyway; beyond that, Umphy could hear the revelry of the people singing and dancing in the city streets. Vestia knelt down by a sewer-hole and removed the grating. Then she slid in first, beckoning Umphy and Arwos to follow her. She slid the lid back over them, and suddenly all three refugees were standing in complete darkness.

From her bag, Vestia produced an enchanted candle that stayed lit and never burned down the wax. The candle produced quite a light, revealing the long dark tunnels of the underground sewer-passages. The walls were wet and slimy, and the air was cold. Except for the noise above their heads, the sewers were quiet.

"Stay with me," Vestia whispered. Together they navigated through the tunnels. Vestia seemed to know precisely where she was going, and spoke quietly to calm her companions. "These sewers are relatively new. We must take the passages beneath them to find the old temple of Ankharam within the mountains. The temple houses the oldest secret in the North: an enchanted portal-well. Nobody knows of it but the wizards and those they choose to tell."

"And how is that going to help us?" Arwos whispered.

"When we reach the well, we must leap into it together and think of the place we most want to visit. If we think of the Evantyri, we'll be transported there."

"Well, that's handy!" Arwos said cheerfully. Umphy was feeling sick.

"Did you say there are passages beneath the sewers?" he asked. "I'm not feeling very well."

Vestia put a hand over his forehead and checked his mouth. "Dragons are not meant to live beneath-ground," she said with concern. "You feel ill because you're not used to being so far below the surface of the earth. Guardians are creatures of light, not darkness. You'll feel better when we reach the Evantyri. I'm afraid we'll have to go even lower now, but if you feel like fainting, I will carry you."

Umphy swallowed and tried to control his swimming head. Very soon they came to a dark, slimy corner. Vestia squatted down and held her candle close to the floor, illuminating a heavy iron grate. Wrapping her fingers around the handles, she pulled with all her strength. Umphy helped to shove the grate aside and then put both paws over his nose. "Ugh!"

"It isn't going to smell very pleasant," Vestia apologized. "The sewers were built over the ancient Northern catacombs."

"Hold on a minute," Arwos protested. "Catacombs? Open tombs? I'm not going down there with a bunch of dead bodies!"

"Oh, don't be such a baby. I'll go first and Umphy will follow. Bring up the rear if you please, Master Ebonfeather."

Slowly, they descended.

The air was thick and cold and silent. Vestia's boots landed on solid rock, and as she stretched out her hand with the candle, the flame illuminated a great stone archway with runes carved into it. Beyond the archway lay a single tunnel that branched off into several directions. Umphy felt very sick, being so far underground, but there was enough air yet. Arwos perched on Vestia's shoulder and closed his eyes.

"Arwos, what *is* the matter with you?" Vestia asked.

"I was born in a graveyard," Arwos whispered. "And once I saw a ghost rise from the grave. I never got over it. Ugh, it was all cold and white and skeletal."

"Do you know where you're going?" Umphy asked Vestia.

"Yes. Galdermyn has brought me here on several occasions."

Umphy thought that to bring anyone into such a dark, cold place was the equivalent of torture. The stony dirt walls were rough and cold, and water dripped from somewhere over head. They took the main tunnel leading straight, and passed into a chamber with two large caverns on either side. Arwos gave a low moan and buried his head into Vestia's hair. Umphy shivered. Each cavern had little shelves carved into them, onto which were placed various urns. On the ground of one of the caverns lay a fully-clothed skeleton clutching a bag of gold coins. His jacket was decayed, but small darts could still be seen clinging to the frayed scraps of cloth. Vestia raised an eyebrow.

"There are traps laid in the tombs for those who would try and steal from the dead," she said quietly. Umphy swallowed and put his paw into Vestia's free hand.

When Tarragon awoke in the mouth of his cave, the first thing he saw was Tworgar curled up in a furry ball at his side. The dragon rose softly, taking care not to awaken his friend, and sniffed the air. There was something alive in the area—and if it was edible, Tarragon had every intention of hunting it.

He had never explored the Galtic Mountains, but he was sure that there were many tasty things to eat. Lumbering down into the forest, he came to a halt in a small clearing. A sandy bank stretched in a ring around a pool of stagnant water. A sludge of dead leaves and algae floated at the top of the dark water. Tarragon's eyes watered at the revolting odor. He poked his tongue out. There was something alive in the water.

As he drew closer, the dragon's warning instincts blared like lightning, and with twice that speed, he jerked backwards as the pool exploded in a shower of repugnant drops and foam. Sharp teeth snapped onto empty air. A behemoth roared in anger as its morsel leapt out of reach. It was much smaller than Tarragon, but the powerful jaws and well-muscled fins could well have dragged any animal twice its size underwater to drown. Yet Tarragon did not give his opponent a second chance to lunge again. This time he did not scorch his victim, but make a violent jab at the exposed throat.

The behemoth slid backwards, and Tarragon's jaws closed around its snout. He ripped savagely, and the behemoth howled in pain. It tried to wriggle free, but the dragon heaved and pulled the creature's fat, oily bulk onto dry land. Before the behemoth could wriggle back down into the water, Tarragon bit into the back of its neck and severed the artery. Within moments, the behemoth lay at the water's edge, twitching in the final death spasms.

"Tarragon! What's happened? What's going on?" Tworgar bounded into view. "Are you hurt?"

"Me? No," Tarragon replied. He smiled proudly. "Are you hungry? Look what I caught!"

The young wolf sniffed the carcass. "Smells fishy to me!" But Tworgar had no problems eating his fill, and even Tarragon admitted that the behemoth tasted much better than a horse or cow. When they had eaten and drunk their fill and rested again, Tarragon hoisted Tworgar over his shoulder and began the journey to the spirit's cave. It took only an hour to find the break in the mountains that Tworgar had spoken of earlier; the mountains were divided by a canyon that shot down to a rushing river below. Tarragon flew between the walls of the canyon and then swooped beneath a majestic stone arch that bridged the mountains together. The canyon twisted and turned in every direction until finally Tarragon broke free from between its walls where the river emptied out from a waterfall into a magnificent valley below. Here among the hills stood giant monoliths, and no roads could be seen for miles.

"We're still in the Galtic Mountains," Tworgar said, pleased with his navigational skills. "But we are now in the Galtic Valley. This used to be a volcanic crater, but the volcano has been dead for over three thousand years. The valley grew in overtop of it. The spirit lives over there in the tallest monolith!"

A small pathway led up into the monolith. The passage was steep and narrow, and Tarragon had some difficulty in climbing through, but when at last he wriggled free, Tworgar held up a paw. Tarragon perked his ears up. From around the corner, he heard the sound of strange, sing-song gurgling and muttering. The sight took Tarragon's breath away. This side of the monolith was an optical illusion, seeming like a wall of solid rock, but actually a tunnel cut into the rock. The narrow passage was a valley of rock, with an uneven path, and sharp, jagged rocks surrounding them. Tworgar climbed carefully over these rocks, and then called Tarragon's attention to where the path narrowed. A small fountain bubbled up from a spring hidden within the rock. The path sloped dangerously into a cave, and here the fountain rushed into a river, frothing madly down into the darkness. Tworgar peered down into the cave and then looked at Tarragon.

"She's gone down into her lair," he murmured. "To follow her means death. We'll go around and meet her on the other side."

Tarragon raised his head as if seeking patience. It was certainly taking a long time to find just one spirit that could have the answer to where his family and friends might be hiding! As he squinted upwards, Tarragon fancied he could see something glittering in the air—and it was not the sun playing tricks in between the clouds. He halted and pointed it out to Tworgar.

"Funny sparkles!" the young wolf yelped with glee. "They're getting closer!"

"What the—"

Tarragon had no idea what happened next. It was as if something had materialized out of thin air and smashed directly into his face, clobbering him and dropping down to the ground below. Tarragon shook his head in disbelief. Tworgar sniffed at the bundle on the ground.

"It's a man!"

Tarragon examined him. Despite his beard, he was still young, with copper hair and a traveling cloak. The fall had knocked him out. As he came to, he groaned and sat up, and

Tarragon noticed that he was bleeding from a cut in his arm. The man looked around dazedly and then, noticing Tarragon for the first time, leapt to his feet and tried to scramble away, but Tarragon neatly hooked him with one claw. He held him up close, watching with amusement as the man struggled.

"PUT ME DOWN AND FIGHT FAIR!! YOU'LL NEVER TAKE ME TO HEBARUIN! GO ON, TRY IT, YOU BIG LIZARD'S SPAWN!!"

"Oh, shut up!" Tarragon snapped. "You're the one who knocked into me; I think I'll be doing the inquisition, thank you! Where in the name of the Brown Dragon did you come from? We were here first!"

"I don't have to answer any of your questions!" the young man spat. "I am a free man!"

"I don't care if you're a stick in the mud. You whalloped right into my face, and I demand to know where you came from, squirt!"

"He means you no harm!" Tworgar barked up. "He is a *Guardian!*"

"Oh yes? Well, if he's a Guardian, why isn't he guarding?" shrieked the young man. He glared at Tarragon. "You're a fine specimen of a coward! Where are all of you when we need you? Villages getting attacked left and right—Black Dragons on the loose—Southerners beating and enslaving everyone in sight—and here I find a Guardian doing everything but what he's supposed to be doing!"

Tarragon was flabbergasted. "You *are* a bold fellow!" he snapped. "How dare you make such long-winded accusations against me? If you don't tell me who you are, where you came from, and what your business is here, I'll bury you right here and now!"

The young man stopped struggling. "My name is Erastil Anthelion. I come from the southeastern village of Hadrake, which has recently been overrun by the Southerners and a Black Dragon. I come to the spirit who haunts these mountains in order to seek out and join the Jacerin!"

Tarragon set Erastil down. He had heard of the Jacerin and understood that they were a respected group of mercenaries skilled in the arts of war and healing. They were most famous for purging villages of demons and witches. "Hadrake, you said? But that's very far inland. The Black Dragon's path continued along the coastlines—at least, I thought it did. So the villages are being overrun and you want to become a Jacerin in order to be a hero, eh?" Tarragon looked thoughtfully at the young man bristling before him.

"They are bullies and cowards, and I nearly lost my life coming here," said Erastil. "I used a portal-ghost. It is very important that I see the spirit! Now if you'll excuse me—"

"Just a minute," Tarragon snapped. "We were here first."

"Do you need to see the spirit, too?"

"Yes, I do! The Black Dragon attacked my clan, but there are survivors, and I must know where they are hiding now. So if you don't mind, I think your errand can wait about ten minutes!"

Tworgar chuckled. "Look at you two, squaring off like to duelists! I've never seen anything so funny: a man facing down a dragon! Sir, my name is Tworgar, and this is my friend Tarragon. It seems that the two of you have very urgent questions for the spirit, but you must remember that she takes only one customer at a time. Perhaps if we all went in as one group, she can see us together as a single customer. There's no harm in that, is there? Now come on, you two; be friends. We're all fighting the same enemy!"

Erastil shuffled his feet. "My apologies, Master Tarragon."

"Accepted, Sir Erastil."

The trio climbed around the cave, taking care to mind their footing. The rocky valley sloped downward and leveled slightly before sloping down again, and here, between the rocks, spurted a jet of water from the underground river. It flowed down the rocks and filled a small, lonely pool of water in the crown of the mountain-peak. Tarragon strained. He couldn't see anything particular. Then, he heard a strange sound, like deep, guttural muttering and then high-pitched, crackled singing. An old woman came slowly around the bend, laden heavily by a massive pile of rags upon her back. She lifted her face, and squinted in the sun. Tarragon's jaw dropped.

"The Bha-Nigh?" he hissed at Tworgar.

"Gaahh!" the old hag shrieked. "Visitors, I think. Yes, that be young Erastil, son of a Jacerin, a wild dog, and—a Guardian, aye, a Guardian!" She chuckled in her throat and moved closer. One of her eyes was swollen shut with a red blister; the other was wide open, staring around with a milky-blue orb. She had only three sharp fangs. Coming closer, the old woman dropped her pile of rags at the pool's edge and began scrubbing them, one by one, muttering all the time. "What do they want of old Bha-Nigh, eh? What do they want of the haunts of the wraith?"

"We have questions about our futures, lady." Erastil said politely.

"The three of ye?"

"Two," Tarragon replied.

"Two, aye, two—thou art wise to come see me," Nigh cackled. She plunged a rag into the water and brought it out, streaming with blood. She laughed. "This man not so wise."

Tarragon felt his own blood run cold. "Will you answer our questions?"

"What would ye give old Nigh?" the woman stretched out a clawed, bloody hand. Tarragon snorted.

"Payment? This was not a part of the deal."

The old woman's eye narrowed. "I make no deal. Ye come to Bha-Nigh haunts, ye suffer consequences. Even thee, Guardian! Wraiths are not thy business."

"I'm about to make 'em my business," Tarragon glared at her. He held her gaze steadily, until the milky-blue eye fell, and the spirit fell back to muttering.

"Thou art brave, Guardian. For speaking to me thus, any other would be dead. But I see great strength in ye. There is a brand of greatness on thy brow. Even Bha-Nigh cannot pit herself against thee. Again, the claw drew forth a tattered rag and plunged it into the pool. It came out dripping blood. "So many die," the spirit said again, sounding sad this time. "Evil's abroad. Mischief runs amok. I see the bodies of many men upon a red field, and the corpses of many more slaughtered in their homes."

"Can you stop it?" Tarragon asked, feeling bold. "You're a very powerful spirit, known to everyone! Is there a way for you to stop the evil?"

"Bha-Nigh is only the washer-woman," the wraith chuckled. "Not good, not bad. I see the fate of men, and I wash the cloth of their life." She held up a clean, white, silk cloth. "This is but a newborn babe." She plunged it into the water and drew it out, unstained. "May she live to grow old!"

"What of the survivors of the Black Dragon attack on the Firespring Clan?" Tarragon asked. "Where have they gone?"

Another cloth was plunged into the water and brought out dripping blood. "Bha-Nigh sees many dragons, many Guardians killed. The survivors are scattered. They have no place of refuge; they go where they will to escape the wrath of Poisonscales. Old Morbane!" Bha-Nigh searched among her bag and brought out another rag. She held it up. "Is this thy sweetheart?" she gurgled ominously. "Is this thy lady-friend?" She dipped the rag, and Tarragon's heart pounded; the rag came up clean. "Alive! Thy heart's alive, Tarragon the Mighty, but to seek her for thee means death. Thy rag I shall not wash until it comes into contact with thy foe. Thy enemy is Morbane, Tarragon. Only thou art his equal, for in ye resides the spirit of the One beneath the Tree of Life."

"I—I have the spirit of the Brown Dragon?" Tarragon said softly. It sounded fantastic, unreal. He had never imagined himself to carry the spirit of the Brown Dragon within him! It meant he was a Chosen One, destined to fulfill the time-honored prophecy of the Guardians. How many times had he listened to the Matriarch give the speech at every keldora ceremony—his included? Why the fates should have chosen him for the task, however, he did not know and he did not care. "Whether that's true or not, I still have to find my kin. I must know if my family is alive. And I'll discover that for myself," he said abruptly as the Bha-Nigh held up two more rags: his mother and father. "Do not show me yet, lady."

The old hag shook her head sadly. "No fool art thou, and yet a fool's errand ye run. Tarragon. Thy journey must take thee North, where the Black Dragon goes."

Tarragon shook his head. "I cannot do that."

"Then do what ye will, Tarragon; thy fate will still lead thee North. It is thy destiny, for I'll not wash thy rag until ye meet with thy foe, even if it be a thousand years from now and ye both are gray and staggering old."

Erastil stepped forward. "And me, noble lady? Who is my foe?"

"Aha!" Bha-Nigh chuckled almost fondly. "Thy foe is not mine to tell thee of, Erastil Anthelion. Start not; I knew thy father. Nay, not thy shopkeeper; thou art not his son. Thy heritage is the very one ye seek. Thy true father is the descendant of the Original Healer, and thou art a Jacerin's son, born of a princess and her lover on the plains of the North! A sister thou hast, too, Erastil, of similar age and height and gray eyes—thy mother's eyes. Thy spirit is all thy father's. Where you seek your father you shalt find connection to thy unseen foe. Thy journey also lies North."

Erastil looked as though Tarragon had punched the air out of him; his face was white, his eyes wide, and he sat down hard, blinking owlishly. The Bha-Nigh chuckled over and over again, as if she found the situation amusing. "Aye, thy two fates are woven in one tapestry—man and dragon! Come not here again. Soon, soon, Guardian, my pool will run red with blood, and the rags I carry will be a bonfire in the night." The old hag shook her head. "Beware the unchained and undead of the wild. The Babasi is loose, and her sister, the green-faced howler. Many behemoths, too. They return to savagery. Few are governed by the laws of magic anymore. Be wary! Protect what is yours."

She turned her back, and Tworgar quietly motioned to his companions. "She won't say anything else," he murmured. "She's made her point, and now we must go."

Chapter 20

Vestia carried Umphy piggy-back; the little dragon had fainted away from being underground. Arwos perched between Umphy's wings and hid his face. The trio were making their way up and out of the catacombs, but the walls were still lined with horizontal holes in which rested the bones of ancient Northerners. A stairway led up to the temple of Ankharam. It had been built deep in the mountains as a pagan altar in the old days, and the new temple had been built over it. When Arwos finally peeked out from over Vestia's shoulder, he noted with horror that the temple still held the remains of some of the sacrificial victims, several urns, and a cracked altar. The stone floor was overgrown with weeds and vines, and the crumbling pillars were laden with dust and spider-webs. At the far end of the room was a large spa-like well that bubbled and frothed with a clear, luminescent liquid. Runes were carved into the stone that rimmed the outside. Vestia set Umphy down and read the inscription.

"This is it," she said. "Come on, let's—"

A noise made her turn.

Arwos squawked and fluttered up to take refuge on one of the statues. Vestia stood over Umphy and drew her sword. The creature standing before them had heaved its gargantuan bulk from out of the shadows in a corner and now stood towering over them—a legend of old.

Langertherums were once counted among the rare behemoths that still inhabited the earth, but ancient scholars had placed them under line of extinct animals when they ceased to be prominent. They were most historically noted for their reptilian features, and runes and scrolls had written of their amphibious nature, carnivorous appetite, and great stature, which surpassed all other animals—except dragons. At eighteen feet in length and nine feet high, the Lang was an impressive creature. But time and age had worn him down. Rolls of dirty gray-blue fat completely squashed the once-elegant, shapely creature into some sort of putty-doll. He had no neck, and only a hump of flesh between his shoulder blades served as a reminder of the placement of his backbone. Flukes and powerful front flippers both aided in hoisting himself out of the water. His conical snout and mouth bore razor-sharp teeth, and his eyes were cloudy. Vestia realized he was blind. Nevertheless, she kept her sword drawn. The Lang sniffed the air and tested it with a forked tongue.

"Vissssitors!" he hissed. "I've not had visssssitorsss for many yearsssss . . ."

"I am Vestia Anthelion, daughter of the Jacerin," Vestia said firmly. "I've come here many times with Galdermyn, but I've never seen you. Who are you?"

The Langertherum laughed.

"You need not know my name; indeed, I wonder if I even have a name," he chuckled. "But I am of the ancient race, and such would be my name then . . . that it isssss not for you to know now. It would sssssstrike terror to your heart," he said, and coughed. "What bringsssssss you to this lonely place?"

"We wish to use the well-portal."

"Ah," sighed the creature. "But I am itsssssss guard. I have sworn that no man or beasssssst may ussssssse it. I have been here for yearssssssss. Galdermyn I have ssssssseen—and perhaps you, lady, I have sssssseen, too, but you have never ussssssed to the well. I left you alone. But I cannot let you passsss tonight."

"But you must!" Vestia argued. "We are on an errand of great emergency. Our mission will affect the entire land of Balské. It is extremely important. You must let us pass!"

"It is a dead end."

Vestia whirled around.

Gurthur stood behind her by one of the pillars, his hands clasped in front of him, his hypnotic eyes fixed upon the young woman's face. But there was no passion there now; his face was contorted in rage, and his eyes burned feverishly. Gurthur stepped forward. Vestia swung her sword in his direction.

"Come no further, coward!" she snapped. "I know who you are. And I swear by the sword I hold that I will strike clean through your heart if you come any closer!"

"You have no need for swords," Gurthur said calmly, though his face betrayed his anger. "Why not defend the dragon and yourself with the proper incantation? It is possible, you know, to block me with that powerful mind of yours."

"Yes, and I know what will happen if I curse you," Vestia replied, holding her sword at the ready. "I'm not stupid, Gurthur—or should I call you Uncle Boranthion? How long have you deceived me? Did you perhaps think to spare me my feelings? You needn't have worried—I don't care how we're related; I still destest you all the same!"

"And yet you refuse to curse me. Perhaps that's wisest."

"Where is Adenile?"

"You worry about that spoiled brat when I have you and the little dragon at my mercy?"

"I suppose you think that if I hand myself over to you, you will let Umphy get away freely," Vestia held her head high. "I think you're a liar."

"Vestia, my dear niece—I would not even dream of going back on my word."

"You betrayed my father. I've no reason to trust you! I reject you utterly and completely; you have no part in my life and hold nothing of my heart! Now go away before I set this demon's bane to you."

Gurthur's face twisted in fury.

"*Magoloth i-torogoloth!*"

The Langertherum suddenly went rigid. His milky-white eyes became amber-hued, and he drew himself up to his full height. Gurthur drew back, a thin smile on his face.

Without warning, the Langertherum struck!

Vestia leapt backwards, grabbing Umphy and dragging him to one side as the massive creature thundered forward, snapping down into thin air. It ignored the inert form of the little dragon, concentrating all its efforts on the young woman. For its age and bulk, the behemoth moved quickly. Vestia whirled left to avoid the sharp teeth and struck with her sword. The blade did not bite deep; time had provided such thick skin that the Langertherum did not even bleed. Again Vestia leapt back to avoid the jaws that came within a hair's breadth of her torso; she fell backwards over a loose crack in the floor and rolled to one side as a massive flipper came down. Springing up again, Vestia ran nimbly behind the creature, and before it could react, she had scampered up its back and brought the blade down between its shoulders. Roaring in pain, the Langertherum crashed forward, knocking over pillars and statues, and plunged itself into a pool of water at the far end of the temple. Vestia came floating up to the top, sputtering. Still clutching her sword, she swam to the side and started to hoist herself out. Then her face twisted in agony, and the behemoth dragged her back under.

Arwos screamed and hopped back from one foot to the other. Gurthur walked quickly over to where Umphy lay and reached down to pick him up. All at once the loyal raven swooped down from his perch and attacked the man, pecking and scratching furiously. "UMPHY, WAKE UP!!"

"*Molunda!*"

Arwos felt himself freeze and drop to the floor. His glazed eyes watched helplessly as Gurthur picked Umphy up like a baby, cradling him almost tenderly.

Suddenly, Umphy's eyes shot open. Seeing Gurthur's face bending over his, the little dragon squealed with fright and did the first thing he could think of: he squirted flame at the man's face like a child squirts water from its loaded mouth. Gurthur screamed in agony and dropped Umphy immediately, who squealed in pain and ran for cover. Over by the pool, the Langertherum was jerking Vestia up and down like a rag doll;

her head broke the surface several times and she gasped for air before being dragged back under. When she broke the surface again, Umphy grabbed at her arms and pulled hard. Vestia shot free, her gown ripped and her leg badly bitten. Picking up her sword, she pushed Umphy back down into a hole by the altar. Gurthur clawed madly at his face; the flames had burned away his beard and much of his skin, and in his agony, he raced to the pool and flung himself in.

"Look out!" Umphy cried. Vestia turned and swung her sword; the Langertherum was right behind her. Crippled in her leg, Vestia managed to fend off the jaws.

"Umphy, come on! Grab Arwos and take my hand!"

They raced towards the portal-well. When the Langertherum saw what they were about to do, he roared in anger and hurled himself forward just as Vestia gathered up Umphy and Arwos in one swoop and leapt into the portal. Umphy felt warm, bubbling water close about his head; he had a brief thought of his mother and of home, and then darkness enveloped him once again.

Chapter 21

Tarragon, Tworgar, and Erastil sat at the base of the monolith. They said nothing to each other, but none of them wanted to part company so soon.

"Somehow I didn't think that fat old widower was really my father," Erastil commented weakly. "But my God! My real father, a Jacerin! What a shock!"

Tarragon didn't say anything. He was just as stunned with the truth about himself, though he was not ready to admit to it yet. The Bha-Nigh must have made a mistake—he was no match for a Black Dragon. He was only a keldora. How could he possibly take on and defeat the deadliest of all creatures?

"It seems I have a long journey ahead of me," Erastil said. "The North! That's a long way from here. I have no horse and no ghost-transport. Where will I find a ride?"

"Well, don't look at me," snapped Tarragon. "I'm going to search for my kin."

"I didn't look at you and wouldn't ask you if you were the last resource," Erastil made a face.

"Oho, preferential, are we?"

"You're the one who would rather go look for your friends and family than obey the dictates of a powerful spirit!"

"Gentlemen, please!" Tworgar yelped unhappily. "This won't get us anywhere. It seems like we have two different paths to take, but surely we could help Erastil a little bit, couldn't we, Tarragon? I mean, really, he needs some kind of horse—or another one of those helpful little ghosts."

"The bartender in my village had dozens of them—ghosts, I mean," said Erastil. "And there were horses, too. But there's no way I could go back there now. It's overrun by Southerners."

"You've made that point extremely clear," Tarragon snapped.

"So I suppose it's no use asking if you'll come back and run them off!"

"No, it's not!"

Tworgar whined and covered his eyes with his paws. "Well, I think it might be a good idea," he whimpered. Tarragon whirled on him.

"What do you mean, a good idea? Look, I'm not about to go about rescuing villages when my people are in danger—"

"But they *are* in danger!" Erastil yelled, leaping to his feet and facing Tarragon down boldly. "Your people are the people of Balské—the same ones the Guardians have protected for centuries until you were driven into hiding by the Black Dragons! It's about time you great lizards stopped skulking about and recognized the great history of your ancestors! You are a Guardian—well, why aren't you guarding? What's to stop you? If you don't come now and prove yourself, you'll be no better than a Black Dragon—serving your own selfish purposes, instead of thinking of someone or something outside of yourself!"

Tarragon grabbed Erastil and dangled him neatly in front of his jaws. "If you weren't protected by the code of dragons, I'd eat you here and—" he stopped. Erastil was not flinching; he faced the dragon with eyes of fire. And Tarragon suddenly saw himself reflected in the young man. How could he forget that only a month ago he had challenged Razot with the same fire in his eyes, with no regard for rules or codes? And why had he done so? Because Razot had been a bully. Tarragon hated bullies. This young man obviously hated bullies, too. And suddenly, Tarragon found himself chuckling, and he could not stop. He had to set Erastil down; he was laughing so hard. Tworgar hid behind the young man's legs.

"When a dragon laughs, it usually isn't funny!" he whimpered. Tarragon shook his head, great tears streaming down his cheeks.

"It's—ooohahahahooo—it's nothing—ohahahahooo! Really, I'm—hee-hee—I'm alright!"

"Are you sure?" Tworgar peered up at Tarragon as if expecting his mood to change violently at any minute. Tarragon shook his head.

"No, I'm not sure. I'm really not positive about anything, anymore. Right, Erastil, you want to frighten off a bunch of cowardly nincompoops who haven't got anything else to do besides bully your people, is that it?"

"I'd be much obliged for some assistance," Erastil replied, bewildered at the strange behavior of this dragon. Tarragon giggled like a naughty dragonet about to pour cold water on his sibling's head.

"Then I'd better lend a paw. Oh, quit cringing, Tworgar, you're in this, too!" He leaned down and permitted the others to get on his back. "Now, Erastil, if you'll point me in the right direction, we'll see if we can change the attitudes of those miserable Southern devilmen!"

Umphy awoke to the sound of Arwos' unearthly screech of anger.

"FABULOUS, JUST FABULOUS!! WHERE IN THE NAME OF ENOVAN HAVE YOU TAKEN US, WOMAN?! THIS IS NOT THE EVANTYRI!!"

"Well, if that's all the thanks I get for taking the ice-charm off you—"

"But where are we? Where the devil have you taken us? This isn't the Evantyri; it's not even close!"

"Well, *I* was *thinking* about the Evantyri!" Vestia snapped.

Umphy opened his eyes. It was morning. He could feel sand beneath his chin, and as he regained consciousness, his ears were filled with the familiar sound of waves crashing against the shoreline, and he smelled the well-known, salty odor of dried seaweed, dead crabs, and empty shells. Arwos was hopping up and down in a rage; Vestia was sitting on the sand beside him. She had torn her skirt in order to bandage her leg, which had been wounded in the battle with the Langertherum.

"Umphy! What were *you* thinking of?" Arwos demanded.

"Leave him alone; it's not his fault!"

"Will you stay out of this, woman? Umphy, when we hit the pool, what were you thinking of?"

"I—I thought of home," the little dragon admitted a bit sheepishly. "I used to live on the Western Seashore. What's wrong? Where are we?"

"The Western Seashore, or so it appears," Vestia groaned. "And neither at your home nor anywhere near the Evantyri—somewhere in between, I'd wager. It's my fault—I forgot to tell you to clear your mind before jumping."

"There was no time. You saved us!" Umphy gave Arwos a warning look.

"Thank you, but if you hadn't burned Gurthur's face like that, we would still have him to contend with."

"Won't he follow us?" Arwos asked. "He found us before. He could find us again!"

"I don't think he'll waste his time," Vestia said heavily. "Nevertheless, he will alert others to our whereabouts. We have to find a way to the Evantyri from here. We'll be very safe there; it's protected. Arwos, you said you were familiar with a way?"

"Well, condsidering the fact that I'm not even sure where we are, I can't exactly give you precise directions, now can I?"

"Oh, stop muttering!" Umphy cried, covering his ears. "We're all safe and sound, aren't we? Count your blessings; it could be worse!"

A low chuckled made them all turn. Standing behind them were ten of the most ragged-looking men Umphy had ever seen, all bearing knives, swords, and poison-pipes. They were barefoot and burned almost black by the sun, and the majority of them bore frightful scars. Their leader, a tall man with a short gray beard and plumed cap strode forward.

"Well, well, what have we here?" he said pleasantly, neither looking nor sounding pleasant at all. "This be quite an interestin' sight fer sore eyes, mates. A pretty lass with a talking raven and a wee bit of a lizard for companions. Now ain't that somethin' yer don't see every day!"

Vestia gripped the hilt of her sword. "Nobody asked you, ruffian!"

"Oho, spice now, is it, me liddle darlin'? Well, there'll be less spice an' more sugar by the time I'm done with yer. I'd leave that blade alone, me beauty; these lads o' mine'll be more than happy to spit yer loverly guts iffen yer make one wrong move. It's ten to three, liddle missie."

Vestia had heard of pirates. They were typically foreigners to Balské, trading only at the major ports around the coasts but hardly ever setting foot on land. The majority of them hailed from islands, but some came from reputable cities in the North, and a few had relatives in the palaces. They were dangerous men but Vestia's training with Galdermyn had not prepared her to face them down. She tried reasoning.

"Good sirs, we're trying to find our way to the Evantyri. If you could point us in the right direction, we'd be much obliged."

"Didjer 'ear that, lads?" the captain roared. "They'd be much obliged if we could point them in the right direction! Ain't that fine and proper, now! And, pray, madam, what sort of reward might we humble gentlemen o' fortune be entitled to?" His men howled with laughter as their captain mocked the lady. Vestia was downright helpless. Suddenly, Arwos flew forward.

"You big bullies, don't you have anything else better to do with your miserable time than pick on helpless females and little dragons? If I were a man, I'd kick you right in the—"

"Hold on there, little black chatterbox," the captain held up a hand. "Did y'say 'dragon'?"

"So what if I did?"

"That there's a dragon!" One of the men pointed at Umphy. "I knowed 'e looked familiar, cap'n, sir; 'e's got wings, an' prob'ly breathes fire, too!"

The pirates looked considerably cowed, if not in awe of the little blue dragon who looked at them with huge frightened eyes and shuffled his feet awkwardly in the sand.

"Well, ain't this a lucky day fer us, mates," the captain sneered. "Just the right size fer show-an'-tell on the loverly islands. I'll wager we could set up our own liddle circus if we catch some singing squids, too!"

"Don't you laugh at him!" Vestia cried, outraged. "And he is not going to be a part of any side-show you ragged lot of boors conjure up! We'll find the Elven Realm alone, if you won't help us!"

The captain whistled. Nine swords were drawn and set around the helpless trio, forcing Vestia to drop her sword. Umphy clutched his tail fearfully, but did not dare breathe any more fire. The captain walked forward and leered into Vestia's face.

"The Elven Realm can wait, me pretty liddle darlin'. We're goin' fer a liddle ride first."

The ship lay anchored in a tiny cove just around the corner. The three prisoners, surrounded by the wicked-looking men, had no choice but to board the craft. They were searched for weapons, and the captain took Vestia's sword, dagger, and pack containing her medicines and food parcels. Arwos was put in a cage. Umphy, who had nothing but his flute in its leather strap, sobbed brokenly as it was taken from him.

"My sister gave that to me!" he wailed. "Please don't take it away!"

"Arrgh, did she, now?" the captain leered. "Poor liddle fellow—what does a dragon need with a flute anyways?" And with a single snap, he broke the flute in two. It was as if he'd stabbed the little dragon straight through the heart. That his last tie to his family should be broken enraged Umphy. Without warning he charged the captain, knocking him backwards and biting madly at his face.

"YEEEEAAARRRGHHH—GET THE LIDDLE DEMON OFF ME!!"

It took five strong men to pull Umphy off their captain, who staggered to his feet, holding his nose. Blood leaked from between his fingers.

"Yew liddle son of a—I'll get yew fer that! Throw 'im into the galley-cage!"

Umphy struggled bravely as he was led off. Arwos shrieked and flapped madly within his cage. The captain put the tip of his blade beneath Vestia's chin, tilting her head up.

"Now then, me loverly liddle plum-puddin', what's t'be done with yer? I think if we chained yer in my cabin—"

"Captain, sir!" a man stepped forward and saluted.

"What is it, Rhun?" the captain snapped.

"Sir, with all due respect, I think we should hold her for ransom. After all, what peasant-girl ever carried such beautiful weapons? Clearly this is a princess from the Northern Realm, and her father would pay dearly to get her back."

"On that you may depend!" Vestia shouted angrily, a plan leaping into her mind. "I am the Princess Adenile of the Fifth Kingdom of the North, and you will unhand me at once, or my father will send a legion of soldiers to attack and destroy you!"

The pirates gazed at her in awe. They had obviously heard of the famous beauty of the North, but they had no idea what she looked like. Vestia tried to look haughty, though she could not bear to throw a fit as Adenile would have clearly done in this situation. The captain took a good look at her.

"A legion of soldiers, eh?" he grunted. "Tell me, princey-princess, would these soldiers know how to sail a craft—or swim?" He burst out laughing. "Yew don't fool us. Landlubbers was always landlubbers, through an' through. Besides, how would yew be a-tellin' yer dear ol' pappy about us? By the time 'e got yer message, we'll be far away on the islands, an' you'll make some foreign king very happy!"

Vestia focused her mind. Summoning the powers within, she gazed into the captain's eyes—the mirrors of his soul—and scrolled through his thoughts like a librarian through a book. She captured one thought and twisted it.

'Then again, maybe we could take yer to the Evantyri," the captain said abruptly. The crew was silent, looking at each other in bewilderment. A smile tugged at the corner's of the young woman's lips, and she twisted the thought again.

"We could provide yer with safe passage," the captain said again. The crew looked stunned.

"Aye, for just think of the ransom the *Elves* would pay!" shrieked the captain.

That made more sense. The crew roared with approval and hustled Vestia away. Opening the hatchway to the hold below, they pushed the "princess" inside and slammed the door shut, locking it securely.

The light was dim and the air was stuffy. Vestia heard coughing behind her and she turned to see a hundred or more slaves lined on either side of the ship, chained to wooden blocks that also served as seats. Their hands were manacled to great wooden oars. Here were men and women, but also children, too! Vestia gasped and put a hand over her mouth, her eyes wide.

Umphy sat beside one of the children, wringing his tail anxiously. The oarslaves looked at him with huge, awed eyes. "Ves, what do we do now? They're pirates—they might never let us go!"

"Keep your chin up, Umphy," Vestia comforted him. "I played with the mind of the captain a bit, and he'll take us to the Evantyri to sell us. Until that time, we have free transportation."

"Don't be so sure of that," said one of the slaves, a man with black hair and clear blue eyes. "I'll wager all the gold of the North that you'll be chained down here like the rest of us.

They might sell you, lass. But they'll keep the dragon for a bigger profit on the islands. Captain Blackfang's a cruel, pitiless master. All he cares about is what might be in it for him."

'Which is why his mind is so pliable," Vestia replied. "Who are all of you, and how did you come here?"

The black-haired man gestured. "We come from different parts of Balské and all over the world. Some you see here came from the islands and don't understand a word of the common tongue. Others went sailing for the experience and were captured. The slave trade is rampant among the islands as it is in Hebaruin."

Vestia sat down beside him. "My name is Vestia Anthelion, daughter of Novanthelion the Jacerin. My friends and I seek the Evantyri. I have twisted the mind of the captain so that he will take us there. But if there's any way I can help you to escape—"

"Escape is impossible," said the man. "The locks to our chains have only one key, and it is kept by the captain in a very secret pouch on his person. I'm Lernar, by the way—pleased to meet you, Lady Vestia. Did you say that young dragon is your companion? Is he a Guardian?"

"Yes," Umphy spoke up for himself. Lernar's eyes filled with tears and he put his head down upon his oar.

"We have waited for the Guardians to rise all our lives. For us to see one now, in the presence of a Jacerin herself gives us great hope."

Umphy did not know how to handle the situation, for in the next instant the captain bellowed down at the oarslaves to get rowing. There was a scurry of feet overhead, and then a harsh grinding noise as the sailors drew up the anchor.

"We're setting sail," said Lernar. "Lady Vestia, will you help us? The children are very weak, but if they do not row, they are beaten and starved."

Umphy immediately sat down by the skinniest-looking child and grabbed his oar. He was enraged at the brutal treatment of the little ones; never in his life had he ever imagined such cruelty and vice. He and Vestia rowed with all their strength, pulling the ship out of the cove and onto the open sea. A small hatch opened, and one of the pirates came down. He leered at the slaves and settled himself down on a stool to watch them work. At his side was a nasty-looking whip with ten leather cords and spiked metal knotted at the ends. The slaves pulled with all their might, their terrified eyes riveted on the pirate and his whip.

"That's Garg the slavemaster," whispered Lernar to Vestia. "He's a cruel one to beware of. But you'll find that some of the pirates are not so bad. The first mate Rhun, now, he's got a better heart than manners or hygiene."

"He was the one who rescued me from being tied up in the captain's cabin," Vestia whispered.

"Aye, he might have taken a fancy to you. Rhun's a Rogue Elf—the child of an Elf and a Human. He's clever, educated, and deadly in battle. You'll find him to be a fair mate. But don't ever let the captain get his slimy hands on you. He's a vicious man who twists everything and everyone to his advantage. You're lucky you escaped him this once. If you're down here long enough, he may forget all about you."

"I hope he doesn't," Vestia said gloomily. "If only for the sake of getting to the Evantyri!"

Chapter 22

In the village of Hadrake, trouble was brewing.

Since the fabled escape of young Erastil, the Southerners were taking extra precautions in their security. They went from door to door with their troops, ransacking houses and barns and stables for any valuables the villagers possessed—including portal-ghosts and other enchanted transportation devices. Carts were filled with beloved heirlooms and treasures. Anyone who protested was slain on the spot.

Razot watched the proceedings from his post outside the village and felt good about himself. Since his appointment by the Black Dragon, he had felt increasingly important. Bullying and frightening others was his strongest talent, and his hideous looks were his most valuable asset. He had little need of strength. Nobody had any need to challenge the vicious dragon whose veins flowed with black blood. He smirked. Finally, a chance to stop sulking on the seashore and take part in the history of Balské! It was only a matter of time before Fordomt had all eight Orbs—the one who carried the White Orb could not run forever from his enemy, and once Fordomt completed his crown, there was nothing to stop him from taking over the land and rewarding his faithful servants with authority and power. Razot grinned wickedly. Power! The word had a certain ring to it, like a sudden flash of lightning across the sky. Oh yes, when the time was right, he and the others would be held in honor beside Morbane—and who knew? Morbane was getting old. Surely another would be appointed to take his place beneath the Tree of Death. Razot almost trembled with the thought of it. Sacrificial victims every month and honors beyond measure! What a life!

He pinpointed a woman who was trundling a wheelbarrow along the ground close to the village gates. Inhaling deeply, Razot lazily squirted fire as casually as a man spitting tobacco juice. The woman screamed and dropped to the ground, rolling this way and that. Razot laughed as a group of men scrambled to help her, beating out the flames with their cloaks. The woman was only injured with minor burns. Razot shrugged. He couldn't wait to *really* set the village on fire—to listen to the screams of the people begging for mercy and know that he had the power and skill and authority that they did not.

He watched as the woman got to her feet and staggered away, helped upright by the men at her side. Chuckling nastily, Razot blew fire-bubbles behind her. "Get moving faster, granny! You'll have to move faster than that in the mines of Hebaruin!"

"You pick easy targets, don't you, Razot?"

The other dragon stiffened. No, it couldn't be . . .

The voice was all too familiar, and to Razot's shame and disgust, it also sent a chill of fear down his spine. He had not heard the voice in weeks, though it often haunted his dreams. He turned.

"Well, well. If it isn't little Tarragon. How does a life of banishment suit you, keldora?"

Tarragon had flown a full day to reach Erastil's village. Just before crossing the last hill leading down to the settlement, the Guardian had caught sight of Razot in the act of setting fire to the woman. A dragon who used fire to bully others was as good as dead, for fire was the sacred symbol of warmth and protection, not destruction. Razot had lived among Guardians; he knew of this all-important code. Seeing him break it was no surprise to Tarragon, but what really got his blood running was the act itself—the attack on a defenseless village and its innocent inhabitants.

"I see you're still picking the weakest targets to play with," Tarragon growled. "Some things never change, do they, Razot? If courage was gold, you'd be the poorest dragon on the face of the planet."

"And if insolence was gold, you'd be the richest," Razot sneered. "Obviously you haven't learned your lesson. Well, what brings you here, anyway?"

"That's none of your business. What happened to the Firespring Clan?"

"Oh, *that*!" Razot laughed scornfully. "Such a sad chain of unfortunate circumstances, Tarragon. It's too bad you weren't around to save us all from the attack—oh, but I'm forgetting, they didn't *want* you. You were a threat, just like me. The only difference between us is that I always played fair and square, and you were more interested in breaking more rules than you kept."

The two dragons began to circle each other while they spoke. Southerners lined the walls of the village to watch the conversation. They had never seen anything like it—a Guardian facing down the spawn of a Black Dragon! Such a sight had been nonexistent for centuries, and now . . . Tarragon looked every inch the worthy opponent to fight against Razot, and the Southerners wanted to see what would happen. They did not see Erastil slip in with Tworgar along the back gate.

Tarragon locked eyes with Razot and did not drop his gaze. "You ran like a coward!"

"I am the Black Dragon's chosen lieutenant!"

"Then he's going to have to look for another," Tarragon snarled. "Because he's about to lose you!"

"Big words from a little keldora," Razot taunted. "I can remember when you hatched, Tarragon. Do you really think you have the strength or the skills to defeat me?"

"No. Just more intelligence."

Razot pawed the ground angrily, making the entire village shudder. "Are you offering me a challenge?"

"There is no challenge," Tarragon spat. "I have not seen you for a month, Razot, but I know better than to offer you a challenge! We still have a battle unfinished between the two of us—you remember, don't you? You insulted my mother and attacked my father at my graduation ceremony—for no good reason besides the fact that you hated my father and coveted my mother and despised me! I interrupted the battle and offered you a challenge, and I don't regret it. So that challenge remains open. Why don't you pick on someone your own size? Come on, I ought to be more of a *challenge* than a pathetic village full of helpless, tiny humans."

Razot hesitated. Tarragon was no easy kill, nor was he a combantant to underestimate. For the first time ever, Razot questioned his ability to strike and kill another dragon.

Tarragon saw the hesitancy in his opponent and lowered his guard slightly.

Suddenly, Razot struck!

Tarragon was bowled over by the ferocity of the attack; Razot had sensed his guard lowering and took full advantage of it, striking with his claws into the armored belly of the keldora. Tarragon retaliated by grabbing Razot's head and twisting viciously; his oppontent screamed in pain and wrenched free. Again they stood glaring at each other, Razot panting for breath. If Tarragon had applied the full force of his arms, he'd have snapped Razot's neck. But Tarragon had never killed before, and he was hesitant to do so now, even if it was his hated enemy. He only wanted to ensure the safety of the village.

Razot charged him again, and Tarragon stood up on his hind legs to meet him. As he had done a month ago, the keldora met the force of the blow with matched strength, the two bodies slamming together in a sound like thunder, causing the ground to tremble. Muscles bulged like shifting boulders on the limbs of the two dragons as they tussled for the upper hand.

Erastil snuck around the back of the gate and crept into the bar.

"Lucca!"

The fat bartender was tied to a chair and gagged with one end of a bottle, tears leaking from his eyes. Erastil unbound him and carefully removed the heavy glass bottle.

"They take my daughters, they beat me and tie me up like this—Erastil, why you no go? Get out of here, friend, run for your life!"

"Tide's turned," Erastil said easily. "I brought back a little souvenir."

Together they rushed outside. The Southerners were watching, slack-jawed, as their "defense" of the village struggled to overcome his foe, a huge Green Dragon, a pure-bred Guardian, through and through! The bartender laughed and cried and jumped up and down all at the same time, clapping his fat little hands and cheering.

"Silence!" A nearby Southerner shrieked and slammed his fist into the bartender's face. There was a sharp crack, and blood spurted from Lucca's nose as he sat down heavily. Erastil grabbed the Southerner and landed a blow across his jaw, felling him like a young sapling. He leapt upon a barrel and addressed the people.

"Hadrake!" he cried. "Grab weapons—anything you can find—rocks, wooden stakes, irons, whatever—take back the village! The Guardian will defeat the Black Dragon's spawn; let us help him and get rid of the Southerners!"

"DOWN WITH THE SOUTHERNERS!! DOWN WITH THE DEVILMEN!!" screamed the villagers. Though the troops of the Southerners numbered at least a hundred to fifty, the rage of the villagers was up, kindled by the wild cries of Erastil, who grabbed a sword from a slain Southerner and whirled with it, wielding the blade as though it was a part of him. The Bha-Nigh had been correct; he was the son of one of the most powerful Jacerin in Balské, and he could not deny his heritage.

Neither could the incredible Guardian who now fought on the offensive, driving Razot back away from the village. Tarragon's blood and adrenaline were up and boiling, and his muscles knotted and bunched as protective warrior instincts took over, surging through his body like a powerful river. The instinct that ran through the dragon's entire being was unlike anything he had felt before. That same nature had been dormant for many years, and now it rose up and lit Tarragon's eyes with an unearthly fire. His whole self knew, in that moment, the same spirit of his ancestor, the Brown Dragon, whose heart and soul beat inside the young keldora.

Razot saw the change come over his opponent's face and fear numbed his mind. For a moment it seemed as though he faced not a young, insolent keldora, but a full-grown Guardian of prestige and strength and power unlike anything the earth had ever seen before. He tried to scramble away.

Tarragon bore down on him and struck, his sharp teeth penetrating between the protective plates of Razot's hide and piercing the flesh beneath. Razot screamed in terror; no dragon had ever drawn blood from him before in battle. He twisted, trying to evade Tarragon's claws and teeth. Instead, the Guardian grabbed his opponent's hind leg and applied all his strength, snapping the limb to cripple—not kill. Pain sliced through Razot's body and he lay on the ground as wave after wave of agnony flooded though his leg, up his spine, and in his head. Tarragon slammed his footpaw down on Razot's back, pinning him to the ground.

"I won't kill you," Tarragon snarled. "It's more than you deserve—permitting you to live is probably the one mistake I will live to regret, but I am not a murderer like your kin."

"You might as well kill me," Razot choked. "When he discovers my failure, he'll do worse to me than you've done today!"

"Who's 'he'?"

"The Black Dragon, Morbane," Razot gasped. "He killed your clan and told me to help him in his work—you don't understand; he would have killed me if I hadn't—"

"Save your excuses for the devil who records your name in his little black book," Tarragon growled. "I'm not interested in them or in you. You'd sell your soul to save your worthless hide because you believe in nothing except yourself! Pride, honor, dignity, life—it means nothing to you or Hebaruin and everything to the Guardians. You're a descendant of Green Dragons, Razot, despite your black blood. If Morbane comes back to slay you, try to die like a Guardian, will you?"

He turned his attention to the village.

The minute his back was turned, Razot's eyes burned with hatred and he inhaled deeply. Tarragon heard the noise and whipped around just in time to meet the incredible blast of fire with his own, driving the purple-black flames back with his golden-red ones, forcing them closer and closer, concentrating fully. Razot was too weak to hold onto the struggle, and his flame was driven back completely until it exploded around him in a powerful burst of fire and sparks. The body of Razot shattered like a fragile glass vase, his own fire forced down his throat. Pieces of him evaporated like mist in the sun, and the ashes were scattered on the wind. What remained of the corpse on the ground burned down until nothing was left but bits of bone and a large pile of ash. The ground beneath was burned black.

But Tarragon was untouched.

When he turned around to peer in at the village, a number of Southerners crashed through the gate and high-tailed it for the hills, running away in mortal terror. Never before had they seen such a display of power and force—not even in Hebaruin had they seen anything to rival the battle they had just witnessed between a Black Dragon's spawn and a Guardian! Tarragon let them run. The village was safe.

Erastil came out, Tworgar at his side, and the villagers following behind. They looked up timidly at the Guardian, who blushed red. He wanted to stammer that it was nothing, he was only doing his job, but he was so overwhelmed by the new feeling of gratitude of the people that he only shuffled his feet and blushed even redder.

"Oh Enovan," Tworgar whispered. "Not a scratch on him."

"Are you alright?" Tarragon asked the wolf.

"Never better! Why, that was even better than chasing behemoths around or jumping off cliffs into the sea! But I missed all the action out here! I told you you could rip a behemoth into shredded wheat! You, my friend, need to listen to me more often. With you loose in the land, there's not a soul who will stand against you!"

"Except the Black Dragon," Tarragon said thoughtfully. Razot's death seemed like a dream. Tarragon felt nothing, only a sense of fulfillment in himself, as though he had accomplished something he was meant to do—but there was still something more. "I must find my kin," he said softly.

"Tarragon," Erastil called up to him. "We must escort the villagers to the city of Curanon. It is a powerful kingdom that will take them in, listen to their tale, and learn how to act against Fordomt. The king must be warned about the threat of the South. And I must go North to find my father." He held up a bottled ghost. "I have my transport, thanks to Lucca the bartender. But will you see these people safely off to Curanon? That is all I ask, and then you may do as you wish. Time is against us. The Black Dragon has employed one of his kin, and may do so again—and he will attack other villages and dragon clans."

Tarragon opened his mouth to protest, but the words that came out hardly seemed his own. "Go and do what you must, Master Anthelion. Seek your father in the North and fulfill your destiny. I will take care of these people and see them delivered safely to Curanon."

Erastil reached up with a hand, and Tarragon picked him up. Erastil pressed his hand against the dragon's nose-horn.

"My Guardian, I swear my service to you. When next we meet, may it be on the field of victory!"

"When next we meet, please don't run into my face," Tarragon laughed. "I accept your service—and your friendship. It was an odd meeting and it's an odd parting, but the Bha-Nigh did say our paths were intertwined. I'll see you on that field of victory, Erastil!"

"And I'll meet you there, my Guardian!"

Chapter 23

Arwos sat sulking in his cage. The large raven had been teased, spat at, and cruelly poked during the first day of captivity by the pirates. He knew that his little blue friend and the Jacerin were down in the hold, but he wished he knew how they were doing.

The stars glittered overhead as the ship glided smoothly through the waters off the Western Coast. Looking up, Arwos could detect the great bear, the cooking-pan, the archer, and the great dragon. He stared long and hard at the dragon. How had it all happened? Only a month ago he had become friends with a dragon, and now he was inevitably bound in the mission to safeguard the powerful treasure his fuzzy blue friend held. And somewhere out there was Umphy's brother, another dragon chosen by fate to be the one to destroy Morbane. The two dragons were the hope of all Balské, and the fulfillers of the prophecy of the Guardians in their bid for victory against the forces of evil.

They were the Heirs of the Brown Dragon.

Arwos ruffled his feathers and settled down to sleep. The pirates could not keep a Brown Dragon heir captive forever—nor could anything stand against the dragon who, unbeknownst to the raven, guided an entire village like a shepherd with his flock.

The raven smiled and remembered the words of the story in the Elbib:

"The Guardians will rise again."